STAR LIGHT,
THE GREAT

Also by Alfred Bester

THE DEMOLISHED MAN

THE STARS MY DESTINATION

THE RAT RACE (WHO HE?)

THE DARK SIDE OF THE EARTH

STARBURST

THE LIFE AND DEATH OF A SATELLITE

THE LIGHT FANTASTIC

Volume I of the Great Short Fiction

of Alfred Bester

STAR BRIGHT

SHORT FICTION OF ALFRED BESTER

VOLUME II

Published by
BERKLEY PUBLISHING CORPORATION
Distributed by
G. P. PUTNAM'S SONS, NEW YORK

COPYRIGHT © 1976, by ALFRED BESTER

SBN: 399-11816-0

Library of Congress Catalog Card Number: 76-17377

PRINTED IN THE UNITED STATES OF AMERICA

Contents

STAR LIGHT, STAR BRIGHT

Adam and No Eve

Introduction

THIS is the first of my "quality" science fiction stories. I put "quality" in quotes because I think it's rather jejune. Nevertheless it had and still has its admirers, who are more or less on a nostalgia kick. They like to remember the impact the story made on them when it first appeared in Campbell's *Astounding Stories*. Campbell was a tough, critical editor, and it was quite an honor for a young writer to have him buy a story.

At this distance of time I remember scattered, unrelated things. My wife and I had become friendly with a man who was a linotypist on *The Daily Worker*, despite the fact that he was a violent anti-Communist and used to berate the editors constantly. He was safe because his job was protected by his powerful union. His hostility went so far that he would slip deliberate typos into his copy, things like "Commrat" for Comrade. He was very kind to me and used to bring me huge reams of the yellow $8\frac{1}{2} \times 15$ copy paper used in the editorial offices. This was a godsend to a poor writer. "Adam and No Eve" was typed on that paper which, unfortunately, was no damned good for filing. It crumbled after a year or so.

The genesis of the story came out of irritation. Very often stories arise because I get fed up with a cliché, and I'd about had it with the Adam and Eve device in science fiction. I'd just finished my formal schooling (one's education never stops) and had studied almost all the branches of the scientific disciplines. It occurred to me that you didn't need a man and a woman to repopulate the earth after a disaster. Just dump a body into the ocean, let nature take its course, and the whole thing will start all over again. (No, repeat, *no* apology to the lunatic anti-evolutionists.) It must be remembered that the story was written long before Urey and Miller performed their epochal experiment demonstrating that amino acids, the basic building blocks of life, could be produced by subjecting a simulation of early terrestrial atmosphere to electric discharges. I'm amused today to realize that all the elements necessary for the regeneration of life were present in the environment of the story, and I didn't need any dying Adam.

For the life of me I can't remember why I found it necessary to incinerate the corpse of the dead dog. Most probably because I wanted to keep the thesis clean; life would regenerate from Adam alone; the title couldn't read, "Adam and His Faithful Dog." The story gave me extraordinary pleasure twenty years after it was published. I was lunching with an NBC producer to discuss a new show he wanted me to write. It was to be a sort of fantasy pilot, which is why he called me in; he knew I'd been a science fiction writer before I sold out to the networks.

"There's one story I've never forgotten," he said, "and I'm hoping you can tell me who wrote it. I'd like to get hold of that man." And he proceded to tell me all about "Adam and No Eve." It was the moment of my life.

Krane knew this must be the seacoast. Instinct told him; but more than instinct, the few shreds of knowledge that clung to his torn brain told him; the stars that had shown at night through the rare breaks in the clouds, and his compass that still pointed a trembling finger north. That was strangest of all, Krane thought. The rubbled Earth still retained its polarity.

It was no longer a coast; there was no longer any sea. Only the faint line of what had been a cliff stretched north and south for endless miles. It was a line of grey ash; the same grey ash and cinders that lay behind him and stretched before him. . . . Fine silt, knee-deep, that swirled up at every motion and choked him; cinders that scudded in dense night clouds when the mad winds blew; black dust that was churned to mud when the frequent rains fell.

The sky was jet overhead. The heavy clouds rode high and were pierced with shafts of sunlight that marched swiftly over the Earth. Where the light struck a cinder storm, it was filled with gusts of dancing, gleaming particles. Where it played through rain it brought the arches of rainbows into being. Rain fell; cinder-storms blew; light thrust down—together, alternately and continually in a jigsaw of black and white violence. So it had been for months. So it was over every mile of the broad Earth.

Krane passed the edge of the ashen cliffs and began crawling down the even slope that had once been the ocean bed. He had been traveling so long that pain had become part of him. He braced elbows and dragged his body forward. Then he brought his right knee under him and reached forward with elbows again. Elbows, knee, elbows, knee—He had forgotten what it was to walk.

Life, he thought dazedly, is miraculous. It adapts itself to anything. If it must crawl, it crawls, Callus forms on the elbows and knees. The neck and shoulders toughen. The nostrils learn to snort away the ashes before they breathe. The bad leg swells and festers. It numbs, and presently it will rot and fall off.

"I beg pardon?" Krane said, "I didn't quite get that—"

He peered up at the tall figure before him and tried to understand the words. It was Hallmyer. He wore his stained lab coat and his grey hair was awry. Hallmyer stood delicately on top of the ashes and Krane wondered why he could see the scudding cinder clouds through his body.

"How do you like your world, Steven?" Hallmyer asked.

Krane shook his head miserably.

"Not very pretty, eh?" said Hallmyer. "Look around you. Dust, that's all; dust and ashes. Crawl, Steven, crawl. You'll find nothing but dust and ashes—"

Hallmyer produced a goblet of water from nowhere. It was clear and cold. Krane could see the fine mist of dew on its surface and his mouth was suddenly coated with grit.

"Hallmyer!" he cried. He tried to get to his feet and reach for the water, but the jolt of pain in his right leg warned him. He crouched back.

Hallmyer sipped and then spat in his face. The water felt warm.

"Keep crawling," said Hallmyer bitterly. "Crawl round and round the face of the Earth. You'll find nothing but dust and ashes—" He emptied the goblet on the ground before Krane. "Keep crawling. How many miles? Figure it out for yourself. Pi-times D. The diameter is eight thousand or so—"

He was gone, coat and goblet. Krane realized that rain was falling again. He pressed his face into the warm cinder mud, opened his mouth and tried to suck the moisture. Presently he began crawling again.

There was an instinct that drove him on. He had to get somewhere. It was associated, he knew, with the sea—with the edge of the sea. At the shore of the sea something waited for him. Something that would help him understand all this. He had to get to the sea—that is, if there was a sea any more.

The thundering rain beat his back like heavy planks. Krane paused and yanked the knapsack around to his side where he probed in it with one hand. It contained exactly three things. A gun, a bar of chocolate, and a can of peaches. All that was left of two months' supplies. The chocolate was pulpy and spoiled. Krane knew he had best eat it before all value rotted away. But in another day he would lack the strength to open the can. He pulled it out and attacked it with the opener. By the time he had pierced and pried away a flap of tin, the rain had passed.

As he munched the fruit and sipped the juice, he watched the wall of rain marching before him down the slope of the ocean bed. Torrents of water were gushing through the mud. Small channels had already been cut—channels that would be new rivers some day; a day he would never see; a day that no living thing would ever see. As he flipped the empty can aside, Krane thought: The last living thing on Earth eats its last meal. Metabolism begins the last act.

Wind would follow the rain. In the endless weeks that he had been crawling, he had learned that. Wind would come in a few minutes and flog him with its clouds of cinders and ashes. He crawled forward, bleary eyes searching the flat grey miles for cover.

Evelyn tapped his shoulder.

Krane knew it was she before he turned his head. She stood alongside, fresh and gay in her bright dress, but her lovely face was puckered with alarm.

"Steven," she said, "you've got to hurry!"

He could only admire the way her smooth hair waved to her shoulders.

"Oh, darling!" she said, "you've been hurt!" Her quick gentle hands touched his legs and back. Krane nodded.

"Got it landing," he said. "I wasn't used to a parachute. I always thought you came down gently—like plumping onto a bed. But the earth came up at me like a fist—And Umber was fighting around in my arms. I couldn't let him drop, could I?"

"Of course not, dear," Evelyn said.

"So I just held on to him and tried to get my legs under me," Krane said. "And then something smashed my legs and side—"

He hesitated, wondering how much she knew of what really had happened. He didn't want to frighten her.

"Evelyn, darling—" he said, trying to reach up his arms.

"No, dear," she said. She looked back in fright. "You've got to hurry. You've got to watch out behind!"

"The cinder-storms?" He grimaced. "I've been through them before."

"Not the storms!" Evelyn cried. "Something else. Oh, Steven—"

Then she was gone, but Krane knew she had spoken the truth. There was something behind—something that had been following him. In the back of his mind he had sensed the menace. It was closing in on him like a shroud. He shook his head. Somehow that was impossible. He was the last living thing on Earth. How could there be a menace?

The wind roared behind him, and an instant later came the heavy clouds of cinders and ashes. They lashed over him, biting his skin. With dimming eyes, he saw the way they coated the mud and covered it with a fine dry carpet. Krane drew his knees under him and covered his head with his arms. With the knapsack as a pillow, he prepared to wait out the storm. It would pass as quickly as the rain.

The storm whipped up a great bewilderment in his sick head. Like a child he pushed at the pieces of his memory, trying to fit them together. Why was Hallmyer so bitter toward him? It couldn't have been that argument, could it?

What argument?

Why, that one before all this happened.

Oh, that!

Abruptly, the pieces locked together.

Krane stood alongside the sleek lines of his ship and admired it tremendously. The roof of the shed had been removed and the nose of the ship hoisted so that it rested on a cradle pointed toward the sky. A workman was carefully burnishing the inner surfaces of the rocket jets.

The muffled sounds of swearing came from within the ship and then a heavy clanking. Krane ran up the short iron ladder to the port and thrust his head inside. A few feet beneath him, two men were clamping the long tanks of ferrous solution into place.

"Easy there," Krane called. "Want to knock the ship apart?"

One looked up and grinned. Krane knew what he was thinking. That the ship would tear itself apart. Everyone said that. Everyone except Evelyn. She had faith in him. Hallmyer never said it either, but Hallmyer thought he was crazy in another way. As he descended the ladder, Krane saw Hallmyer come into the shed, lab coat flying.

"Speak of the devil!" Krane muttered.

Hallmyer began shouting as soon as he saw Krane. "Now, listen—"

"Not all over again," Krane said.

Hallmyer dug a sheaf of papers out of his pocket and waved it under Krane's nose.

"I've been up half the night," he said, "working it through again. I tell you I'm right. I'm absolutely right—"

Krane looked at the tight-written equations and then at Hallmyer's bloodshot eyes. The man was half-mad with fear.

"For the last time," Hallmyer went on. "You're using your new catalyst on iron solution. All right. I grant that it's a miraculous discovery. I give you credit for that."

Miraculous was hardly the word for it. Krane knew that without conceit, for he realized he'd only stumbled on it. You had to stumble on a catalyst that would induce atomic disintegration of iron and give 10×10^{10} foot-pounds of energy for every gram of fuel. No man was smart enough to think all that up by himself.

"You don't think I'll make it?" Krane asked.

"To the Moon? Around the Moon? Maybe. You've got a fifty-fifty chance." Hallmyer ran fingers through his lank hair. "But for God's sake, Steven, I'm not worried about you. If you want to kill yourself, that's your own affair. It's the Earth I'm worried about—"

"Nonsense. Go home and sleep it off."

"Look—" Hallmyer pointed to the sheets of paper with a shaky hand—"No matter how you work the feed and mixing system, you can't get one hundred percent efficiency in the mixing and discharge."

"That's what makes it a fifty-fifty chance," Krane said. "So what's bothering you?"

"The catalyst that will escape through the rocket tubes. Do you realize what it'll do if a drop hits the Earth? It'll start a chain of disintegration that'll envelop the globe. It'll reach out to every iron atom—and there's iron everywhere. There won't be any Earth left for you to return to—"

"Listen," Krane said wearily, "we've been through all this before."

He took Hallmyer to the base of the rocket cradle. Beneath the iron framework was a two-hundred-foot pit, fifty feet wide and lined with firebrick.

"That's for the initial discharge flames. If any of the catalyst goes through, it'll be trapped in this pit and taken care of by the secondary reactions. Satisfied now?"

"But while you're in flight," Hallmyer persisted, "you'll be endangering the Earth until you're beyond Roche's limit. Every drop of nonactivated catalyst will eventually sink back to the ground and—"

"For the very last time," Krane said grimly, "the flame of the rocket discharge takes care of that. It will envelop any escaped particles and destroy them. Now get out. I've got work to do."

As Krane pushed him to the door, Hallmyer screamed and waved his arms. "I won't let you do it!" he repeated over and over. "I won't let you risk it—"

Work? No, it was sheer intoxication to labor over the ship. It had the fine beauty of a well-made thing. The beauty of polished armor, of a balanced swept-hilt rapier, of a pair of matched guns. There was no thought of danger and death in Krane's mind as he wiped his hands with waste after the last touches were finished.

She lay in the cradle ready to pierce the skies. Fifty feet of slender steel, the rivet heads gleaming like jewels. Thirty feet were given over to fuel and catalyst. Most of the forward compartment contained the spring hammock Krane had devised to absorb the acceleration strain. The ship's nose was a porthole of natural crystal that stared upward like a cyclopean eye.

Krane thought: She'll die after this trip. She'll return to the Earth and smash in a blaze of fire and thunder, for there's no way yet of devising a safe landing for a rocket ship. But it's worth it. She'll have had her one great flight, and that's all any of us should want. One great beautiful flight into the unknown—

As he locked the workshop door, Krane heard Hallmyer shouting from the cottage across the fields. Through the evening gloom he could see him waving urgently. He trotted through the crisp stubble, breathing the sharp air deeply, grateful to be alive.

"It's Evelyn on the phone," Hallmyer said.

Krane stared at him. Hallmyer refused to meet his eyes.

"What's the idea?" Krane asked. "I thought we agreed that she wasn't to call—wasn't to get in touch with me until I was ready to start? You been putting ideas into her head? Is this the way you're going to stop me?"

Hallmyer said, "No—" and studiously examined the darkening horizon.

Krane went into his study and picked up the phone.

"Now listen, darling," he said without preamble, "there's no sense getting alarmed now. I explained everything very carefully. Just before the ship crashes, I take to a parachute. I love you very much and I'll see you Wednesday when I start. So long—"

"Good-bye, sweetheart," Evelyn's clear voice said, "and is that what you called me for?"

"Called you!"

A brown hulk disengaged itself from the hearth rug and

lifted itself to strong legs. Umber, Krane's mastiff, sniffed and cocked an ear. Then he whined.

"Did you say I called you?" Krane repeated.

Umber's throat suddenly poured forth a bellow. He reached Krane in a single bound, looked up into his face and whined and roared all at once.

"Shut up, you monster!" Krane said. He pushed Umber away with his foot.

"Give Umber a kick for me," Evelyn laughed. "Yes, dear. Someone called and said you wanted to speak to me."

"They did, eh? Look, honey, I'll call you back—"

Krane hung up. He arose doubtfully and watched Umber's uneasy actions. Through the windows, the late evening glow sent flickering shadows of orange light. Umber gazed at the light, sniffed and bellowed again. Suddenly struck, Krane leaped to the window.

Across the fields a mass of flame thrust high into the air, and within it were the crumbling walls of the workshop. Silhouetted against the glaze, the figures of half a dozen men darted and ran.

Krane shot out of the cottage and with Umber hard at his heels, sprinted toward the shed. As he ran he could see the graceful nose of the spaceship within the fire, still looking cool and untouched. If only he could reach it before the flames softened its metal and started the rivets.

The workmen trotted up to him, grimy and panting. Krane gaped at them in a mixture of fury and bewilderment.

"Hallmyer!" he shouted. "Hallmyer!"

Hallmyer pushed through the crowd. His eyes gleamed with triumph.

"Too bad," he said, "I'm sorry, Steven—"

"You bastard!" Krane shouted. He grasped Hallmyer by the lapels and shook him once. Then he dropped him and started into the shed.

Hallmyer snapped orders to the workmen and an instant later a body hurtled against Krane's calves and spilled him to the ground. He lurched to his feet, fists swinging. Umber was alongside, growling over the roar of the flames. Krane battered a man in the face, and saw him stagger back against a second. He lifted a knee in a vicious drive that sent the last workman crumpling to the ground. Then he ducked his head and plunged into the shop.

The scorch felt cool at first, but when he reached the ladder and began mounting to the port, he screamed with the agony of his burns. Umber was howling at the foot of the ladder, and Krane realized that the dog could never escape from the rocket blasts. He reached down and hauled Umber into the ship.

Krane was reeling as he closed and locked the port. He retained consciousness barely long enough to settle himself in the spring hammock. Then instinct alone prompted his hands to reach out toward the control board; instinct and the frenzied refusal to let his beautiful ship waste itself in the flames. He would fail—yes. But he would fail trying.

His fingers tripped the switches. The ship shuddered and roared. And blackness descended over him.

How long was he unconscious? There was no telling. Krane awoke with cold pressing against his face and body, and the sound of frightened yelps in his ears. Krane looked up and saw Umber tangled in the springs and straps of the hammock. His first impulse was to laugh, then suddenly he realized; he had looked *up!* He had looked up at the hammock.

He was lying curled in the cup of the crystal nose. The ship had risen high—perhaps almost to Roche's zone, to the limit of the Earth's gravitational attraction, but then without guiding hands at the controls to continue its flight, had turned and was dropping back toward Earth. Krane peered through the crystal and gasped.

Below him was the ball of the Earth. It looked three times the size of the Moon. And it was no longer his Earth. It was a globe of fire mottled with black clouds. At the northernmost pole there was a tiny patch of white, and even as Krane watched, it was suddenly blotted over with hazy tones of red, scarlet and crimson. Hallmyer had been right.

Krane lay frozen in the cup of the nose as the ship descended, watching the flames gradually fade away to leave nothing but the dense blanket of black around the Earth. He lay numb with horror, unable to understand—unable to reckon up a people snuffed out, a green, fair planet reduced to ashes and cinders. Everything that was once dear and close to him—gone. He could not think of Evelyn.

Air whistling outside, awoke some instinct in him. The few shreds of reason left told him to go down with his ship and forget everything in the thunder and destruction, but the instinct of life forced him to action. He climbed up to the store chest and prepared for the landing. Parachute, a small oxygen tank—a knapsack of supplies. Only half-aware of what he was doing he dressed for the descent, buckled on the 'chute and opened the port. Umber whined pathetically, and he took the heavy dog in his arms and stepped out into space.

But space hadn't been so clogged, the way it was now. Then it had been difficult to breathe. But that was because the air had been rare—not filled with clogging grit like now.

Every breath was a lungful of ground glass—or ashes—or cinders—He had returned to a suffocating black present that hugged him with soft weight and made him fight for breath. Krane struggled in panic, and then relaxed.

It had happened before. A long time past he'd been buried deep under ashes when he'd stopped to remember. Weeks ago—or days—or months. Krane clawed with his hands, inching out of the mound of cinders that the wind had thrown over him. Presently he emerged into the light again. The wind had died away. It was time to begin his crawl to the sea once more.

The vivid pictures of his memory scattered again before the grim vista that stretched out ahead. Krane scowled. He remembered too much, and too often. He had the vague hope that if he remembered hard enough, he might change one of the things he had done—just a very little thing—and then all this would become untrue. He thought: It might help if everyone remembered and wished at the same time—but there isn't any everyone. I'm the only one. I'm the last memory on Earth. I'm the last life.

He crawled. Elbows, knee, elbows, knee—And then Hallmyer was crawling alongside and making a great game of it. He chortled and plunged in the cinders like a happy sea lion.

Krane said: "But why do we have to get to the sea?"

Hallmyer blew a spume of ashes.

"Ask her," he said, pointing to Krane's other side.

Evelyn was there, crawling seriously, intently, mimicking Krane's smallest action.

"It's because of our house," she said. "You remember our house, darling? High on the cliff. We were going to live there forever and ever. I was there when you left. Now you're coming back to the house at the edge of the sea. Your beautiful flight is over, dear, and you're coming back to me. We'll live together, just we two, like Adam and Eve—"

Krane said, "That's nice."

Then Evelyn turned her head and screamed, "Oh, Steven! Watch out!" and Krane felt the menace closing in on him again. Still crawling, he stared back at the vast grey plains of ash, and saw nothing. When he looked at Evelyn again he saw only his shadow, sharp and black. Presently, it too, faded away as the marching shaft of sunlight passed.

But the dread remained. Evelyn had warned him twice, and she was always right. Krane stopped and turned, and settled himself to watch. If he was really being followed, he would see whatever it was, coming along his tracks.

There was a painful moment of lucidity. It cleaved through his fever and bewilderment, bringing with it the sharpness and strength of a knife.

I'm mad, he thought. The corruption in my leg has spread to my brain. There is no Evelyn, no Hallmyer, no menace. In all this land there is no life but mine—and even ghosts and spirits of the underworld must have perished in the inferno that girdled the planet. No—there is nothing but me and my sickness. I'm dying—and when I perish, everything will perish. Only a mass of lifeless cinders will go on.

But there was a movement.

Instinct again—Krane dropped his head and lay still. Through slitted eyes he watched the ashen plains, wondering if death was playing tricks with his eyes. Another facade of rain was beating down toward him, and he hoped he could make sure before all vision was obliterated.

Yes. There.

A quarter mile back, a grey-brown shape was flitting along the grey surface. Despite the drone of the distant rain, Krane could hear the whisper of trodden cinders and see the little clouds kicking up. Stealthily he groped for the revolver in the knapsack as his mind reached feebly for explanations and recoiled from fear.

The thing approached, and suddenly Krane squinted and understood. He recalled Umber kicking with fear and springing away from him when the 'chute landed them on the ashen face of the Earth.

"Why, it's Umber," he murmured. He raised himself. The dog halted. "Here, boy!" Krane croaked gaily. "Here, boy!"

He was overcome with joy. He realized that loneliness had hung over him, a horrible sensation of oneness in emptiness. Now his was not the only life. There was another. A friendly life that could offer love and companionship. Hope kindled again.

"Here, boy!" he repeated. "Come on, boy—"

After a while he stopped trying to snap his fingers. The mastiff hung back, showing fangs and a lolling tongue. The dog was emaciated and its eyes gleamed red in the dusk. As

Krane called once more, the dog snarled. Puffs of ash leaped beneath its nostrils.

He's hungry, Krane thought, that's all. He reached into the knapsack and at the gesture the dog snarled again. Krane withdrew the chocolate bar and laboriously peeled off the paper and silver foil. Weakly he tossed it toward Umber. It fell far short. After a minute of savage uncertainty, the dog advanced slowly and snapped up the food. Ashes powdered its muzzle. It licked its chops ceaselessly and continued to advance on Krane.

Panic jerked within him. A voice persisted: This is no friend. He has no love or companionship for you. Love and companionship have vanished from the land along with life. Now there is nothing left but hunger.

"No—" Krane whispered. "That isn't right that we should tear at each other and seek to devour—"

But Umber was advancing with a slinking sidle, and his teeth showed sharp and white. And even as Krane stared at him, the dog snarled and lunged.

Krane thrust up an arm under the dog's muzzle, but the weight of the charge carried him backward. He cried out in agony as his broken, swollen leg was struck by the weight of the dog. With his free hand he struck weakly, again and again, scarcely feeling the grind of teeth on his left arm. Then something metallic was pressed under him and he realized he was lying on the revolver he had let fall.

He groped for it and prayed the cinders had not clogged it. As Umber let go his arm and tore at his throat, Krane brought the gun up and jabbed the muzzle blindly against the dog's body. He pulled and pulled the trigger until the roars died away and only empty clicks sounded. Umber shuddered in the ashes before him, his body nearly shot in two. Thick scarlet stained the grey.

Evelyn and Hallmyer looked down sadly at the broken animal. Evelyn was crying, and Hallmyer reached nervous fingers through his hair in the same old gesture.

"This is the finish, Steven," he said. "You've killed part of yourself. Oh—you'll go on living, but not all of you. You'd best bury that body, Steven. It's the corpse of your soul."

"I can't," Krane said. "The wind will blow the cinders away."

"Then burn it," Hallmyer ordered with dream-logic.

It seemed that they helped him thrust the dead dog into his knapsack. They helped him take off his clothes and packed them underneath. They cupped their hands around the matches until the cloth caught fire, and blew on the weak flame until it sputtered and burned limply. Krane crouched by the fire and nursed it. Then he turned and once again began crawling down the ocean bed. He was naked now. There was nothing left of what-had-been but his flickering little life.

He was too heavy with sorrow to notice the furious rain that slammed and buffeted him, or the searing pains that were searing through his blackened leg and up his hip. He crawled. Elbows, knee, elbows, knee— Woodenly, mechanically, apathetic to everything . . . to the latticed skies, the dreary ashen plains and even the dull glint of water that lay far ahead.

He knew it was the sea—what was left of the old, or a new one in the making. But it would be an empty, lifeless sea that someday would lap against a dry, lifeless shore. This would be a planet of stone and dust, of metal and snow and ice and water, but that would be all. No more life. He, alone, was useless. He was Adam, but there was no Eve.

Evelyn waved gaily to him from the shore. She was standing alongside the white cottage with the wind snapping her dress to show the slender lines of her figure. And when he came a little closer, she ran out to him and helped him. She said nothing—only placed her hands under his shoulders and helped him lift the weight of his heavy, pain-ridden body. And so at last he reached the sea.

It was real. He understood that. For even after Evelyn and

the cottage had vanished, he felt the cool waters bathe his face.

Here's the sea, Krane thought, and here am I. Adam and no Eve. It's hopeless.

He rolled a little farther into the waters. They laved his torn body. He lay with face to the sky, peering at the high menacing heavens, and the bitterness within him welled up.

"It's not right!" he cried. "It's not right that all this should pass away. Life is too beautiful to perish at the mad act of one mad creature—"

Quietly the waters laved him. Quietly . . . Calmly . . .

The sea rocked him gently, and even the death that was reaching up toward his heart was no more than a gloved hand. Suddenly the skies split apart—for the first time in all those months—and Krane stared up at the stars.

Then he knew. This was not the end of life. There could never be an end to life. Within his body, within the rotting tissues rocking gently in the sea was the source of ten million-million lives. Cells—tissues—bacteria—amoeba— Countless infinities of life that would take new root in the waters and live long after he was gone.

They would live on his rotting remains. They would feed on each other. They would adapt themselves to the new environment and feed on the minerals and sediments washed into this new sea. They would grow, burgeon, evolve. Life would reach out to the lands once more. It would begin again the same old repeated cycle that had begun perhaps with the rotting corpse of some last survivor of interstellar travel. It would happen over and over in the future ages.

And then he knew what had brought him back to the sea. There need be no Adam—no Eve. Only the sea, the great mother of life was needed. The sea had called him back to her depths that presently life might emerge once more, and he was content.

Quietly   the   waters   comforted   him.   Quietly . . . Calmly . . . The mother of life rocked the last-born of the old cycle who would become the first-born of the new. And with glazing eyes Steven Krane smiled up at the stars, stars that were sprinkled evenly across the sky. Stars that had not yet formed into the familiar constellations, and would not for another hundred million centuries.

Time Is the Traitor

Introduction

I READ an interview with a top management executive in which he said he was no different from any other employee of the corporation; as a matter of fact, he did less work than most. What he was paid an enormous salary for was making decisions. And he added rather wryly that his decisions had no better than a fifty-fifty chance of being correct.

That stayed with me. I began to think about decision making, and since my habit is to look at characters from the Freudian point of view first—other points of view receive equal time later—I thought that decisions might well be an aspect of compulsion. My wife and I, who are quick and firm deciders, are often annoyed by the many hesitating, vacillating people we see in action. What's the answer? The others are the normals and we're the compelled. Fair enough. Good, at least for a story.

But are you born a compulsive or are you kicked into it by background and/or a traumatic experience? Both, probably, but it's better for a story to have a single shattering event trigger the decision compulsion, provided the event ties into the body of the story. I thought of an amusing couplet Manly Wade Wellman had written to the effect that if your girl is one girl in a million, there must be at least six like her in a city of any size. Good. It'll work and lock in to give us a chase quality. It will also provide conflict, mystery and suspense.

And all this is a damned tissue of lies. I don't coolly block a story in progressive steps like an attorney preparing a brief for the supreme court. I'm more like Zerah Colburn, the American idiot-savant, who could perform mathematical marvels mentally and recognize prime numbers at sight. He did it, but he didn't know how he did it. I write stories, but as a rule I don't know how I do it. There are occasional exceptions, but this isn't one.

All I do know is that the ingredients mentioned above went into the stockpot along with a lot of others. I don't know in what order. I don't know why some were fished out a moment after they went in while others were permitted to remain and "marry." This is why most authors agree that writing can't be taught; it can be mastered only through trial and error, and the more errors the better. Youngsters have a lot of damned bad writing to get out of their systems before they can find their way.

The purpose of trial and error, imitations and experiments, constant slaving through uncertainty and despair is twofold: to acquire merciless self-discipline; to acquire conscious story patterns and reduce them to unconscious practice. I've often said that you become a writer when you *think* story, not *about* a story.

When a writer tells you how he wrote something, he's usually second-guessing. He's telling you what he figures may have happened, after the fact. He can't report on what went on deep under the surface; the unconscious matrix which shapes the story, the unconscious editing, the unconscious revelation of his own character. All he can do is give you the things that went on consciously and gussy them up to make them sound logical and sensible. But writing isn't logical and sensible. It's an act of insane violence committed against yourself and the rest of the world . . . at least it is with me.

You can't go back and you can't catch up. Happy endings are always bittersweet.

There was a man named John Strapp; the most valuable, the most powerful, the most legendary man in a world containing seven hundred planets and seventeen hundred billion people. He was prized for one quality alone. He could make Decisions. Note the capital D. He was one of the few men who could make Major Decisions in a world of incredible complexity, and his Decisions were 87 percent correct. He sold his Decisions for high prices.

There would be an industry named, say, Bruxton Biotics, with plants on Deneb Alpha, Mizar III, Terra, and main offices on Alcor IV. Bruxton's gross income was Cr. 270 billions. The involutions of Bruxton's trade relations with consumers and competitors required the specialized services of two hundred company economists, each an expert on one tiny facet of the vast overall picture. No one was big enough to coordinate the entire picture.

Bruxton would need a Major Decision on policy. A research expert named E. T. A. Goland in the Deneb laboratories had discovered a new catalyst for biotic synthesis. It was an embryological hormone that rendered nucleonic molecules as plastic as clay. The clay could be modeled and developed in any direction. Query: Should Bruxton abandon the old culture methods and retool for this new technique? The Decision involved an intricate ramification of interreacting factors: cost, saving, time, supply, demand, training, patents, patent legislation, court actions and so on. There was only one answer: Ask Strapp.

The initial negotiations were crisp. Strapp Associates replied that John Strapp's fee was Cr. 100,000 plus 1 percent of the voting stock of Bruxton Biotics. Take it or leave it. Bruxton Biotics took it with pleasure.

The second step was more complicated. John Strapp was very much in demand. He was scheduled for Decisions at the rate of two a week straight through to the first of the year.

Could Bruxton wait that long for an appointment? Bruxton could not. Bruxton was TT'd a list of John Strapp's future appointments and told to arrange a swap with any of the clients as best he could. Bruxton bargained, bribed, blackmailed and arranged a trade. John Strapp was to appear at the Alcor central plant on Monday, June 29, at noon precisely.

Then the mystery began. At nine o'clock that Monday morning, Aldous Fisher, the acidulous liaison man for Strapp, appeared at Bruxton's offices. After a brief conference with Old Man Bruxton himself, the following announcement was broadcast through the plant: ATTENTION! ATTENTION! URGENT! URGENT! ALL MALE PERSONNEL NAMED KRUGER REPORT TO CENTRAL. REPEAT. ALL MALE PERSONNEL NAMED KRUGER REPORT TO CENTRAL. URGENT! REPEAT. URGENT!

Forty-seven men named Kruger reported to Central and were sent home with strict instructions to stay at home until further notice. The plant police organized a hasty winnowing and, goaded by the irascible Fisher, checked the identification cards of all employees they could reach. Nobody named Kruger should remain in the plant, but it was impossible to comb out 2,500 men in three hours. Fisher burned and fumed like nitric acid.

By eleven-thirty, Bruxton Biotics was running a fever. Why send home all the Krugers? What did it have to do with the legendary John Strapp? What kind of man was Strapp? What did he look like? How did he act? He earned Cr. 10 millions a year. He owned 1 percent of the world. He was so close to God in the minds of the personnel that they expected angels and golden trumpets and a giant bearded creature of infinite wisdom and compassion.

At eleven-forty Strapp's personal bodyguard arrived—a security squad of ten men in plainclothes who checked doors and halls and cul-de-sacs with icy efficiency. They gave orders. This had to be removed. That had to be locked. Such and such had to be done. It was done. No one argued with John Strapp. The security squad took up positions and waited. Bruxton Biotics held its breath.

Noon struck, and a silver mote appeared in the sky. It approached with a high whine and landed with agonizing speed and precision before the main gate. The door of the ship snapped open. Two burly men stepped out alertly, their eyes busy. The chief of the security squad made a sign. Out of the ship came two secretaries, brunette and redheaded, striking, chic, efficient. After them came a thin, fortyish clerk in a baggy suit with papers stuffed in his side pockets, wearing horn-rimmed spectacles and a harassed air. After him came a magnificent creature, tall, majestic, clean-shaven but of infinite wisdom and compassion.

The burly men closed in on the beautiful man and escorted him up the steps and through the main door. Bruxton Biotics sighed happily. John Strapp was no disappointment. He was indeed God, and it was a pleasure to have 1 percent of yourself owned by him. The visitors marched down the main hall to Old Man Bruxton's office and entered. Bruxton had waited for them, poised majestically behind his desk. Now he leaped to his feet and ran forward. He grasped the magnificent man's hand fervently and exclaimed, "Mr. Strapp, sir, on behalf of my entire organization, I welcome you."

The clerk closed the door and said, "I'm Strapp." He nodded to his decoy, who sat down quietly in a corner. "Where's your data?"

Old Man Bruxton pointed faintly to his desk. Strapp sat down behind it, picked up the fat folders and began to read. A thin man. A harassed man. A fortyish man. Straight black hair. China-blue eyes. A good mouth. Good bones under the skin. One quality stood out—a complete lack of self-consciousness. But when he spoke there was a hysterical undercurrent in his voice that showed something violent and possessed deep inside him.

After two hours of breakneck reading and muttered comments to his secretaries, who made cryptic notes in Whitehead symbols, Strapp said, "I want to see the plant."

"Why?" Bruxton asked.

"To feel it," Strapp answered. "There's always the nuance involved in a Decision. It's the most important factor."

They left the office and the parade began: the security squad, the burly men, the secretaries, the clerk, the acidulous Fisher and the magnificent decoy. They marched everywhere. They saw everything. The "clerk" did most of the legwork for "Strapp." He spoke to workers, foremen, technicians, high, low and middle brass. He asked names, gossiped, introduced them to the great man, talked about their families, working conditions, ambitions. He explored, smelled and felt. After four exhausting hours they returned to Bruxton's office. The "clerk" closed the door. The decoy stepped aside.

"Well?" Bruxton asked. "Yes or No?"

"Wait," Strapp said.

He glanced through his secretaries' notes, absorbed them, closed his eyes and stood still and silent in the middle of the office like a man straining to hear a distant whisper.

"Yes," he Decided, and was Cr. 100,000 and 1 percent of the voting stock of Bruxton Biotics richer. In return, Bruxton had an 87 percent assurance that the Decision was correct. Strapp opened the door again, the parade reassembled and marched out of the plant. Personnel grabbed its last chance to take photos and touch the great man. The clerk helped promote public relations with eager affability. He asked names, introduced, and amused. The sound of voices and laughter increased as they reached the ship. Then the incredible happened.

"You!" the clerk cried suddenly. His voice screeched horribly. "You sonofabitch! You goddamned lousy murdering bastard! I've been waiting for this. I've waited ten years!" He pulled a flat gun from his inside pocket and shot a man through the forehead.

Time stood still. It took hours for the brains and blood to burst out of the back of the head and for the body to crumple. Then the Strapp staff leaped into action. They hurled the clerk into the ship. The secretaries followed, then the decoy. The two burly men leaped after them and slammed the door. The ship took off and disappeared with a fading whine. The ten men in plainclothes quietly drifted off and vanished. Only Fisher, the Strapp liason man, was left alongside the body in the center of the horrified crowd.

"Check his identification," Fisher snapped.

Someone pulled the dead man's wallet out and opened it.

"William F. Kruger, biomechanic."

"The damned fool!" Fisher said savagely. "We warned him. We warned all the Krugers. All right. Call the police."

That was John Strapp's sixth murder. It cost exactly Cr. 500,000 to fix. The other five had cost the same, and half the amount usually went to a man desperate enough to substitute for the killer and plead temporary insanity. The other half went to the heirs of the deceased. There were six of these substitutes languishing in various penitentiaries, serving from twenty to fifty years, their families Cr. 250,000 richer.

In their suite in the Alcor Splendide, the Strapp staff consulted gloomily.

"Six in six years," Aldous Fisher said bitterly. "We can't keep it quiet much longer. Sooner or later somebody's going to ask why John Strapp always hires crazy clerks."

"Then we fix him too," the redheaded secretary said. "Strapp can afford it."

"He can afford a murder a month," the magnificent decoy murmured.

"No." Fisher shook his head sharply. "You can fix so far and no further. You reach a saturation point. We've reached it now. What are we going to do?"

"What the hell's the matter with Strapp anyway?" one of the burly men inquired.

"Who knows?" Fisher exclaimed in exasperation. "He's got a Kruger fixation. He meets a man named Kruger—any man named Kruger. He screams. He curses. He murders. Don't ask me why. It's something buried in his past."

"Haven't you asked him?"

"How can I? It's like an epileptic fit. He never knows it happened."

"Take him to a psychoanalyst," the decoy suggested.

"Out of the question."

"Why?"

"You're new," Fisher said. "You don't understand."

"Make me understand."

"I'll make an analogy. Back in the nineteen hundreds, people played card games with fifty-two cards in the deck. Those were simple times. Today everything's more complex. We're playing with fifty-two hundred in the deck. Understand?"

"I'll go along with it."

"A mind can figure fifty-two cards. It can make decisions on that total. They had it easy in the nineteen hundreds. But no mind is big enough to figure fifty-two hundred—no mind except Strapp's."

"We've got computers."

"And they're perfect when only cards are involved. But when you have to figure fifty-two hundred cardplayers, too, their likes, dislikes, motives, inclinations, prospects, tendencies and so on—what Strapp calls the nuances—then Strapp can do what a machine can't do. He's unique, and we might destroy his uniqueness with psychoanalysis."

"Why?"

"Because it's an unconscious process in Strapp," Fisher explained irritably. "He doesn't know how he does it. If he did he'd be one hundred percent right instead of eighty-seven percent. It's an unconscious process, and for all we know it may be linked up with the same abnormality that makes him murder Krugers. If we get rid of one, we may destroy the other. We can't take the chance."

"Then what do we do?"

"Protect our property," Fisher said, looking around ominously. "Never forget that for a minute. We've put in too much work on Strapp to let it be destroyed. We protect our property!"

"I think he needs a friend," the brunette said.

"Why?"

"We could find out what's bothering him without destroying anything. People talk to their friends. Strapp might talk."

"We're his friends."

"No, we're not. We're his associates."

"Has he talked with you?"

"No."

"You?" Fisher shot at the redhead.

She shook her head.

"He's looking for something he never finds."

"What?"

"A woman, I think. A special kind of woman."

"A woman named Kruger?"

"I don't know."

"Damn it, it doesn't make sense." Fisher thought a moment. "All right. We'll have to hire him a friend, and we'll have to ease off the schedule to give the friend a chance to make Strapp talk. From now on we cut the program to one Decision a week."

"My God!" the brunette exclaimed. "That's cutting five million a year."

"It's got to be done," Fisher said grimly. "It's cut now or take a total loss later. We're rich enough to stand it."

"What are you going to do for a friend?" the decoy asked.

"I said we'd hire one. We'll hire the best. Get Terra on the TT. Tell them to locate Frank Alceste and put him through urgent."

"Frankie!" the redhead squealed. "I swoon."

"Ooh! Frankie!" The brunette fanned herself.

"You mean Fatal Frank Alceste? The heavyweight champ?" the burly man asked in awe. "I saw him fight Lonzo Jordan. Oh, man!"

"He's an actor now," the decoy explained. "I worked with him once. He sings. He dances. He—"

"And he's twice as fatal," Fisher interrupted. "We'll hire him. Make out a contract. He'll be Strapp's friend. As soon as Strapp meets him, he'll—"

"Meets who?" Strapp appeared in the doorway of his bedroom, yawning, blinking in the light. He always slept deeply after his attacks. "Who am I going to meet?" He looked around, thin, graceful, but harassed and indubitably possessed.

"A man named Frank Alceste," Fisher said. "He badgered us for an introduction, and we can't hold him off any longer."

"Frank Alceste?" Strapp murmured. "Never heard of him."

Strapp could make Decisions; Alceste could make friends. He was a powerful man in his middle thirties, sandy-haired, freckle-faced, with a broken nose and deep-set grey eyes. His voice was high and soft. He moved with the athlete's lazy poise that is almost feminine. He charmed you without knowing how he did it, or even wanting to do it. He charmed Strapp, but Strapp also charmed him. They became friends.

"No, it really is friends," Alceste told Fisher when he returned the check that had been paid him. "I don't need the money, and old Johnny needs me. Forget you hired me original-like. Tear up the contract. I'll try to straighten Johnny out on my own."

Alceste turned to leave the suite in the Rigel Splendide and passed the great-eyed secretaries. "If I wasn't so busy, ladies," he murmured, "I'd sure like to chase you a little."

"Chase me, Frankie," the brunette blurted.

The redhead looked caught.

And as Strapp Associates zigzagged in slow tempo from city to city and planet to planet, making the one Decision a week, Alceste and Strapp enjoyed themselves while the magnificent decoy gave interviews and posed for pictures. There were interruptions when Frankie had to return to Terra to make a picture, but in between they golfed, tennised, brubaged, bet on horses, dogs and dowlens, and went to fights and routs. They hit the night spots and Alceste came back with a curious report.

"Me, I don't know how close you folks been watching Johnny," he told Fisher, "but if you think he's been sleeping every night, safe in his little trundle, you better switch notions."

"How's that?" Fisher asked in surprise.

"Old Johnny, he's been sneaking out nights all along when you folks thought he was getting his brain rest."

"How do you know?"

"By his reputation," Alceste told him sadly. "They know him everywhere. They know old Johnny in every bistro from here to Orion. And they know him the worst way."

"By name?"

"By nickname. Wasteland, they call him."

"Wasteland!"

"Uh-huh. Mr. Devastation. He runs through women like a prairie fire. You don't know this?"

Fisher shook his head.

"Must pay off out of his personal pocket," Alceste mused and departed.

There was a terrifying quality to the possessed way that Strapp ran through women. He would enter a club with Alceste, take a table, sit down and drink. Then he would stand up and coolly survey the room, table by table, woman by woman. Upon occasion men would become angered and offer to fight. Strapp disposed of them coldly and viciously, in a manner that excited Alceste's professional admiration. Frankie never fought himself. No professional ever touches an amateur. But he tried to keep the peace, and failing that, at least kept the ring.

After the survey of the women guests, Strapp would sit down and wait for the show, relaxed, chatting, laughing. When the girls appeared, his grim possession would take over again and he would examine the line carefully and dispassionately. Very rarely he would discover a girl that interested him; always the identical type—a girl with jet hair, inky eyes, and clear, silken skin. Then the trouble began.

If it was an entertainer, Strapp went backstage after the show. He bribed, fought, blustered and forced his way into her dressing room. He would confront the astonished girl, examine her in silence, then ask her to speak. He would listen to her voice, then close in like a tiger and make a violent and unexpected pass. Sometimes there would be shrieks, sometimes a spirited defense, sometimes compliance. At no time was Strapp satisfied. He would abandon the girl abruptly, pay off all complaints and damages like a gentleman, and leave to repeat the performance in club after club until curfew.

If it was one of the guests, Strapp immediately cut in, disposed of her escort, or if that was impossible, followed the girl home and there repeated the dressing-room attack. Again he would abandon the girl, pay like a gentleman and leave to continue his possessed search.

"Me, I been around, but I'm scared by it," Alceste told Fisher. "I never saw such a hasty man. He could have most any woman agreeable if he'd slow down a little. But he can't. He's driven."

"By what?"

"I don't know. It's like he's working against time."

After Strapp and Alceste became intimate, Strapp permitted him to come along on a daytime quest that was even stranger. As Strapp Associates continued its round through the planets and industries, Strapp visited the Bureau of Vital Statistics in each city. There he bribed the chief clerk and presented a slip of paper. On it was written:

Height	5'6"
Weight	110
Hair	Black
Eyes	Black
Bust	34
Waist	26
Hips	36
Size	12

"I want the name and address of every girl over twenty-one who fits this description," Strapp would say. "I'll pay ten credits a name."

Twenty-four hours later would come the list, and off Strapp would chase on a possessed search, examining, talking, listening, sometimes making the terrifying pass, always paying off like a gentleman. The procession of tall, jet-haired, inky-eyed, busty girls made Alceste dizzy.

"He's got an idee fix," Alceste told Fisher in the Cygnus Splendide, "and I got it figured this much. He's looking for a special particular girl and nobody comes up to specifications."

"A girl named Kruger?"

"I don't know if the Kruger business comes into it."

"Is he hard to please?"

"Well, I'll tell you. Some of those girls—me, I'd call them sensational. But he don't pay any mind to them. Just looks and moves on. Others—dogs, practically; he jumps like old Wasteland."

"What is it?"

"I think it's a kind of test. Something to make the girls react hard and natural. It ain't that kind of passion with old Wasteland. It's a cold-blooded trick so he can watch 'em in action."

"But what's he looking for?"

"I don't know yet," Alceste said, "but I'm going to find out. I got a little trick figured. It's taking a chance, but Johnny's worth it."

It happened in the arena where Strapp and Alceste went to watch a pair of gorillas tear each other to pieces inside a glass cage. It was a bloody affair, and both men agreed that gorill-fighting was no more civilized than cockfighting and left in disgust. Outside, in the empty concrete corridor, a shriveled man loitered. When Alceste signaled to him, he ran up to them like an autograph hound.

"Frankie!" the shriveled man shouted. "Good old Frankie! Don't you remember me?"

Alceste stared.

"I'm Blooper Davis. We was raised together in the old precinct. Don't you remember Blooper Davis?"

"Blooper!" Alceste's face lit up. "Sure enough. But it was Blooper Davidoff then."

"Sure." The shriveled man laughed. "And it was Frankie Kruger then."

"Kruger!" Strapp cried in a thin, screeching voice.

"That's right," Frankie said. "Kruger. I changed my name when I went into the fight game." He motioned sharply to the shriveled man, who backed against the corridor wall and slid away.

"You sonofabitch!" Strapp cried. His face was white and twitched hideously. "You goddamned lousy murdering bastard! I've been waiting for this. I've waited ten years."

He whipped a flat gun from his inside pocket and fired. Alceste sidestepped barely in time and the slug ricocheted down the corridor with a high whine. Strapp fired again, and the flame seared Alceste's cheek. He closed in, caught Strapp's wrist and paralyzed it with his powerful grip. He pointed the gun away and clinched. Strapp's breath was hissing. His eyes rolled. Overhead sounded the wild roars of the crowd.

"All right, I'm Kruger," Alceste grunted. "Kruger's the name, Mr. Strapp. So what? What are you going to do about it?"

"Sonofabitch!" Strapp screamed, struggling like one of the gorillas. "Killer! Murderer! I'll rip your guts out!"

"Why me? Why Kruger?" Exerting all his strength, Alceste dragged Strapp to a niche and slammed him into it. He caged him with his huge frame. "What did I ever do to you ten years ago?"

He got the story in hysterical animal outbursts before Strapp fainted.

After he put Strapp to bed, Alceste went out into the lush living room of the suite in the Indi Splendide and explained to the staff.

"Old Johnny was in love with a girl named Sima Morgan," he began. "She was in love with him. It was big romantic stuff. They were going to be married. Then Sima Morgan got killed by a guy named Kruger."

"Kruger! So that's the connection. How?"

"This Kruger was a drunken no-good. Society. He had a bad driving record. They took his license away from him, but that didn't make any difference to Kruger's kind of money. He bribed a dealer and bought a hot-rod jet without a license. One day he buzzed a school for the hell of it. He smashed the roof in and killed thirteen children and their teacher . . . . This was on Terra in Berlin.

"They never got Kruger. He started planet-hopping and he's still on the lam. The family sends him money. The police can't find him. Strapp's looking for him because the school-teacher was his girl, Sima Morgan."

There was a pause, then Fisher asked, "How long ago was this?"

"Near as I can figure, ten years eight months."

Fisher calculated intently. "And ten years three months ago, Strapp first showed he could make decisions. The Big Decisions. Up to then he was nobody. Then came the tragedy, and with it the hysteria and the ability. Don't tell me one didn't produce the other."

"Nobody's telling you anything."

"So he kills Kruger over and over again," Fisher said coldly. "Right. Revenge fixation. But what about the girls and the Wasteland business?"

Alceste smiled sadly. "You ever hear the expression 'One girl in a million'?"

"Who hasn't?"

"If your girl was one in a million, that means there ought to be nine more like her in a city of ten million, yes?"

The Strapp staff nodded, wondering.

"Old Johnny's working on that idea. He thinks he can find Sima Morgan's duplicate."

"How?"

"He's worked it out arithmetic-wise. He's thinking like so: There's one chance in sixty-four billion of fingerprints matching. But today there's seventeen hundred billion people. That means there can be twenty-six with one matching print, and maybe more."

"Not necessarily."

"Sure, not necessarily, but there's the chance and that's all old Johnny wants. He figures if there's twenty-six chances of one print matching, there's an outside chance of one person matching. He thinks he can find Sima Morgan's duplicate if he just keeps on looking hard enough."

"That's outlandish!"

"I didn't say it wasn't, but it's the only thing that keeps him going. It's a kind of life preserver made out of numbers. It keeps his head above water—the crazy notion that sooner or later he can pick up where death left him off ten years ago."

"Ridiculous!" Fisher snapped.

"Not to Johnny. He's still in love."

"Impossible."

"I wish you could feel it like I feel it," Alceste answered. "He's looking . . . looking. He meets girl after girl. He hopes. He talks. He makes the pass. If it's Sima's duplicate, he knows she'll respond just the way he remembers Sima responding ten years ago. 'Are you Sima?' he asks himself. 'No,' he says and moves on. It hurts, thinking about a lost guy like that. We ought to do something for him."

"No," Fisher said.

"We ought to help him find his duplicate. We ought to coax him into believing some girl's the duplicate. We ought to make him fall in love again."

"No," Fisher repeated emphatically.

"Why no?"

"Because the moment Strapp finds his girl, he heals himself. He stops being the great John Strapp, the Decider. He turns back into a nobody—a man in love."

"What's he care about being great? He wants to be happy."

"Everybody wants to be happy," Fisher snarled. "Nobody is. Strapp's no worse off than any other man, but he's a lot richer. We maintain the *status quo*."

"Don't you mean *you're* a lot richer?"

"We maintain the *status quo*," Fisher repeated. He eyed Alceste coldly. "I think we'd better terminate the contract. We have no further use for your services."

"Mister, we terminated when I handed back the check. You're talking to Johnny's friend now."

"I'm sorry, Mr. Alceste, but Strapp won't have much time for his friends from now on. I'll let you know when he'll be free next year."

"You'll never pull it off. I'll see Johnny when and where I please."

"Do you want him for a friend?" Fisher smiled unpleasantly. "Then you'll see him when and where I please. Either you see him on those terms or Strapp sees the contract we gave you. I still have it in the files, Mr. Alceste. I did not tear it up. I never part with anything. How long do you imagine Strapp will believe in your friendship after he sees the contract you signed?"

Alceste clenched his fists. Fisher held his ground. For a moment they glared at each other, then Frankie turned away.

"Poor Johnny," he muttered. "It's like a man being run by his tapeworm. I'll say so long to him. Let me know when you're ready for me to see him again."

He went into the bedroom, where Strapp was just awakening from his attack without the faintest memory, as usual. Alceste sat down on the edge of the bed.

"Hey, old Johnny." He grinned.

"Hey, Frankie." Strapp smiled.

They punched each other solemnly, which is the only way that men friends can embrace and kiss.

"What happened after that gorilla fight?" Strapp asked. "I got fuzzy."

"Man, you got plastered. I never saw a guy take on such a load." Alceste punched Strapp again. "Listen, old Johnny. I got to get back to work. I got a three-picture-a-year contract, and they're howling."

"Why, you took a month off six planets back," Strapp said in disappointment. "I thought you caught up."

"Nope. I'll be pulling out today, Johnny. Be seeing you real soon."

"Listen," Strapp said. "To hell with the pictures. Be my partner. I'll tell Fisher to draw up an agreement." He blew his nose. "This is the first time I've had laughs in—in a long time."

"Maybe later, Johnny. Right now I'm stuck with a contract. Soon as I can get back, I'll come a-running. Cheers."

"Cheers," Strapp said wistfully.

Outside the bedroom, Fisher was waiting like a watchdog. Alceste looked at him with disgust.

"One thing you learn in the fight game," he said slowly. "It's never won till the last round. I give you this one, but it isn't the last."

As he left, Alceste said, half to himself, half aloud, "I want him to be happy. I want every man to be happy. Seems like every man could be happy if we'd all just lend a hand."

Which is why Frankie Alceste couldn't help making friends.

So the Strapp staff settled back into the same old watchful vigilance of the murdering years, and stepped up Strapp's Decision appointments to two a week. They knew why Strapp had to be watched. They knew why the Krugers had to be protected. But that was the only difference. Their man was miserable, hysteric, almost psychotic; it made no difference. That was a fair price to pay for 1 percent of the world.

But Frankie Alceste kept his own counsel, and visited the Deneb laboratories of Bruxton Biotics. There he consulted with one E. T. A. Goland, the research genuis who had discovered that novel technique for molding life which first brought Strapp to Bruxton, and was indirectly responsible for his friendship with Alceste. Ernst Theodor Amadeus Goland was short, fat, asthmatic and enthusiastic.

"But yes, yes," he sputtered when the layman had finally made himself clear to the scientist. "Yes, indeed! A most ingenious notion. Why it never occurred to me, I cannot think. It could be accomplished without any difficulty whatsoever." He considered. "Except money," he added.

"You could duplicate the girl that died ten years ago?" Alceste asked.

"Without any difficulty, except money." Goland nodded emphatically.

"She'd look the same? Act the same? Be the same?"

"Up to ninety-five percent, plus or minus point nine seven five."

"Would that make any difference? I mean, ninety-five percent of a person as against one hundred percent."

"Ach! No. It is a most remarkable individual who is aware of more than eighty percent of the total characteristics of another person. Above ninety percent is unheard of."

"How would you go about it?"

"Ach? So. Empirically we have two sources. One: complete psychological pattern of the subject in the Centaurus Master Files. They will TT a transcript upon application and payment of one hundred credits through formal channels. I will apply."

"And I'll pay. Two?"

"Two: the embalmment process of modern times, which— She is buried, yes?"

"Yes."

"Which is ninety-eight percent perfect. From remains and psychological pattern we re-clone body and psyche by the equation sigma equals the square root of minus two over— We do it without any difficulty, except money."

"Me, I've got the money," Frankie Alceste said. "You do the rest."

For the sake of his friend, Alceste paid Cr. 100 and expedited the formal application to the Master Files on Centaurus for the transcript of the complete psychological pattern of Sima Morgan, deceased. After it arrived, Alceste returned to Terra and a city called Berlin, where he blackmailed a gimpster named Augenblick into turning grave robber. Augenblick visited the *Staats-Gottesacker* and removed the porcelain coffin from under the marble headstone that read SIMA MORGAN. It contained what appeared to be a black-haired, silken-skinned girl in deep sleep. By devious routes, Alceste got the porcelain coffin through four customs barriers to Deneb.

One aspect of the trip of which Alceste was not aware, but which bewildered various police organizations, was the series of catastrophes that pursued him and never quite caught up. There was the jetliner explosion that destroyed the ship and an acre of docks half an hour after passengers and freight were discharged. There was a hotel holocaust ten minutes after Alceste checked out. There was the shuttle disaster that extinguished the pneumatic train for which Alceste had unexpectedly canceled passage. Despite all this he was able to present the coffin to biochemist Goland.

"Ach!" said Ernst Theodor Amadeus. "A beautiful creature. She is worth re-creating. The rest now is simple, except money."

For the sake of his friend, Alceste arranged a leave of absence for Goland, bought him a laboratory and financed an incredibly expensive series of experiments. For the sake of his friend, Alceste poured forth money and patience until at last, eight months later, there emerged from the opaque maturation chamber a black-haired, inky-eyed, silken-skinned creature with long legs and a high bust. She answered to the name of Sima Morgan.

"I heard the jet coming down toward the school," Sima said, unaware that she was speaking eleven years later. "Then I heard a crash. What happened?"

Alceste was jolted. Up to this moment she had been an objective . . . a goal . . . unreal, unalive. This was a living woman. There was a curious hesitation in her speech, almost a lisp. Her head had an engaging tilt when she spoke. She arose from the edge of the table, and she was not fluid or graceful as Alceste had expected she would be. She moved boyishly.

"I'm Frank Alceste," he said quietly. He took her shoulders. "I want you to look at me and make up your mind whether you can trust me."

Their eyes locked in a steady gaze. Sima examined him gravely. Again Alceste was jolted and moved. His hands began to tremble and he released the girl's shoulders in panic.

"Yes," Sima said. "I can trust you."

"No matter what I say, you must trust me. No matter what I tell you to do, you must trust me and do it."

"Why?"

"For the sake of Johnny Strapp."

Her eyes widened. "Something's happened to him," she said quickly. "What is it?"

"Not to him, Sima. To you. Be patient, honey. I'll explain. I had it in my mind to explain now, but I can't. I—I'd best wait until tomorrow."

They put her to bed and Alceste went out for a wrestling match with himself. The Deneb nights are soft and black as velvet, thick and sweet with romance—or so it seemed to Frankie Alceste that night.

"You can't be falling in love with her," he muttered. "It's crazy."

And later, "You saw hundreds like her when Johnny was hunting. Why didn't you fall for one of them?"

And last of all, "What are you going to do?"

He did the only thing an honorable man can do in a situation like that, and tried to turn his desire into friendship. He came into Sima's room the next morning, wearing tattered old jeans, needing a shave, with his hair standing on end. He hoisted himself up on the foot of her bed, and while she ate the first of the careful meals Goland had prescribed, Frankie chewed on a cigarette and explained to her. When she wept, he did not take her in his arms to console her, but thumped her on the back like a brother.

He ordered a dress for her. He had ordered the wrong size, and when she showed herself to him in it, she looked so adorable that he wanted to kiss her. Instead he punched her, very gently and very solemnly, and took her out to buy a wardrobe. When she showed herself to him in proper clothes, she looked so enchanting that he had to punch her again. Then they went to a ticket office and booked immediate passage for Ross-Alpha III.

Alceste had intended delaying a few days to rest the girl, but he was compelled to rush for fear of himself. It was this alone that saved both from the explosion that destroyed the private home and private laboratory of biochemist Goland, and destroyed the biochemist too. Alceste never knew this. He was already on board ship with Sima, frantically fighting temptation.

One of the things that everybody knows about space travel but never mentions is its aphrodisiac quality. Like the ancient days when travelers crossed oceans on ships, the passengers are isolated in their own tiny world for a week. They're cut off from reality. A magic mood of freedom from ties and responsibilities pervades the jetliner. Everyone has a fling. There are thousands of jet romances every week—quick, passionate affairs that are enjoyed in complete safety and ended on landing day.

In this atmosphere, Frankie Alceste maintained a rigid self-control. He was not aided by the fact that he was a celebrity with a tremendous animal magnetism. While a dozen handsome women threw themselves at him, he persevered in the role of big brother and thumped and punched Sima until she protested.

"I know you're a wonderful friend to Johnny and me," she said on the last night out. "But you are exhausting, Frankie. I'm covered with bruises."

"Yeah. I know. It's habit. Some people, like Johnny, they think with their brains. Me, I think with my fists."

They were standing before the starboard crystal, bathed in the soft light of the approaching Ross-Alpha, and there is nothing more damnably romantic than the velvet of space illuminated by the white-violet of a distant sun. Sima tilted her head and looked at him.

"I was talking to some of the passengers," she said. "You're famous, aren't you?"

"More notorious-like."

"There's so much to catch up on. But I must catch up on you first."

"Me?"

Sima nodded. "It's all been so sudden. I've been bewildered—and so excited that I haven't had a chance to thank you, Frankie. I do thank you. I'm beholden to you forever."

She put her arms around his neck and kissed him with parted lips. Alceste began to shake.

"No," he thought. "No. She doesn't know what she's doing. She's so crazy happy at the idea of being with Johnny again that she doesn't realize . . ."

He reached behind him until he felt the icy surface of the crystal, which passengers are strictly enjoined from touching. Before he could give way, he deliberately pressed the backs of his hands against the subzero surface. The pain made him start. Sima released him in surprise and when he pulled his hands away, he left six square inches of skin and blood behind.

So he landed on Ross-Alpha III with one girl in good condition and two hands in bad shape and he was met by the acid-faced Aldous Fisher, accompanied by an official who requested Mr. Alceste to step into an office for a very serious private talk.

"It has been brought to our attention by Mr. Fisher," the official said, "that you are attempting to bring in a young woman of illegal status."

"How would Mr. Fisher know?" Alceste asked.

"You fool!" Fisher spat. "Did you think I would let it go at that? You were followed. Every minute."

"Mr. Fisher informs us," the official continued austerely, "that the woman with you is traveling under an assumed name. Her papers are fraudulent."

"How fraudulent?" Alceste said. "She's Sima Morgan. Her papers say she's Sima Morgan."

"Sima Morgan died eleven years ago," Fisher answered. "The woman with you can't be Sima Morgan."

"And unless the question of her true identity is cleared up," the official said, "she will not be permitted entry."

"I'll have the documentation on Sima Morgan's death here within the week," Fisher added triumphantly.

Alceste looked at Fisher and shook his head wearily. "You don't know it, but you're making it easy for me," he said. "The one thing in the world I'd like to do is take her out of here and never let Johnny see her. I'm so crazy to keep her for myself that—" He stopped himself and touched the bandages on his hands. "Withdraw your charge, Fisher."

"No," Fisher snapped.

"You can't keep 'em apart. Not this way. Suppose she's interned? Who's the first man I subpoena to establish her identity? John Strapp. Who's the first man I call to come and see her? John Strapp. D'you think you could stop him?"

"That contract," Fisher began. "I'll—"

"To hell with the contract. Show it to him. He wants his girl, not me. Withdraw your charge, Fisher. And stop fighting. You've lost your meal ticket."

Fisher glared malevolently, then swallowed. "I withdraw the charge," he growled. Then he looked at Alceste with blood in his eyes. "It isn't the last round yet," he said and stamped out of the office.

Fisher was prepared. At a distance of light-years he might be too late with too little. Here on Ross-Alpha III he was protecting his property. He had all the power and money of John Strapp to call on. The floater that Frankie Alceste and Sima took from the spaceport was piloted by a Fisher aide who unlatched the cabin door and performed steep banks to tumble his fares out into the air. Alceste smashed the glass partition and hooked a meaty arm around the driver's throat until he righted the floater and brought them safely to earth. Alceste was pleased to note that Sima did not fuss more than was necessary.

On the road level they were picked up by one of a hundred cars that had been pacing the floater from below. At the first shot, Alceste clubbed Sima into a doorway and followed her at the expense of a burst shoulder, which he bound hastily with strips of Sima's lingerie. Her dark eyes were enormous, but she made no complaint. Alceste complimented her with mighty thumps and took her up to the roof and down into the adjoining building, where he broke into an apartment and telephoned for an ambulance.

When the ambulance arrived, Alceste and Sima descended to the street, where they were met by uniformed policemen who had official instructions to pick up a couple answering to their description. "Wanted for floater robbery with assault. Dangerous. Shoot to kill." The police Alceste disposed of, and also the ambulance driver and intern. He and Sima departed in the ambulance, Alceste driving like a fury, Sima operating the siren like a banshee.

They abandoned the ambulance in the downtown shopping district, entered a department store, and emerged forty minutes later as a young valet in uniform pushing an old man in a wheelchair. Outside the difficulty of the bust, Sima was boyish enough to pass as a valet. Frankie was weak enough from assorted injuries to simulate the old man.

They checked into the Ross Splendide, where Alceste barricaded Sima in a suite, had his shoulder attended to and bought a gun. Then he went looking for John Strapp. He found him in the Bureau of Vital Statistics, bribing the chief clerk and presenting him with a slip of paper that gave the same description of the long-lost love.

"Hey, old Johnny," Alceste said.

"Hey, Frankie!" Strapp cried in delight.

They punched each other affectionately. With a happy grin, Alceste watched Strapp explain and offer further bribes to the chief clerk for the names and addresses of all girls over twenty-one who fitted the description on the slip of paper. As they left, Alceste said, "I met a girl who might fit that, old Johnny."

That cold look came into Strapp's eyes. "Oh?" he said.

"She's got a kind of half lisp."

Strapp looked at Alceste strangely.

"And a funny way of tilting her head when she talks."

Strapp clutched Alceste's arm.

"Only trouble is, she isn't girlie-girlie like most. More like a fella. You know what I mean? Spunky-like."

"Show her to me, Frankie," Strapp said in a low voice.

They hopped a floater and were taxied to the Ross Spen-
dide roof. They took the elevator down to the twentieth floor
and walked to suite 20-M. Alceste code-knocked on the door.
A girl's voice called, "Come in." Alceste shook Strapp's hand
and said, "Cheers, Johnny." He unlocked the door, then
walked down the hall to lean against the balcony balustrade.
He drew his gun just in case Fisher might get around to
last-ditch interruptions. Looking out across the glittering city,
he reflected that every man could be happy if everybody
would just lend a hand; but sometimes that hand was expensive.

John Strapp walked into the suite. He shut the door, turned
and examined the jet-haired inky-eyed girl, coldly, intently.
She stared at him in amazement. Strapp stepped closer,
walked around her, faced her again.

"Say something," he said.

"You're not John Strapp?" she faltered.

"Yes."

"No!" she exclaimed. "No! My Johnny's young. My Johnny
is—"

Strapp closed in like a tiger. His hands and lips savaged her
while his eyes watched coldly and intently. The girl screamed
and struggled, terrified by those strange eyes that were alien,
by the harsh hands that were alien, by the alien compulsions of
the creature who was once her Johnny Strapp but was now
aching years of change apart from her.

"You're someone else!" she cried. "You're not Johnny
Strapp. You're another man."

And Strapp, not so much eleven years older as eleven years
other than the man whose memory he was fighting to fulfill,
asked himself, "Are you my Sima? Are you my love—my lost,
dead love?" And the change within him answered, "No, this
isn't Sima. This isn't your love yet. Move on, Johnny. Move on
and search. You'll find her someday—the girl you lost."

He paid like a gentleman and departed.

From the balcony, Alceste saw him leave. He was so

astonished that he could not call to him. He went back to the suite and found Sima standing there, stunned, staring at a sheaf of money on a table. He realized what had happened at once. When Sima saw Alceste, she began to cry—not like a girl, but boyishly, with her fists clenched and her face screwed up.

"Frankie," she wept. "My God! Frankie!" She held out her arms to him in desperation. She was lost in a world that had passed her by.

He took a step, then hesitated. He made a last attempt to quench the love within him for this creature, searching for a way to bring her and Strapp together. Then he lost all control and took her in his arms.

"She doesn't know what she's doing," he thought. "She's so scared of being lost. She's not mine. Not yet. Maybe never."

And then, "Fisher's won, and I've lost."

And last of all, "We only remember the past; we never know it when we meet it. The mind goes back, but time goes on, and farewells should be forever."

Oddy and Id

Introduction

WHEN I was a mystery writer I went mad digging up gimmicks for my scripts. A gimmick is any odd fact, not very well known to the public (but of course known by the detective) which can be used as a vital clue. Here's a simple example: did you know that the United States minted no silver dollars between 1910 and 1920? If you come across one dated 1915 it has to be a counterfeit, and that's a gimmick.

I usually needed three per script; one for an opening hook, a second for the big twist at the halfway mark, and a third for "The Morris" which would wrap everything up. I'd better give the derivation of the expression, which was used in the business to describe the final explanation of the mystery.

There was a speakeasy in Philadelphia back in the twenties which preyed on innocent transients. Stranger would come in for lunch, order a sandwich and a couple of beers, and when the waiter presented the bill it was like for twenty dollars. The customer would scream and demand an explanation of the outrage. The waiter would answer, "Yes, sir. Morris will explain." When Morris came to the table, he turned out to be the bouncer; six foot six, two hundred and fifty pounds and ugly mean. That was all the explanation the victim required.

As I was saying, my life was a constant search for fresh

gimmicks, and I haunted the reading rooms of the main library at 42nd and Fifty Avenue. I'd speed-read through four or five books an hour and count myself lucky if I averaged one solid gimmick per book. Eventually I got onto psychiatry and discovered that the field was rich in behavior gimmicks, which were far more interesting than silver dollars with the wrong date.

It was as a result of this purely pragmatic research that I became hooked on psychiatry and started writing about compulsives and their corrosive conflicts. I also became a worshiper of Freud, and I can't tell you how crushed I was when his correspondence with Jung was published and I realized that my god was only human after all. The most laughable aspect of my deep belief in psychiatry is the fact that I've never been in analysis.

Well, "Oddy and Id" was the first science fiction story I wrote after my conversion (I'd already written acres of scripts using psychiatric material) and it led to my first meeting with the great John W. Campbell, Jr., editor of the trailblazing *Astounding Science Fiction*. I'd submitted the story by mail and Campbell phoned me a few weeks later, said he liked the story and would buy it, but wanted a few changes made. Would I come to his office and discuss it? I was delighted to accept. A chance to meet the Great Man! Like wow!

It was a harrowing encounter. I won't go into the details here (you'll find them in "My Affair with Science Fiction, p. 220) but I can confess my guilt. All my experience in the entertainment business had taught me that it's folly to go backstage after you've been enchanted by a show. Don't meet the author, the performers, the director, the designer, the producer . . . anybody who's created the brilliance that grabbed you. You're sure to be disillusioned. Never confuse the artist with his work.

Well, I should have known better, but I went through the stage door of *Astounding Science Fiction,* met its director, and it was a disaster. As a result, I listen to my writing colleagues' worship of John Campbell, and I feel guilty as hell because I can't join in. Understand that I speak as a writer, not a reader. As a reader, I, too, worship him. I also feel guilty because I believe the *antipatico* between us was entirely my fault. I think I was contemptuous because we were reflections of each other; both arrogant, know-it-all, and unyielding. End of *Apologia Pro Vita Sua.*

Anyway, the crux of that story conference was Campbell's pronouncement that the entire field of psychiatry had been exploded by L. Ron Hubbard's discovery of a new, earthshaking science called "dianetics," and he wanted all references to Freud, and His Merry Men (including the title) to be removed. Understand, please; he didn't ask me to make a pitch for dianetics; he just wanted me to get the antiquated vocabulary of Freud out of Hubbard's way.

I thought this was absurd, but I agreed anyway. The changes would not affect the point of the story, so it was easy to go along with the Great Man. And right here I should mention something about my kind of writer that isn't easily understood: I see a story as a whole, I have omnivision. Example: A director will say to me, "Hey, Alf, we need time. Can't we cut that scene with the locksmith?" I know instantly that the locksmith scene controls two scenes that precede it and three that follow, that four of the five can be easily patched, but the fifth is a holdout which will require an entirely new approach. I don't have to puzzle it out; I know it instantly. Lightningsville.

So I knew instantly that the changes Campbell asked for weren't important to the story and could easily be sloughed. I agreed and got the hell out of there. Naturally, the first time the story was reprinted, I went back to the original version. I don't know whether Campbell ever knew, but my guess is that he did. He was very shrewd and aware, when he wasn't riding his latest scientific hobbyhorse.

"Oddy and Id" was generated by an argument I had with a close friend who was extremely intolerant of what he called "sin." He could neither understand nor forgive intelligent people who did wrong. I argued that people aren't always in conscious control of their actions; very often the unconscious takes over.

"There are times," I said, "when all the good sense in a man shouts a warning that what he's about to do will only create grief, but he goes ahead and does it anyway. Something deep down inside is driving him. Hasn't that happened to you?"

"Never."

"Well, can you see it happening to other people?"

"Not intelligent people. No."

"Intelligence has nothing to do with it. Can't you concede that a nice guy who only wants to do right can be compelled by his within to do wrong?"

"No."

A stubborn sonofabitch, but the impasse generated the story through a very easy extrapolation. A writer is always opportunistic; he lets nothing go to waste. This makes people think we're insincere. We're not. We're just minding the store.

This is the story of a monster.

They named him Odysseus Gaul in honor of Papa's favorite hero, and over Mama's desperate objections; but he was known as Oddy from the age of one.

The first year of life is an egotistic craving for warmth and security. Oddy was not likely to have much of that when he was born, for Papa's real estate business was bankrupt, and Mama was thinking of divorce. But an unexpected decision by United Radiation to build a plant in the town made Papa wealthy, and Mama fell in love with him all over again. So Oddy had warmth and security.

The second year of life is a timid exploration. Oddy crawled and explored. When he reached for the crimson coils inside the nonobjective fireplace, an unexpected short circuit saved him from a burn. When he fell out the third-floor window, it was into the grass filled hopper of the Mechano-Gardener. When he teased the Phoebus Cat, it slipped as it snapped at his face, and the brilliant fangs clicked harmlessly over his ear.

"Animals love Oddy," Mama said. "They only pretend to bite."

Oddy wanted to be loved, so everybody loved Oddy. He was petted, pampered and spoiled through preschool age. Shopkeepers presented him with largess, and acquaintances showered him with gifts. Of sodas, candy, tarts, chrystons, bobble-trucks, freezies, and various other comestibles, Oddy consumed enough for an entire kindergarten. He was never sick.

"Takes after his father," Papa said. "Good stock."

Family legends grew about Oddy's luck. . . . How a perfect stranger mistook him for his own child just as Oddy was about to amble into the Electronic Circus, and delayed him long enough to save him from the disastrous explosion of '98. . . . How a forgotten library book rescued him from the Rocket Crash of '99. . . . How a multitude of odd incidents saved him from a multitude of assorted catastrophes. No one realized he was a monster . . . yet.

At eighteen, he was a nice-looking boy with seal-brown hair, warm brown eyes, and a wide grin that showed even white teeth. He was strong, healthy, intelligent. He was completely uninhibited in his quiet, relaxed way. He had charm. He was happy. So far, his monstrous evil had only affected the little Town Unit where he was born and raised.

He came to Harvard from a Progressive School, so when one of his many new friends popped into the dormitory room and said: "Hey Oddy, come down to the Quad and kick a ball around." Oddy answered: "I don't know how, Ben."

"Don't know how?" Ben tucked the football under his arm and dragged Oddy with him. "Where you been, laddie?"

"They didn't think much of football back home," Oddy grinned. "Said it was old-fashioned. We were strictly Huxley-Hob."

"Huxley-Hob! That's for eggheads," Ben said. "Football is still the big game. You want to be famous? You got to be on that gridiron on TV every Saturday."

"So I've noticed, Ben. Show me."

Ben showed Oddy, carefully and with patience. Oddy took the lesson seriously and industriously. His third punt was caught by a freakish gust of wind, traveled seventy yards through the air, and burst through the third-floor window of Proctor Charley (Gravy-Train) Stuart. Stuart took one look out the window and had Oddy down to Soldier Stadium in half an hour. Three Saturdays later, the headlines read: Oddy Gaul 57—Army 0.

"Snell and Rumination!" Coach Hig Clayton swore. "How does he do it? There's nothing sensational about that kid. He's just average. But when he runs, they fall down chasing him. When he kicks, they fumble. When they fumble, he recovers."

"He's a negative player," Gravy-Train answered. "He lets you make the mistakes, and then he cashes in."

They were both wrong. Oddy Gaul was a monster.

With his choice of any eligible young woman, Oddy Gaul went stag to the Observatory Prom, wandered into a dark-room by mistake, and discovered a girl in a smock bending over trays in the hideous green safe-light. She had cropped black hair, icy blue eyes, strong features, and a sensuous, boyish figure. She ordered him out and Oddy fell in love with her . . . temporarily.

His friends howled with laughter when he told them. "Shades of Pygmalion, Oddy, don't you know about *her*? The girl is frigid. A statue. She loathes men. You're wasting your time."

But through the adroitness of her analyst, the girl turned a neurotic corner one week later and feel deeply in love with Oddy Gaul. It was sudden, devastating and enraptured for

two months. Then just as Oddy began to cool, the girl had a
relapse and everything ended on a friendly, convenient basis.

So far only minor events made up the response to Oddy's
luck, but the shock wave of reaction was spreading. In September of his sophomore year, Oddy competed for the Political Economy Medal with a thesis entitled: "Causes of Mutiny."
The striking similarity of his paper to the Astraean mutiny
that broke out the day his paper was entered won him the
prize.

In October, Oddy contributed twenty dollars to a pool
organized by a crackpot classmate for speculating on the
Exchange according to "Stock Market Trends," an ancient
superstition. The prophet's calculations were ridiculous, but a
sharp panic nearly ruined the Exchange as it quadrupled the
pool. Oddy made one hundred dollars.

And so it went . . . worse and worse. The monster.

Now, a monster can get away with a lot when he's studying a
speculative philosophy where causation is rooted in history
and the Present is devoted to statistical analysis of the Past; but
the living sciences are bulldogs with their teeth clamped on
the phenomena of Now. So it was Jesse Migg, physiologist and
spectral physicist, who first trapped the monster . . . and he
thought he'd found an angel.

Old Jess was one of the Sights. In the first place he was
young . . . not over forty. He was a malignant knife of a man,
an albino, pink-eyed, bald, pointed-nosed, and brilliant. He
affected twentieth-century clothes and twentieth-century
vices . . . tobacco and potation so C_2H_5OH. He never
talked . . . He spat. He never walked . . . He scurried. And he
was scurrying up and down the aisles of the laboratory of
Tech I (General Survey of Spatial Mechanics—Required for
All General Arts Students) when he ferreted out the monster.

One of the first experiments in the course was EMF Elec-
trolysis. Elementary stuff. A U-Tube containing water was
passed between the poles of a stock Remosant Magnet. After
sufficient voltage was transmitted through the coils, you drew

off hydrogen and oxygen in two-to-one ratio at the arms of the tube and related them to the voltage and the magnetic field.

Oddy ran his experiment earnestly, got the approved results, entered them in his lab book and then waited for the official check-off. Little Migg came hustling down the aisle, darted to Oddy and spat: "Finished?"

"Yes, sir."

Migg checked the book entries, glanced at the indicators at the ends of the tube, and stamped Oddy out with a sneer. It was only after Oddy was gone that he noticed the Remosant Magnet was obviously shorted. The wires were fused. There hadn't been any field to electrolyze the water.

"Hell and Damnation!" Migg grunted (he also affected twentieth-century vituperation) and rolled a clumsy cigarette.

He checked off possibilities in his comptometer head. 1. Gaul cheated. 2. If so, with what apparatus did he portion out the H_2 and O_2? 3. Where did he get the pure gases? 4. Why did he do it? Honesty was easier. 5. He didn't cheat. 6. How did he get the right results? 7. How did he get *any* results?

Old Jess emptied the U-Tube, refilled it with water, and ran off the experiment himself. He, too, got the correct result without a magnet.

"Christ on a raft!" he swore, unimpressed by the miracle, and infuriated by the mystery. He snooped, darting about like a hungry bat. After four hours he discovered that the steel bench supports were picking up a charge from the Greeson Coils in the basement and had thrown just enough field to make everything come out right.

"Coincidence," Migg spat. But he was not convinced.

Two weeks later, in Elementary Fission Analysis, Oddy completed his afternoon's work with a careful listing of resultant isotopes from selenium to lanthanum. The only trouble, Migg discovered, was that there had been a mistake in the stock issued to Oddy. He hadn't received any U^{235} for neutron bombardment. His sample had been a leftover from a Stefan-Boltzmann black-body demonstration.

"God in Heaven!" Migg swore, and double-checked. Then he triple-checked. When he found the answer—a remarkable coincidence involving improperly cleaned apparatus and a defective cloud-chamber—he swore further. He also did some intensive thinking.

"There are accident-prones," Migg snarled at the reflection in his Self-Analysis Mirror. "How about good-luck prones? Horse manure!"

But he was a bulldog with his teeth sunk in phenomena. He tested Oddy Gaul. He hovered over him in the laboratory, cackling with infuriated glee as Oddy completed experiment after experiment with defective equipment. When Oddy successfully completed the Rutherford Classic—getting $_8O^{17}$ after exposing nitrogen to alpha radiation, but in this case without the use of nitrogen or alpha radiation—Migg actually clapped him on the back in delight. Then the little man investigated and found the logical, improbable chain of coincidences that explained it.

He devoted his spare time to a check-back on Oddy's career at Harvard. He had a two-hour conference with a lady astronomer's faculty analyst, and a ten-minute talk with Hig Clayton and Gravy-Train Stuart. He rooted out the Exchange Pool, the Political Economy Medal, and half a dozen other incidents that filled him with malignant joy. Then he cast off his twentieth-century affectation, dressed himself properly in formal leotards, and entered the Faculty Club for the first time in a year.

A four-handed chess game on a transparent toroid board was in progress in the Diathermy Alcove. It had been in progress since Migg joined the faculty, and would probably not be finished before the end of the century. In fact, Johansen, playing Red, was already training his son to replace him in the likely event of his dying before the completion of the game.

As abrupt as ever, Migg marched up to the glowing board, sparkling with vari-colored pieces, and blurted: "What do you know about accidents?"

"Ah?" said Bellanby, *Philosopher in Res* at the University. "Good evening, Migg. Do you mean the accident of substance, or the accident of essence? If, on the other hand, your question implies—"

"No, no," Migg interrupted. "My apologies, Bellanby. Let me rephrase the question. Is there such a thing as Compulsion of Probability?"

Hrrdnikkisch completed his move and gave full attention to Migg, as did Johansen and Bellanby. Wilson continued to study the board. Since he was permitted one hour to make his move and would need it, Migg knew there would be ample time for the discussion.

"Compulthon of Probability?" Hrrdnikkisch lisped. "Not a new conthept, Migg. I recall a thurvey of the theme in "The Integraph' Vol. LVIII, No. 9. The calculuth, if I am not mithtaken—"

"No," Migg interrupted again. "My respects, Signoid. I'm not interested in the mathematics of probability, nor the philosophy. Let me put it this way. The accident-prone has already been incorporated into the body of psychoanalysis. Paton's Theorem of the Least Neurotic Norm settled that. But I've discovered the obverse. I've discovered a Fortune-Prone."

"Ah?" Johansen chuckled. "It's to be a joke. You wait and see, Signoid."

"No," answered Migg. "I'm perfectly serious. I've discovered a genuinely lucky man."

"He wins at cards?"

"He wins at everything. Accept this postulate for the moment. . . . I'll document it later. . . . There is a man who is lucky. He is a Fortune-Prone. Whatever he desires, he receives. Whether he has the ability to achieve it or not, he receives it. If his desire is totally beyond the peak of his accomplishment, then the factors of chance, coincidence, hazard, accident . . . and so on, combine to produce his desired end."

"No." Bellanby shook his head. "Too farfetched."

"I've worked it out empirically," Migg continued. "It's something like this. The future is a choice of mutually exclusive possibilities, one or other of which must be realized in terms of favorability of the events and number of the events. . . ."

"Yes, yes," interrupted Johansen. "The greater the number of favorable possibilities, the stronger the probability of an event maturing. This is elementary, Migg. Go on."

"I continue," Milg spat indignantly. "When we discuss probability in terms of throwing dice, the predictions or odds are simple. There are only six mutually exclusive possibilities to each die. The favorability is easy to compute. Chance is reduced to simple odds-ratios. *But* when we discuss probability in terms of the Universe, we cannot encompass enough data to make a prediction. There are too many factors. Favorability cannot be ascertained."

"All thith ith true," Hrrdnikkisch said, "but what of your Fortune-Prone?"

"I don't know how he does it . . . but merely by the intensity or mere existence of his desire, he can affect the favorability of possibilities. By wanting, he can turn possibility into probability, and probability into certainty."

"Ridiculous," Bellanby snapped. "You claim there's a man farsighted and far-reaching enough to do this?"

"Nothing of the sort. He doesn't know what he's doing. He just thinks he's lucky, if he thinks about it at all. Let us say he wants . . . Oh . . . Name anything."

"Heroin," Bellanby said.

"What's that?" Johansen inquired.

"A morphine derivative," Hrrdnikkisch explained. "Formerly manufactured and thold to narcotic addictth."

"Heroin," Migg said. "Excellent. Say my man desires

heroin, an antique narcotic no longer in existence. Very good. His desire would compel this sequence of possible but improbable events: A chemist in Australia, fumbling through a new organic synthesis, will accidentally and unwittingly prepare six ounces of heroin. Four ounces will be discarded, but through a logical mistake two ounces will be preserved. A further coincidence will ship it to this country and this city, wrapped as powdered sugar in a plastic ball; where the final accident will serve it to my man in a restaurant which he is visiting for the first time on an impulse. . . ."

"La-La-La!" said Hrrdnikkisch. "Thith shuffling of hithtory. Thith fluctuation of inthident and pothibility? All achieved without the knowledge but with the dethire of a man?"

"Yes. Precisely my point," Migg snarled. "I don't know how he does it, but he turns possibility into certainty. And since almost anything is possible, he is capable of accomplishing almost anything. He is godlike but not a god, because he does this without consciousness. He is an angel."

"Who is this angel?" Johansen asked.

And Migg told them all about Oddy Gaul.

"But how does he do it?" Bellanby persisted. "How does he do it?"

"I don't know," Migg repeated again. "Tell me how Espers do it."

"What!" Bellanby exclaimed. "Are you prepared to deny the telepathic pattern of thought? Do you—"

"I do nothing of the sort. I merely illustrate one possible explanation. Man produces events. The threatening War of Resources may be thought to be a result of the natural exhaustion of Terran resources. We know it is not. It is a result of centuries of thriftless waste by man. Natural phenomena are less often produced by nature and more often produced by man."

"And?"

"Who knows? Gaul is producing phenomena. Perhaps

he's unconsciously broadcasting on a telepathic wave-band. Broadcasting and getting results. He wants Heroin. The broadcast goes out—"

"But Espers can't pick up any telepathic pattern further than the horizon. It's direct wave transmission. Even large objects cannot be penetrated. A building, say, or a—"

"I'm not saying this is on the Esper level," Migg shouted. "I'm trying to imagine something bigger. Something tremendous. He wants heroin. His broadcast goes out to the world. All men unconsciously fall into a pattern of activity which will produce that heroin as quickly as possible. That Austrian chemist—"

"No. Australian."

"That Australian chemist may have been debating between half a dozen different syntheses. Five of them could never have produced heroin; but Gaul's impulse made him select the sixth."

"And if he did not anyway?"

"Then who knows what parallel chains were also started? A boy playing Robin Hood in Montreal is impelled to explore an abandoned cabin where he finds the drug, hidden there centuries ago by smugglers. A woman in California collects old apothecary jars. She finds a pound of heroin. A child in Berlin, playing with a defective Radar-Chem Set, manufactures it. Name the most improbable sequence of events, and Gaul can bring it about, logically and certainly. I tell you, that boy is an angel!"

And he produced his documented evidence and convinced them.

It was then that four scholars of various but indisputable intellects elected themselves an executive committee for Fate and took Oddy Gaul in hand. To understand what they attempted to do, you must first understand the situation the world found itself in during that particular era.

It is a known fact that all wars are founded in economic conflict, or to put it another way, a trial by arms is merely the last battle of an economic war. In the pre-Christian centuries, the Punic Wars were the final outcome of a financial struggle between Rome and Carthage for economic control of the Mediterranean. Three thousand years later, the impending War of Resources loomed as the finale of a struggle between the two Independent Welfare States controlling most of the known economic world.

What petroleum oil was to the twentieth century, FO (the nickname for Fissionable Ore) was to the thirtieth; and the situation was peculiarly similar to the Asia Minor crisis that ultimately wrecked the United Nations a thousand years before. Triton, a backward semibarbaric satellite, previously unwanted and ignored, had suddenly discovered it possessed enormous resources of FO. Financially and technologically incapable of self-development, Triton was peddling concessions to both Welfare States.

The difference between a Welfare State and a Benevolent Despot is slight. In times of crisis, either can be traduced by the sincerest motives into the most abominable conduct. Both the Comity of Nations (bitterly nicknamed "The Con Men" by Der Realpolitik aus Terra) and Der Realpolitik aus Terra (sardonically called "The Rats" by the Comity of Nations) were desperately in need of natural resources, meaning FO. They were bidding against each other hysterically, and elbowing each other with sharp skirmishes at outposts. Their sole concern was the protection of their citizens. From the best of motives they were preparing to cut each other's throat.

Had this been the issue before the citizens of both Welfare States, some compromise might have been reached; but Triton, intoxicated as a schoolboy with a newfound prominence and power, confused issues by raising a religious issue and reviving a Holy War which the Family of Planets had long forgotten. Assistance in their Holy War (involving the extermination of a harmless and rather unimportant sect called the Quakers) was one of the conditions of sale. This, both the Comity of Nations and Der Realpolitik aus Terra were prepared to swallow with or without private reservations, but it could not be admitted to their citizens.

And so, camouflaged by the burning issues of Rights of Minority Sects, Priority of Pioneering, Freedom of Religion, Historical Rights to Triton v. Possession in Fact, etc., the two Houses of the Family of Planets feinted, parried, riposted and slowly closed, like fencers on the strip, for the final sortie which meant ruin for both.

All this the four men discussed through three interminable meetings.

"Look here," Migg complained toward the close of the third consultation. "You theoreticians have already turned nine man-hours into carbonic acid with ridiculous dissensions . . ."

Bellanby nodded, smiling. "It's as I've always said, Migg. Every man nurses the secret belief that were he God he could do the job much better. We're just learning how difficult it is."

"Not God," Hrrdnikkisch said, "but hith Prime Minithterth. Gaul will be God."

Johansen winced. "I don't like that talk," he said. "I happen to be a religious man."

"You?" Bellanby exclaimed in surprise. "A Colloid-Therapeutist?"

"I happen to be a religious man," Johansen repeated stubbornly.

"But the boy hath the power of the miracle," Hrrdnikkisch protested. "When he hath been taught to know what he doth, he will be a God."

"This is pointless," Migg rapped out. "We have spent three sessions in piffling discussion. I have heard three opposed views re Mr. Odysseus Gaul. Although all are agreed he must be used as a tool, none can agree on the work to which the tool must be set. Bellanby prattles about an Ideal Intellectual Anarchy, Johansen preaches about a Soviet of God, and Hrrdnikkisch has wasted two hours postulating and destroying his own theorems. . . ."

"Really, Migg . . ." Hrrdnikkisch began. Migg waved his hand.

"Permit me," Migg continued malevolently, "to reduce this discussion to the kindergarten level. First things first, gentlemen. Before attempting to reach cosmic agreement we must make sure there is a cosmos left for us to agree upon. I refer to the impending war. . . .

"Our program, as I see it, must be simple and direct. It is the education of a God or, if Johansen protests, of an angel. Fortunately Gaul is an estimable young man of kindly, honest disposition. I shudder to think what he might have done had he been inherently vicious."

"Or what he might do once he learns what he can do," muttered Bellanby.

"Precisely. We must begin a careful and rigorous ethical education of the boy, but we haven't enough time. We can't educate first, and then explain the truth when he's safe. We must forestall the war. We need a shortcut."

"All right," Johansen said. "What do you suggest?"

"Dazzlement," Migg spat. "Enchantment."

"Enchantment?" Hrrdnikkisch chuckled. "A new thienth, Migg?"

"Why do you think I selected you three of all people for this secret?" Migg snorted. "For your intellects? Nonsense! I can think you all under the table. No. I selected you, gentlemen, for your charm."

"It's an insult," Bellanby grinned, "and yet I'm flattered."

"Gaul is nineteen," Migg went on. "He is at the age when undergraduates are most susceptible to hero-worship. I want you gentlemen to charm him. You are not the first brains of the University, but you are the first heroes."

"I altho am inthulted and flattered," said Hrrdnikkisch.

"I want you to charm him, dazzle him, inspire him with affection and awe . . . as you've done with countless classes of undergraduates."

"Aha!" said Johansen. "The chocolate around the pill."

"Exactly. When he's enchanted, you will make him want to stop the war . . . and then tell him how he can stop it. That will give us breathing space to continue his education. By the time he outgrows his respect for you he will have a sound ethical foundation on which to build. He'll be safe."

"And you, Migg?" Bellanby inquired. "What part do you play?"

"Now? None," Migg snarled. "I have no charm, gentlemen. I come later. When he outgrows his respect for you, he'll begin to acquire respect for me."

All of which was frightfully conceited but perfectly true.

And as events slowly marched toward the final crisis, Oddy Gaul was carefully and quickly enchanted. Bellanby invited him to the twenty-foot crystal globe atop his house . . . the famous hen-roost to which only the favored few were invited. There, Oddy Gaul sunbathed and admired the philosopher's magnificent iron-hard condition at seventy-three. Admiring Bellanby's muscles, it was only natural for him to admire Bellanby's ideas. He returned often to sunbathe, worship the great man, and absorb ethical concepts.

Meanwhile, Hrrdnikkisch took over Oddy's evenings. With the mathematician, who puffed and lisped like some flamboyant character out of Rabelais, Oddy was carried to the dizzy heights of the *haute cuisine* and the complete pagan life. Together they ate and drank incredible foods and liquids and pursued incredible women until Oddy returned to his room each night intoxicated with the magic of the senses and the riotous color of the great Hrrdnikkisch's glittering ideas.

And occasionally . . . not too often, he would find Papa Johansen waiting for him, and then would come the long, quiet talks through the small hours when young men search for the harmonics of life and the meaning of entity. And there was Johansen for Oddy to model himself after . . . a glowing embodiment of Spiritual Good . . . a living example of Faith in God and Ethical Sanity.

The climax came on March 15 . . . The Ides of March, and

they should have taken the date as a sign. After dinner with his three heroes at the Faculty Club, Oddy was ushered into the Foto-Library by the three great men where they were joined, quite casually, by Jesse Migg. There passed a few moments of uneasy tension until Migg made a sign, and Bellanby began.

"Oddy," he said, "have you ever had the fantasy that some day you might wake up and discover you were a king?"

Oddy blushed.

"I see you have. You know, every man has entertained that dream. It's called the Mignon Complex. The usual pattern is: You learn your parents have only adopted you and that you are actually and rightfully the King of . . . of . . ."

"Ruritania," said Hrrdnikkisch, who had made a study of Stone Age Fiction.

"Yes, sir," Oddy muttered. "I've had that dream."

"Well," Bellanby said quietly, "it's come true. You are a king."

Oddy stared while they explained and explained and explained. First, as a college boy, he was wary and suspicious of a joke. Then, as an idolator, he was almost persuaded by the men he most admired. And finally, as a human animal, he was swpet away by the exaltation of security. Not power, not glory, not wealth thrilled him, but security alone. Later he might come to enjoy the trimmings, but now he was released from fear. He need never worry again.

"Yes," exclaimed Oddy. "Yes, yes, yes! I understand. I understand what you want me to do." He surged up excitedly from his chair and circled the illuminated walls, trembling with joy. Then he stopped and turned.

"And I'm grateful," he said. "Grateful to all of you for what you've been trying to do. It would have been shameful if I'd been selfish . . . or mean. . . . Trying to use this for myself. But you've shown me the way. It's to be used for good. Always!"

Johansen nodded happily.

"I'll always listen to you," Oddy went on. "I don't want to

make any mistakes. Ever!" He paused and blushed again. "That dream about being a king . . . I had that when I was a kid. But here at the school I've had something bigger. I used to wonder what would happen if I was the one man who could run the world. I used to dream about the kind, generous things I'd do. . . ."

"Yes," said Bellanby. "We know, Oddy. We've all had that dream too. Every man does."

"But it isn't a dream any more," Oddy laughed. "It's reality. I can do it. I can make it happen."

"Start with the war," Migg said sourly.

"Of course," said Oddy. "The war first; but then we'll go on from there, won't we? I'll make sure the war never starts, but then we'll do big things . . . great things! Just the five of us in private. Nobody'll know about us. We'll be ordinary people, but we'll make life wonderful for everybody. If I'm an angel . . . like you say . . . then I'll spread heaven around me as far as I can reach."

"But start with the war," Migg repeated.

"The war is the first disaster that must be averted, Oddy," Bellanby said. "If you don't want this disaster to happen, it will never happen."

"And you want to prevent that tragedy, don't you?" said Johansen.

"Yes," answered Oddy. "I do."

On March 20, the war broke. The Comity of Nations and Der Realpolitik aus Terra mobilized and struck. While blow followed shattering counterblow, Oddy Gaul was commissioned subaltern in a line regiment, but gazetted to Intelligence on May 3. On June 24 he was appointed A.D.C. to the Joint Forces Council meeting in the ruins of what had been Australia. On July 11, he was brevetted to command of the wrecked Space Force, being jumped 1,789 grades over regular officers. On September 19 he assumed supreme command in the Battle of the Parsec and won the victory that ended the disastrous solar annihilation called the Six Month War.

On September 23, Oddy Gaul made the astonishing Peace Offer that was accepted by the remnants of both Welfare States. It required the scrapping of antagonistic economic theories, and amounted to the virtual abandonment of all economic theory with an amalgamation of both States into a Solar Society. On January 1, Oddy Gaul, by unanimous acclaim, was elected Solon of the Solar Society in perpetuity.

And today . . . still youthful, still vigorous, still handsome, still sincere, idealistic, charitable, kindly and sympathetic, he lives in the Solar Palace. He is unmarried but a mighty lover; uninhibited, but a charming host and devoted friend; democratic, but the feudal overlord of a bankrupt Family of Planets that suffers misgovernment, oppression, poverty, and confusion with a cheerful joy that sings nothing but Hosannahs to the glory of Oddy Gaul.

In a last moment of clarity, Jesse Migg communicated his desolate summation of the situation to his friends in the Faculty Club. This was shortly before they made the trip to join Oddy in the palace as his confidential and valued advisors.

"We were fools," Migg said bitterly. "We should have killed him. He isn't an angel. He's a monster. Civilization and culture . . . philosophy and ethics . . . those were only masks Oddy put on; masks that covered the primitive impulses of his subconscious mind."

"You mean Oddy was not sincere?" Johansen asked heavily. "He wanted this wreckage . . . this ruin?"

"Certainly he was sincere . . . consciously. He still is. He thinks he desires nothing but the most good for the most men. He's honest, kind and generous . . . but only consciously."

"Ah! The Id!" said Hrrdnikkisch with an explosion of breath as though he had been punched in the stomach.

"You understand, Signoid? I see you do. Gentlemen, we were imbeciles. We made the mistake of assuming that Oddy would have conscious control of his power. He does not. The control was and still is below the thinking, reasoning level.

The control lies in Oddy's Id . . . in that deep, unconscious reservoir of primordial selfishness that lies within every man."

"Then he wanted the war," Bellanby said.

"His Id wanted the war, Bellanby. It was the quickest route to what his Id desires . . . to be Lord of the Universe and loved by the Universe . . . and his Id controls the Power. All of us have that selfish, egocentric Id within us, perpetually searching for satisfaction, timeless, immortal, knowing no logic, no values, no good and evil, no morality; and that is what controls the power in Oddy. He will always win, not what he's been educated to desire but what his Id desires. It's the inescapable conflict that may be the doom of our system."

"But we'll be there to advise him . . . counsel him . . . guide him," Bellanby protested. "He asked us to come."

"And he'll listen to our advice like the good child that he is," Migg answered, "agreeing with us, trying to make a heaven for everybody while his Id will be making a hell for everybody. Oddy isn't unique. We all suffer from the same conflict . . . but Oddy has the power."

"What can we do?" Johansen groaned. "What can we do?"

"I don't know," Migg bit his lip, then bobbed his head to Papa Johansen in what amounted to apology for him. "Johansen," he said, "you were right. There must be a God, if only because there must be an opposite to Oddy Gaul, who was most assuredly invented by the Devil."

But that was Jesse Migg's last sane statement. Now, of course, he adores Gaul the Glorious, Gaul the Gauleiter, Gaul the God Eternal who has achieved the savage, selfish satisfaction for which all of us unconsciously yearn from birth, but which only Oddy Gaul has won.

Hobson's Choice

Introduction

THIS was the first short story I wrote after my first science fiction novel, and it brought about my first disagreement with Horace Gold, the splendid editor of *Galaxy*, who had contributed so much to the making of the novel. I can never thank him enough for that, for although I'm a damned good writer, I'm no better than my editor or director. The disagreement arose over the ending or lack of ending of "Hobson's Choice," and it was only one of many similar good-natured differences I've had with my bosses.

You see, I don't believe in a complete point-by-point wrap-up of a story. Very often I'll leave questions unresolved, whether I know the answer or not. I like to leave the reader with something hanging, anything that will make him smile and speculate. I'll do that with the punch line of a joke which is never told, or a phrase from a song which is never sung, and so on.

The device works, as a rule. People are amused because, I think, they enjoy the guessing part of a guessing game more than the solution. If there is no solution it doesn't matter, provided the enigma isn't a crucial part of the story. As a throwaway it's fine, more or less in a class with "Why is a raven like a writing desk?" Chuck Dodgson knew what he was doing when he left *Alice* and us hanging with that one.

On the other hand, if the enigma is the crux of the story, it must be resolved come hell or high water, which is why the Mysterious Message story is so irritating. I can't give its official title because I've read at least three different versions by three different authors, all with different titles. Apparently the original basis for the story must have been in the P.D. You must have read one of them.

Briefly: Traveler in foreign land has written message handed him by a stranger. Can't translate. Asks various natives to translate for him. Each one reads, refuses to translate and reacts violently; horrified, turns away in disgust, knocks him down, calls the cops, etc. Bewilderment. On board ship going home, traveler meets missionary type. Pours out story. Missionary offers to translate mysterious message. Swears as Man of God not to turn ugly. Guy hands over slip of paper. Wind catches same. Blows it overboard. End. This is Cruel and Unusual Punishment.

Well, my ending for "Hobson's Choice" was unresolved in one sense, yet resolved in another. I didn't think the definitive wrap-up which Horace wanted me to decide on would work. It wasn't the point of the story, and if I did lay a decision on the reader it would be a letdown. Try it yourself after you've read this story and see if I'm not right. I think you'll agree that sometimes nothing works better than something.

Now I'll confess the truth. I fell into the answer-trap myself; me, a past master of leaving 'em hanging. In one of the Nero Wolfe mysteries Archie Goodwin says to a girl, "Are you Catholic? What's the difference between a Catholic and a river that runs uphill?" Left unresolved. Left me puzzled for years. When I met Rex Stout at last, I reminded him of the conundrum and asked for the answer. He burst out laughing. "How the hell do I know? I just invented it for the scene."

Hoist by my own petard.

This is a warning to accomplices like you, me, and Addyer.

Can you spare price of one cup coffee, honorable sir? I am indigent organism which are hungering.

By day, Addyer was a statistician. He concerned himself with such matters as Statistical Tables, Averages and Dispersions, Groups That Are Not Homogenous, and Random Sampling. At night, Addyer plunged into an elaborate escape fantasy divided into two parts. Either he imagined himself moved back in time a hundred years with a double armful of the *Encyclopaedia Britannica*, bestsellers, hit plays and gambling records; or else he imagined himself transported forward in time a thousand years to the Golden Age of perfection.

There were other fantasies which Addyer entertained on odd Thursdays, such as (by a fluke) becoming the only man left on earth with a world of passionate beauties to fecundate; such as acquiring the power of invisibility which would enable him to rob banks and right wrongs with impunity; such as possessing the mysterious power of working miracles.

Up to this point you and I and Addyer are identical. Where we part company is in the fact that Addyer was a statistician.

Can you spare cost of one cup coffee, honorable miss? For blessed charitability? I am beholden.

On Monday, Addyer rushed into his chief's office, waving a sheaf of papers. "Look here, Mr. Grande," Addyer sputtered. "I've found something fishy. Extremely fishy . . . In the statistical sense, that is."

"Oh, hell," Grande answered. "You're not supposed to be finding anything. We're in between statistics until the war's over."

"I was leafing through the Interior Department's reports. D'you know our population's up?"

"Not after the Atom Bomb it isn't," said Grande. "We've lost double what our birthrate can replace." He pointed out the window to the twenty-five-foot stub of the Washington Monument. "There's your documentation."

"But our population's up 3.0915 per cent." Addyer displayed his figures. "What about that, Mr. Grande?"

"Must be a mistake somewhere," Grande muttered after a moment's inspection. "You'd better check."

"Yes, sir," said Addyer scurrying out of the office. "I knew you'd be interested, sir. You're the ideal statistician, sir." He was gone.

"Poop," said Grande and once again began computing the quantity of bored respirations left to him. It was his personalized anesthesia.

On Tuesday, Addyer discovered that there was no correlation between the mortality-birthrate ratio and the population increase. The war was multiplying mortality and reducing births; yet the population was minutely increasing. Addyer displayed his discovery to Grande, received a pat on the back, and went home to a new fantasy in which he woke up a million years in the future, learned the answer to the enigma, and decided to remain amidst snow-capped mountains and snow-capped bosoms, safe under the aegis of a culture saner than Aureomycin.

On Wednesday, Addyer requisitioned the comptometer and file and ran a test check on Washington, D.C. To his dismay, he discovered that the population of the former capital was down 0.0029 per cent. This was distressing, and Addyer went home to escape into a dream about Queen Victoria's Golden Age when he amazed and confounded the world with his brilliant output of novels, plays and poetry, all cribbed from Shaw, Galsworthy, and Wilde.

Can you spare price of one coffee, honorable sir? I am distressed individual needful of chariting.

On Thursday, Addyer tried another check, this time on the

city of Philadelphia. He discovered that Philadelphia's population was up 0.0959 per cent. Very encouraging. He tried a
rundown on Little Rock. Population up 1.1329 per cent. He
tested St. Louis. Population up 2.0924 per cent . . . and this
despite the complete extinction of Jefferson County owing to
one of those military mistakes of an excessive nature.

"My God!" Addyer exclaimed, trembling with excitement.
"The closer I get to the center of the country, the greater the
increase. But it was the center of the country that took the
heaviest punishment in the Buz-Raid. What's the answer?"

That night he shuttled back and forth between the future
and the past in his ferment, and he was down at the shop by
seven A.M. He put a twenty-four-hour claim on the Compo
and Files. He followed up his hunch and he came up with a
fantastic discovery which he graphed in approved form. On
the map of the remains of the United States he drew concen-
tric circles in colors illustrating the areas of population
increase. The red, orange, yellow, green and blue circles
formed a perfect target around Finney County, Kansas.

"Mr. Grande," Addyer shouted in a high statistical passion,
"Finney County has got to explain this."

"You go out there and get that explanation," Grande
replied, and Addyer departed.

"Poop," muttered Grande and began integrating his pulse-
rate with his eye-blink.

> *Can you spare price of one coffee, dearly madam? I am starvel-*
> *ing organism requiring nutritiousment.*

Now travel in those days was hazardous. Addyer took ship
to Charleston (there were no rail connections remaining in the
North Atlantic states) and was wrecked off Hatteras by a
rogue mine. He drifted in the icy waters for seventeen hours,
muttering through his teeth: "Oh Christ! If only I'd been born
a hundred years ago."

Apparently this form of prayer was potent. He was picked

up by a Navy Sweeper and shipped to Charleston where he arrived just in time to acquire a subcritical radiation burn from a raid which fortunately left the railroad unharmed. He was treated for the burn from Charleston to Macon (change) from Birmingham to Memphis (bubonic plague) to Little Rock (polluted water) to Tulsa (fallout quarantine) to Kansas City (The O.K. Bus Co. Accepts No Liability for Lives Lost Through Acts of War) to Lyonesse, Finney County, Kansas.

And there he was in Finney County with its great magma pits and scars and radiation streaks; whole farms blackened and razed; whole highways so blasted they looked like dotted lines; whole population 4-F. Clouds of soot and fallout neutralizers hung over Finney County by day, turning it into a Pittsburgh on a still afternoon. Auras of radiation glowed at night, highlighted by the blinking red warning beacons, turning the county into one of those overexposed night photographs, all blurred and crosshatched by deadly slashes of light.

After a restless night in Lyonesse Hotel, Addyer went over to the county seat for a check on their birth records. He was armed with the proper credentials, but the county seat was not armed with the statistics. That excessive military mistake again. It had extinguished the seat.

A little annoyed, Addyer marched off to the County Medical Association office. His idea was to poll the local doctors on births. There was an office and one attendant who had been a practical nurse. He informed Addyer that Finney County has lost its last doctor to the army eight months previous. Midwives might be the answer to the birth enigma, but there was no record of midwives. Addyer would simply have to canvass from door to door, asking if any lady within practiced that ancient profession.

Further piqued, Addyer returned to the Lyonesse Hotel and wrote on a slip of tissue paper: HAVING DATA DIFFICULTIES. WILL REPORT AS SOON AS INFORMATION AVAILABLE. He slipped the message into an aluminum capsule, attached it to his sole surviving carrier pigeon, and dispatched it to Washington with a prayer. Then he sat down at his window and brooded.

He was aroused by a curious sight. In the street below, the O.K. Bus Co. had just arrived from Kansas City. The old coach wheezed to a stop, opened its door with some difficulty and permitted a one-legged farmer to emerge. His burned face was freshly bandaged. Evidently this was a well-to-do burgess who could afford to travel for medical treatment. The bus backed up for the return trip to Kansas City and honked a warning horn. That was when the curious sight began.

From nowhere . . . absolutely nowhere . . . a horde of people appeared. They skipped from back alleys, from behind rubble piles; they popped out of stores, they filled the street. They were all jolly, healthy, brisk, happy. They laughed and chatted as they climbed into the bus. They looked like hikers and tourists, carrying knapsacks, carpetbags, box lunches, and even babies. In two minutes the bus was filled. It lurched off down the road, and as it disappeared Addyer heard happy singing break out and echo from the walls of rubble.

"I'll be damned," he said.

He hadn't heard spontaneous singing in over two years. He hadn't seen a carefree smile in over three years. He felt like a color-blind man who was seeing the full spectrum for the first time. It was uncanny. It was also a little blasphemous.

"Don't those people know there's a war on?" he asked himself.

And a little later: "They looked too healthy. Why aren't they in uniform?"

And last of all: "Who *were* they anyway?"

That night Addyer's fantasy was confused.

Can you spare price of one cup coffee, kindly sir? I am estrangered and faintly from hungering.

The next morning Addyer arose early, hired a car at an exorbitant fee, found he could not buy any fuel at any price, and ultimately settled for a lame horse. He was allergic to horse dander and suffered asthmatic tortures as he began his house-to-house canvass. He was discouraged when he returned to the Lyonesse Hotel that afternoon. He was just in time to witness the departure of the O.K. Bus Co.

Once again a horde of happy people appeared and boarded the bus. Once again the bus hirpled off down the broken road. Once again the joyous singing broke out.

"I *will* be damned," Addyer wheezed.

He dropped into the County Surveyor's Office for a large scale map of Finney County. It was his intent to plot the midwife coverage in accepted statistical manner. There was a little difficulty with the surveyor, who was deaf, blind in one eye, and spectacleless in the other. He could not read Addyer's credentials with any faculty or facility. As Addyer finally departed with the map, he said to himself: "I think the old idiot thought I was a spy."

And later he muttered: "Spies?"

And just before bedtime: "Holy Moses! Maybe *that's* the answer to *them.*"

That night he was Lincoln's secret agent, anticipating Lee's every move, outwitting Jackson, Johnston and Beauregard, foiling John Wilkes Booth, and being elected President of the United States by 1868.

The next day the O.K. Bus Co. carried off yet another load of happy people.

And the next.

And the next.

"Four hundred tourists in five days," Addyer computed. "The country's filled with espionage."

He began loafing around the streets trying to investigate these joyous travelers. It was difficult. They were elusive before the bus arrived. They had a friendly way of refusing to pass the time. The locals of Lyonesse knew nothing about them and were not interested. Nobody was interested in much more than painful survival these days. That was what made the singing obscene.

After seven days of cloak-and-dagger and seven days of counting, Addyer suddenly did the big take. "It adds up," he said. "Eighty people a day leaving Lyonesse. Five hundred a week. Twenty-five thousand a year. Maybe that's the answer to the population increase." He spent fifty-five dollars on a telegram to Grande with no more than a hope of delivery. The Telegram read: "EUREKA. I HAVE FOUND (IT)."

Can you spare price of lone cup coffee, honorable madam? I am not tramp-handler but destitute life-form.

Addyer's opportunity came the next day. The O.K. Bus Co. pulled in as usual. Another crowd assembled to board the bus, but this time there were too many. Three people were refused passage. They weren't in the least annoyed. They stepped back, waved energetically as the bus started, shouted instructions for future reunions and then quietly turned and started off down the street.

Addyer was out of his hotel room like a shot. He followed the trio down the main street, turned left after them onto Fourth Avenue, passed the ruined schoolhouse, passed the demolished telephone building, passed the gutted library, railroad station, Protestant church, Catholic church . . . and finally reached the outskirts of Lyonesse and then open country.

Here he had to be more cautious. It was difficult stalking the spies with so much of the dusky road illuminated by warning lights. He wasn't suicidal enough to think of hiding in radiation pits. He hung back in an agony of indecision and was at last relieved to see them turn off the broken road and enter the old Baker farmhouse.

"Ah-ha!" said Addyer.

He sat down at the edge of the road on the remnants of a missile and asked himself: "Ah-ha what?" He could not answer, but he knew where to find the answer. He waited until dusk deepened to darkness and then slowly wormed his way forward toward the farmhouse.

It was while he was creeping between the deadly radiation glows and only occasionally butting his head against grave markers that he first became aware of two figures in the night. They were in the barnyard of the Baker place and were performing most peculiarly. One was tall and thin. A man. He stood stockstill, like a lighthouse. Upon occasion he took a slow, stately step with infinite caution and waved an arm in slow motion to the other figure. The second was also a man. He was stocky and trotted jerkily back and forth.

As Addyer approached, he heard the tall man say: "Rooo booo fooo mooo hwaaa looo fooo."

Whereupon the trotter chattered: "Wd-nk-kd-ik-md-pd-ld-nk."

Then they both laughed; the tall man like a locomotive, the trotter like a chipmunk. They turned. The trotter rocketed into the house. The tall man drifted in. And that was amazingly that.

"Oh-ho," said Addyer.

At that moment a pair of hands seized him and lifted him from the ground. Addyer's heart constricted. He had time for one convulsive spasm before something vague was pressed against his face. As he lost consciousness, his last idiotic thought was of telescopes.

Can you spare price of solitary coffee for no-loafing unfortunate, honorable sir? Charity will blessings.

When Addyer awoke he was lying on a couch in a small whitewashed room. A grey-haired gentleman with heavy fea-

tures was seated at a desk alongside the couch, busily ciphering on bits of paper. The desk was cluttered with what
appeared to be intricate timetables. There was a small radio
perched on one side.

"L-Listen . . ." Addyer began faintly.

"Just a minute, Mr. Addyer," the gentleman said pleasantly.
He fiddled with the radio. A glow germinated in the middle of
the room over a circular copper plate and coalesced into a girl.
She was extremely nude and extremely attractive. She scurried to the desk, patted the gentleman's head with the speed of
a pneumatic hammer. She laughed and chattered: "Wd-nk-
tk-ik-lt-nk."

The grey-haired man smiled and pointed to the door. "Go
outside and walk it off," he said. She turned and streaked
through the door.

"It has something to do with temporal rates," the gentleman
said to Addyer. "I don't understand it. When they come
forward, they've got accumulated momentum." He began
ciphering again. "Why in the world did you have to come
snooping, Mr. Addyer?"

"You're spies," Addyer said. "She was talking Chinese."

"Hardly. I'd say it was French. Early French. Middle fifteenth century."

"Middle fifteenth century!" Addyer exclaimed.

"That's what I'd say. You begin to acquire an ear for those
stepped-up tempos. Just a minute, please."

He switched the radio on again. Another glow appeared
and solidified into a nude man. He was stout, hairy and
lugubrious. With exasperating slowness he said: "Mooo fooo
blooo wawww hawww pooo."

The grey-haired man pointed to the door. The stout man
departed in slow motion.

"The way I see it," the grey-haired man continued conver-
sationally, "when they come back they're swimming against
the time current. That slows 'em down. When they come
forward, they're swimming with the current. That speeds 'em

up. Of course, in any case it doesn't last longer than a few minutes. It wears off."

"What?" Addyer said. "Time travel?"

"Yes. Of course."

"That thing . . ." Addyer pointed to the radio. "A time machine?"

"That's the idea. Roughly."

"But it's too small."

The grey-haired man laughed.

"What is this place anyway? What are you up to?"

"It's a funny thing," the grey-haired man said. "Everybody used to speculate about time travel. How it would be used for exploration, archaeology, historical and social research and so on. Nobody ever guessed what the real use would be. . . . Therapy."

"Therapy? You mean medical therapy?"

"That's right. Psychological therapy for the misfits who won't respond to any other cure. We let them emigrate. Escape. We've set up stations every quarter century. Stations like this."

"I don't understand."

"This is an immigration office."

"Oh my God!" Addyer shot up from the couch. "Then you're the answer to the population increase. Yes? That's how I happened to notice it. Mortality's up so high and birth's down so low these days that your time-addition becomes significant. Yes?"

"Yes, Mr. Addyer."

"Thousands of you coming here. From where?"

"From the future, of course. Time travel wasn't developed until C/H 127. That's . . . oh, say, 2505 A.D. your chronology. We didn't set up our chain of stations until C/H 189."

"But those fast-moving ones. You said they came forward from the past."

"Oh, yes, but they're all from the future originally. They just decided they went too far back."

"Too far?"

The grey-haired man nodded and reflected. "It's amusing, the mistakes people will make. They become unrealistic when they read history. Lose contact with facts. Chap I knew . . . wouldn't be satisfied with anything less than Elizabethan times. 'Shakespeare," he said. 'Good Queen Bess. Spanish Armada. Drake and Hawkins and Raleigh. Most virile period in history. The Golden Age. That's for me,' I couldn't talk sense into him, so we sent him back. Too bad."

"Well?" Addyer asked.

"Oh, he died in three weeks. Drar.k a glass of water. Typhoid."

"You didn't inoculate him? I mean, the army when it sends men overseas always—"

"Of course we did. Gave him all the immunization we could. But diseases evolve and change, too. New strains develop. Old strains disappear. That's what causes pandemics. Evidently our shots wouldn't take against the Elizabethan typhoid. Excuse me . . ."

Again the glow appeared. Another nude man appeared, chattered briefly and then whipped through the door. He almost collided with the nude girl who poked her head in, smiled and called in a curious accent: "Ie vous prie de me pardonner. Quy estoit cette gentilhomme?"

"I was right," the grey-haired man said. "That's medieval French. They haven't spoken like that since Rabelais." To the girl he said, "Middle English, please. The American dialect."

"Oh. I'm sorry, Mr. Jelling. I get so damned fouled up with my linguistics. Fouled? Is that right? Or do they say—"

"Hey!" Addyer cried in anguish.

"They say it, but only in private these years. Not before strangers."

"Oh, yes. I remember. Who was that gentleman who just left?"

"Peters."

"From Athens?"

"That's right."

"Didn't like it, eh?"

"Not much. Seems the Peripatetics didn't have plumbing."

"Yes. You begin to hanker for a modern bathroom after a while. Where do I get some clothes . . . or don't they wear clothes this century?"

"No, that's a hundred years forward. Go see my wife. She's in the outfitting room in the barn. That's the big red building."

The tall lighthouse-man Addyer had first seen in the farmyard suddenly manifested himself behind the girl. He was now dressed and moving at normal speed. He stared at the girl; she stared at him. "Splem!" they both cried. They embraced and kissed shoulders.

"St'u my rock-ribbering rib-rockery to heart the hearts two," the man said.

"Heart's too, argal, too heart," the girl laughed.

"Eh? Then you st'u too."

They embraced again and left.

"What was that? Future talk?" Addyer asked. "Shorthand?"

"Shorthand?" Jelling exclaimed in a surprised tone. "Don't you know rhetoric when you hear it? That was thirtieth-century rhetoric, man. We don't talk anything else up there. Prosthesis, Diastole, Epergesis, Metabasis, Hendiadys . . . And we're all born scanning."

"You don't have to sound so stuck up," Addyer muttered enviously. "I could scan too if I tried."

"You'd find it damned inconvenient trying at your time of life."

"What difference would that make?"

"It would make a big difference," Jelling said, "because you'd find that living is the sum of conveniences. You might think plumbing is pretty unimportant compared to ancient Greek philosophers. Lots of people do. But the fact is, we already know the philosophy. After a while you get tired of seeing the great men and listening to them expound the material you already know. You begin to miss the conveniences and familiar patterns you used to take for granted."

"That," said Addyer, "is a superficial attitude."

"You think so? Try living in the past by candlelight, without central heating, without refrigeration, canned foods, elementary drugs. . . . Or, future-wise, try living with Berganlicks, the Twenty-Two Commandments. Duodecimal calendars and currency, or try speaking in meter, planning and scanning each sentence before you talk . . . and damned for a contemptible illiterate if you forget yourself and speak spontaneously in your own tongue."

"You're exaggerating," Addyer said. "I'll bet there are times where I could be very happy. I've thought about it for years, and I—"

"Tcha!" Jelling snorted. "The great illusion. Name one."

"The American Revolution."

"Pfui! No sanitation. No medicine. Cholera in Philadelphia. Malaria in New York. No anesthesia. The death penalty for hundreds of small crimes and petty infractions. None of the books and music you like best. None of the jobs or professions for which you've been trained. Try again."

"The Victorian Age."

"How are your teeth and eyes? In good shape? They'd better be. We can't send your inlays and spectacles back with you. How are your ethics? In bad shape? They'd better be, or you'd starve in that cutthroat era. How do you feel about class distinctions? They were pretty strong in those days. What's your religion? You'd better not be a Jew or Catholic or Quaker or Moravian or any minority. What's your politics? If you're a reactionary today, the same opinions would make you a dangerous radical a hundred years ago. I don't think you'd be happy."

"I'd be safe."

"Not unless you were rich; and we can't send money back. Only the flesh. No, Addyer, the poor died at the average age

of forty in those days . . . worked out, worn out. Only the
privileged survived, and you wouldn't be one of the
privileged."

"Not with my superior knowledge?"

Jelling nodded wearily. "I knew *that* would come up sooner
or later. What superior knowledge? Your hazy recollection of
science and invention? Don't be a damned fool, Addyer. You
enjoy your technology without the faintest idea of how it
works."

"It wouldn't have to be hazy recollection. I could prepare."

"What, for instance?"

"Oh . . . say, the radio. I could make a fortune inventing
the radio."

Jelling smiled. "You couldn't invent radio until you'd first
invented the hundred allied technical discoveries that went
into it. You'd have to create an entire new industrial world.
You'd have to discover the vacuum rectifier and create an
industry to manufacture it; the self-heterodyne circuit, the
nonradiating neutrodyne receiver, and so forth. You'd have
to develop electric power production and transmission and
alternating current. You'd have to—but why belabor the obvious? Could you invent internal combustion before the de-
velopment of fuel oils?"

"My God!" Addyer groaned.

"And another thing," Jelling went on grimly. "I've been
talking about technological tools, but language is a tool, too;
the tool of communication. Did you ever realize that all the
studying you might do could never teach you how a language
was really used centuries ago? Do you know how the Romans
pronounced Latin? Do you know the Greek dialects? Could
you learn to speak and think in Gaelic, seventeenth-century
Flemish, Old Low German? Never. You'd be a deaf-mute."

"I never thought about it that way," Addyer said slowly.

"Escapists never do. All they're looking for is a vague excuse
to run away."

"What about books? I could memorize a great book and—"

"And what? Go back far enough into the past to anticipate the real author? You'd be anticipating the public, too. A book doesn't become great until the public's ready to understand it. It doesn't become profitable until the public's ready to buy it."

"What about going forward into the future?" Addyer asked.

"I've already told you. It's the same problem only in reverse. Could a medieval man survive in the twentieth century? Could he stay alive in street traffic? Drive cars? Speak the language? Think in the language? Adapt to the tempo, ideas and coordinations you take for granted? Never. Could someone from the twenty-fifth century adapt to the thirtieth? Never."

"Well, then," Addyer said angrily, "if the past and future are so uncomfortable, what are those people traveling around for?"

"They're not traveling," Jelling said. "They're running."

"From what?"

"Their own time."

"Why?"

"They don't like it."

"Why not?"

"Do you like yours? Does any neurotic?"

"Where are they going?"

"Anyplace but where they belong. They keep looking for the Golden Age. Tramps! Time-stiffs! Never satisfied. Always searching, shifting . . . bumming through the centuries. Pfui! Half the panhandlers you meet are probably time-bums stuck in the wrong century."

"And those people coming here . . . they think *this* is a Golden Age?"

"They do."

"They're crazy," Addyer protested. "Have they seen the ruins? The radiation? The war? The anxiety? The hysteria?"

"Sure. That's what appeals to them. Don't ask me why. Think of it this way: You like the American Colonial period, yes?"

"Among others."

"Well, if you told Mr. George Washington the reasons why you liked his time, you'd probably be naming everything he hated about it."

"But that's not a fair comparison. This is the worst age in all history."

Jelling waved his hand. "That's how it looks to you. Everybody says that in every generation; but take my word for it, no matter when you live and how you live, there's always somebody else somewhere else who thinks you live in the Golden Age."

"Well I'll be damned," Addyer said.

Jelling looked at him steadily for a long moment. "You will be," he said sorrowfully. "I've got bad news for you, Addyer. We can't let you remain. You'll talk and make trouble, and our secret's got to be kept. We'll have to send you out one-way."

"I can talk wherever I go."

"But nobody'll pay attention to you outside your own time. You won't make sense. You'll be an eccentric . . . a lunatic . . . a foreigner . . . safe."

"What if I come back?"

"You won't be able to get back without a visa, and I'm not tattooing any visa on you. You won't be the first we've had to transport, if that's any consolation to you. There was a Jap, I remember—"

"Then you're going to send me somewhere in time? Permanently?"

"That's right. I'm really very sorry."

"To the future or the past?"

"You can take your choice. Think it over while you're getting undressed."

"You don't have to act so mournful," Addyer said. "It's a

great adventure. A high adventure. It's something I've always dreamed."

"That's right. It's going to be wonderful."

"I could refuse," Addyer said nervously.

Jelling shook his head. "We'd only drug you and send you anyway. It might as well be your choice."

"It's a choice I'm delighted to make."

"Sure. That's the spirit, Addyer."

"Everybody says I was born a hundred years too soon."

"Everybody generally says that . . . unless they say you were born a hundred years too late."

"Some people say that too."

"Well, think it over. It's a permanent move. Which would you prefer . . . the phonetic future or the poetic past?"

Very slowly Addyer began to undress, as he undressed each night when he began the prelude to his customary fantasy. But now his dreams were faced with fulfillment and the moment of decision terrified him. He was a little blue and rather unsteady on his legs when he stepped to the copper disc in the center of the floor. In answer to Jelling's inquiry, he muttered his choice. Then he turned argent in the aura of an incandescent glow and disappeared from his time forever.

Where did he go? You know. I know. Addyer knows. Addyer traveled to the land of Our pet fantasy. He escaped into the refuge that is Our refuge, to the time of Our dreams; and in practically no time at all he realized that he had in truth departed from the only time for himself.

Through the vistas of the years every age but our own seems glamorous and golden. We yearn for the yesterdays and to-morrows, never realizing that we are faced with Hobson's Choice . . . that today, bitter or sweet, anxious or calm, is the only day for us. The dream of time is the traitor, and we are all accomplices to the betrayal of ourselves.

Can you spare price of one coffee, honorable sir? No, sir, I am not panhandling organism. I am starveling Japanese transient

*stranded in this so-miserable year. Honorable sir! I beg in tears for
holy charity. Will you donate to this destitute person one ticket to
township of Lyonesse? I want to beg on knees for visa. I want to go
back to year 1945 again. I want to be in Hiroshima again. I want
to go home.*

Star Light, Star Bright
Introduction

THE Chase formula and the Search formula have been with us for a long time and will remain on the scene for a long time to come. They're sure-fire if handled with originality and can make your pulse pound like a Sousa march. I'm a little disappointed in the Hollywood writers, to say the least. Their idea of a chase seems to be one car pursuing another.

Chase and search aren't identical; you can have one without the other, but both totether is best. Back in the carefree comic book days I even tried a tandem; started with an ordinary paper chase and then the paper trail turned into a trail of paper money. I wish I could remember the hero I did it for; "The Green Lantern"? "The Star-Spangled Kid"? "Captain Marvel"? I also wish I could remember how the story turned out.

You've probably noticed that I don't remember my work very well. Frankly, I never look at anything after it's been published, and anyway I'm not unique in that respect. I got it from the best authority, Jed Harris, that our wonderful popular composer, Jerome Kern, could never remember his own songs. In the course of a party, he'd be coaxed to the piano to play his tunes. Everybody would cluster around, but as he played they'd have to correct him. "No, no, Jerry! It doesn't go like that." And they'd be forced to sing his hits to him to refresh his memory.

"Star Light, Star Bright" is a search with a chase tempo. I don't know where I got the central idea but in those days science fiction authors were worrying a lot in print about misunderstood wild talents and child geniuses, so I guess it rubbed off on me. No, that can't be right. I'd tried the recipe many years before with a young nature counselor in a summer camp who is an idiot-genius and terribly misunderstood. But he solves a kidnapping despite the fact that I'd given him the ridiculous name of Erasmus Gaul.

The story-attack and the search techniques in "Star Light" were all from gimmick research. The Heirs of Buchanan swindle was a racket years ago and probably still is, in one form or another. God knows, they never die. In our sophomore year my college roommate got taken for his month's allowance ($20) by a couple of petty cons in Pennsylvania Station. Years later I read the identical racket in Greene's "The Art of Cony Catching" published circa 1592. No, they never die. Also, there's one born every minute.

I rather liked the story while I was writing it, but I don't like the fourth and third paragraphs from the end, counting backward from the end. They're the result of the same old battle which I lost this time to Tony Boucher of *Fantasy & Science Fiction*, again over specifics. He wanted me to wrap up the story by showing precisely what happened to the victims. I wanted to slough it. I lost and had to add the paragraphs.

When I was defeated in the battle of specifics with Horace Gold over "Hobson's Choice," I took the story back and gave it to Tony, who ran it. When I lost the battle with Tony, I should have taken "Star Light" back and sent it to Horace in a plain brown wrapper. I didn't, and now I'm stuck with those two rotten paragraphs. Please read them with your eyes shut.

The man in the car was thirty-eight years old. He was tall, slender, and not strong. His cropped hair was prematurely grey. He was afflicted with an education and a sense of humor. He was inspired by a purpose. He was armed with a phone book. He was doomed.

He drove up Post Avenue, stopped at No. 17 and parked. He consulted the phone book, then got out of the car and entered the house. He examined the mailboxes and then ran up the stairs to apartment 2-F. He rang the bell. While he waited for an answer he got out a small black notebook and a superior silver pencil that wrote in four colors.

The door opened. To a nondescript middle-aged lady, the man said, "Good evening. Mrs. Buchanan?"

The lady nodded.

"My name is Foster. I'm from the Science Institute. We're trying to check some flying saucer reports. I won't take a minute." Mr. Foster insinuated himself into the apartment. He had been in so many that he knew the layout automatically. He marched briskly down the hall to the front parlor, turned, smiled at Mrs. Buchanan, opened the notebook to a blank page, and poised the pencil.

"Have you ever seen a flying saucer, Mrs. Buchanan?"

"No. And it's a lot of bunk, I—"

"Have your children ever seen them? You do have children?"

"Yeah, but they—"

"How many?"

"Two. Them flying saucers never—"

"Are either of school age?"

"What?"

"School," Mr. Foster repeated impatiently. "Do they go to school?"

"The boy's twenty-eight," Mrs. Buchanan said. "The girl's twenty-four. They finished school a long—"

"I see. Either of them married?"

"No. About them flying saucers, you scientist doctors ought to—"

"We are," Mr. Foster interrupted. He made a tic-tac-toe in the notebook, then closed it and slid it into a inside pocket with the pencil. "Thank you very much, Mrs. Buchanan," he said, turned, and marched out.

Downstairs, Mr. Foster got into the car, opened the telephone directory, turned to a page and ran his pencil through a name. He examined the name underneath, memorized the address and started the car. He drove to Fort George Avenue and stopped the car in front of No. 800. He entered the house and took the self-service elevator to the fourth floor. He rang the bell of apartment 4-G. While he waited for an answer he got out the small black notebook and the superior pencil.

The door opened. To a truculent man, Mr. Foster said, "Good evening. Mr. Buchanan?"

"What about it?" the truculent man said.

Mr. Foster said, "My name is Davis. I'm from the Association of National Broadcasters. We're preparing a list of names for prize competitors. May I come in? Won't take a minute."

Mr. Foster/Davis insinuated himself and presently consulted with Mr. Buchanan and his redheaded wife in the living room of their apartment.

"Have you ever won a prize in radio or television?"

"No," Mr. Buchanan said angrily. "We never got a chance. Everybody else does but not us."

"All that free money and iceboxes," Mrs. Buchanan said. "Trips to Paris and planes and—"

"That's why we're making up this list," Mr. Foster/Davis broke in. "Have any of your relatives won prizes?"

"No. It's all a fix. Put-up jobs. They—"

"Any of your children?"

"Ain't got any children."

"I see. Thank you very much." Mr. Foster/Davis played out the tic-tac-toe game in his notebook, closed it and put it away.

He released himself from the indignation of the Buchanans, went down to his car, crossed out another name in the phone book, memorized the address of the name underneath and started the car.

He drove to No. 215 East Sixty-Eighth Street and parked in front of a private brownstone house. He rang the doorbell and was confronted by a maid in uniform.

"Good evening," he said. "Is Mr. Buchanan in?"

"Who's calling?"

"My name is Hook," Mr. Foster/Davis said, "I'm conducting an investigation for the Better Business Bureau."

The maid disappeared, reappeared and conducted Mr. Foster/Davis/Hook to a small library where a resolute gentleman in dinner clothes stood holding a Limoges demitasse cup and saucer. There were expensive books on the shelves. There was an expensive fire in the grate.

"Mr. Hook?"

"Yes, sir," the doomed man replied. He did not take out the notebook. "I won't be a minute, Mr. Buchanan. Just a few questions."

"I have great faith in the Better Business Bureau," Mr. Buchanan pronounced. "Our bulwark against the inroads of—"

"Thank you, sir," Mr. Foster/Davis/Hook interrupted. "Have you ever been criminally defrauded by a businessman?"

"The attempt has been made. I have never succumbed."

"And your children? You do have children?"

"My son is hardly old enough to qualify as a victim."

"How old is he, Mr. Buchanan?"

"Ten."

"Perhaps he has been tricked at school? There are crooks who specialize in victimizing children."

"Not at my son's school. He is well protected."

"What school is that, sir?"

"Germanson."

"One of the best. Did he ever attend a city public school?"

"Never."

The doomed man took out the notebook and the superior pencil. This time he made a serious entry.

"Any other children, Mr. Buchanan?"

"A daughter, seventeen."

Mr. Foster/Davis/Hook considered, started to write, changed his mind and closed the notebook. He thanked his host politely and escaped from the house before Mr. Buchanan could ask for his credentials. He was ushered out by the maid, ran down the stoop to his car, opened the door, entered and was felled by a tremendous blow on the side of his head.

When the doomed man awoke, he thought he was in bed suffering from a hangover. He started to crawl to the bathroom when he realized he was dumped in a chair like a suit for the cleaners. He opened his eyes. He was in what appeared to be an underwater grotto. He blinked frantically. The water receded.

He was in a small legal office. A stout man who looked like an unfrocked Santa Claus stood before him. To one side, seated on a desk and swinging his legs carelessly, was a thin young man with a lantern jaw and eyes closely set on either side of his nose.

"Can you hear me?" the stout man asked.

The doomed man grunted.

"Can we talk?"

Another grunt.

"Joe," the stout man said pleasantly, "a towel."

The thin young man slipped off the desk, went to a corner basin and soaked a white hand towel. He shook it once, sauntered back to the chair where, with a suddeness and savagery of a tiger, he lashed it across the sick man's face.

"For God's sake!" Mr. Foster/Davis/Hook cried.

"That's better," the stout man said. "My name's Herod.

Walter Herod, attorney-at-law." He stepped to the desk where the contents of the doomed man's pockets were spread, picked up a wallet and displayed it. "Your name is Warbeck. Marion Perkin Warbeck. Right?"

The doomed man gazed at his wallet, then at Walter Herod, attorney-at-law, and finally admitted the truth. "Yes," he said. "My name is Warbeck. But I never admit the Marion to strangers."

He was again lashed by the wet towel and fell back in the chair, stung and bewildered.

"That will do, Joe," Herod said. "Not again, please, until I tell you." To Warbeck he said, "Why this interest in the Buchanans?" He waited for an answer, then continued pleasantly, "Joe's been tailing you. You've averaged five Buchanans a night. Thirty, so far. What's your angle?"

"What the hell is this? Russia?" Warbeck demanded indignantly. "You've got no right to kidnap me and grill me like the MVD. If you think you can—"

"Joe," Herod interrupted pleasantly. "Again, please."

Again the towel lashed Warbeck. Tormented, furious and helpless, he burst into tears.

Herod fingered the wallet casually. "Your papers say you're a teacher by profession, principal of a public school. I thought teachers were supposed to be legit. How did you get mixed up in the inheritance racket?"

"The what racket?" Warbeck asked faintly.

"The inheritance racket," Herod repeated patiently. "The Heirs of Buchanan caper. What kind of parlay are you using? Personal approach?"

"I don't know what you're talking about," Warbeck answered. He sat bolt upright and pointed to the thin youth. "And don't start that towel business again."

"I'll start what I please and when I please," Herod said ferociously. "And I'll finish you when I goddamned well please. You're stepping on my toes and I don't buy it. I've got seventy-five thousand a year I'm taking out of this and I'm not going to let you chisel."

There was a long pause, significant for everybody in the room except the doomed man. Finally he spoke. "I'm an educated man," he said slowly. "Mention Galileo, say, or the lesser Cavalier poets, and I'm right up there with you. But there are gaps in my education and this is one of them. I can't meet the situation. Too many unknowns."

"I told you my name," Herod answered. He pointed to the thin young man. "That's Joe Davenport."

Warbeck shook his head. "Unknown in the mathematical sense. X quantities. Solving equations. My education speaking."

Joe looked startled. "Jesus!" he said without moving his lips. "Maybe he *is* legit."

Herod examined Warbeck curiously. "I'm going to spell it out for you," he said. "The inheritance racket is a long-term con. It operates something like so: There's a story that James Buchanan—"

"Fifteenth President of the U.S.?"

"In person. There's a story he died intestate leaving an estate for heirs unknown. That was in 1868. Today at compound interest that estate is worth millions. Understand?"

Warbeck nodded. "I'm educated," he murmured.

"Anybody named Buchanan is a sucker for this setup. It's a switch on the Spanish Prisoner routine. I send them a letter. Tell 'em there's a chance they may be one of the heirs. Do they want me to investigate and protect their cut in the estate? It only costs a small yearly retainer. Most of them buy it. From all over the country. And now you—"

"Wait a minute," Warbeck exclaimed. "I can draw a conclusion. You found out I was checking the Buchanan families. You think I'm trying to operate the same racket. Cut in . . . cut in? Yes? Cut in on you?"

"Well," Herod asked angrily, "aren't you?"

"Oh God!" Warbeck cried. "That this should happen to me. Me! Thank You, God. Thank You. I'll always be grateful." In his happy fervor he turned to Joe. "Give me the towel, Joe," he said. "Just throw it. I've got to wipe my face." He caught the flung towel and mopped himself joyously.

"Well," Herod repeated. "Aren't you?"

"No," Warbeck answered, "I'm not cutting in on you. But I'm grateful for the mistake. Don't think I'm not. You can't imagine how flattering it is for a schoolteacher to be taken for a thief."

He got out of the chair and went to the desk to reclaim his wallet and other possessions.

"Just a minute," Herod snapped.

The thin young man reached out and grasped Warbeck's wrist with an iron clasp.

"Oh stop it," the doomed man said impatiently. "This is a silly mistake."

"I'll tell you whether it's a mistake and I'll tell you if it's silly," Herod replied. "Just now you'll do as you're told."

"Will I?" Warbeck wrenched his wrist free and slashed Joe across the eyes with the towel. He darted around behind the desk, snatched up a paperweight and hurled it through the window with a shattering crash.

"Joe!" Herod yelled.

Warbeck knocked the phone off its stand and dialed Operator. He picked up his cigarette lighter, flicked it and dropped it into the wastepaper basket. The voice of the operator buzzed in the phone. Warbeck shouted, "I want a policeman!" Then he kicked the flaming basket into the center of the office.

"Joe!" Herod yelled and stamped on the blazing paper.

Warbeck grinned. He picked up the phone. Squawking noises were coming out of it. He put one hand over the mouthpiece. "Shall we negotiate?" he inquired.

"You sonofabitch," Joe growled. He took his hands from his eyes and slid toward Warbeck.

"No!" Herod called. "This crazy fool's hollered copper. He's legit, Joe." To Warbeck he said in pleading tones, "Fix it. Square it. We'll make it up to you. Anything you say. Just square the call."

The doomed man lifted the phone to his mouth. He said, "My name is M. P. Warbeck. I was consulting my attorney at this number and some idiot with a misplaced sense of humor made this call. Please phone back and check."

He hung up, finished pocketing his private property and winked at Herod. The phone rang, Warbeck picked it up, reassured the police and hung up. He came around from behind the desk and handed his car keys to Joe.

"Go down to my car," he said. "You know where you parked it. Open the glove compartment and bring up a brown manila envelope you'll find."

"Go to hell," Joe spat. His eyes were still tearing.

"Do as I say," Warbeck said firmly.

"Just a minute, Warbeck," Herod said. "What's this? A new angle? I said we'd make it up to you, but—"

"I'm going to explain why I'm interested in the Buchanans," Warbeck replied. "And I'm going into partnership with you. You've got what I need to locate one particular Buchanan . . . you and Joe. My Buchanan's ten years old. He's worth a hundred times your make-believe fortune."

Herod stared at him.

Warbeck placed the keys in Joe's hand. "Go down and get that envelope, Joe," he said. "And while you're at it you'd better square that broken window rap. Rap? Rap."

The doomed man placed the manila envelope neatly on his lap. "A school principal," he explained, "has to supervise school classes. He reviews work, estimates progress, irons out student problems and so on. This must be done at random. By samplings, I mean. I have nine hundred pupils in my school. I can't supervise them individually."

Herod nodded. Joe looked blank.

"Looking through some fifth-grade work last month," Warbeck continued, "I came across this astonishing document."
He opened the envelope and took out a few sheets of ruled
composition paper covered with blots and scrawled writing.
"It was written by a Stuart Buchanan of the fifth grade. His
age must be ten or thereabouts. The composition is entitled:
My Vacation. Read it and you'll understand why Stuart Buchanan must be found."

He tossed the sheets to Herod who picked them up, took
out a pair of horn-rim spectacles and balanced them on his fat
nose. Joe came around to the back of his chair and peered
over his shoulder.

My Vacatoin
by
Stuart Buchanan

*This sumer I vissited my frends. I have 4 frends and they are
verry nice. First there is Tommy who lives in the contry and he is
an astronnimer. Tommy bilt his own tellescop out of glass 6 inches
acros wich he grond himself. He loks at the stars every nihgt and he
let me lok even wen it was raining cats & dogs . . .*

"What the hell?" Herod looked up, annoyed.
"Read on. Read on," Warbeck said.

*cats & dogs. We cold see the stars becaze Tommy made a thing for
over the end of the tellescop wich shoots up like a serchlite and
makes a hole in the skie to see rite thru the rain and everythinng to
the stars.*

"Finished the astronomer yet?" Warbeck inquired.
"I don't dig it."
"Tommy got bored waiting for clear nights. He invented
something that cuts through clouds and atmosphere . . . a
funnel of vacuum so he can use his telescope all weather. What
it amounts to is a disintegration beam."

"The hell you say."
"The hell I don't. Read on. Read on."

Then I went to AnnMary and staied one hole week. It was fun.
Becaze AnnMary has a spinak chainger for spinak and beats and
strinbeans—
"What the hell is a 'spinak chainger'?"
"Spinach. Spinach changer. Spelling isn't one of Stuart's specialties. 'Beats' are beets. 'Strinbeens' are string beans."

beats and strinbeens. Wen her mother made us eet them AnnMary
presed the buton and they staid the same outside onnly inside they
became cake. Chery and strowbery. I asted AnnMary how & she
sed it was by Enhv.

"This, I don't get."
"Simple. Anne-Marie doesn't like vegetables. So she's just as smart as Tommy, the astronomer. She invented a matter-transmuter. She transmutes spinak into cake. Chery or strowberry. Cake she eats with pleasure. So does Stuart."
"You're crazy."
"Not me. The kids. They're geniuses. Geniuses? What am I saying? They make a genius look imbecile. There's no label for these children."
"I don't believe it. This Stuart Buchanan's got a tall imagination. That's all."
"You think so? Then what about Enhv? That's how Anne-Marie transmutes matter. It took time but I figured Enhv out. It's Planck's quantum equation $E=nhv$. But read on. Read on. The best is yet to come. Wait till you get to lazy Ethel."

My frend Gorge bilds modell airplanes very good and small.
Gorg's hands are clumzy but he makes small men out of moddel-
ling clay and he tels them and they bild for him.

"What's this?"

"George, the plane-maker?"

"Yes."

"Simple. He makes miniature androids . . . robots . . . and they build the planes for him. Clever boy, George, but read about his sister, lazy Ethel."

His sister Ethel is the lazyist girl I ever saw. She is big & fat and she hates to walk. So wen her mothar sends her too the store Ethel thinks to the store and thinks home with all the pakejes and has to hang arownd Gorg's room hiding untill it wil look like she walked both ways. Gorge and I make fun of her becaze she is fat and lazy but she gets into the movees for free and saw Hoppalong Casidy sixteen times.

The End

Herod stared at Warbeck.

"Great little girl, Ethel," Warbeck said. "She's too lazy to walk, so she teleports. Then she has a devil of a time covering up. She has to hide with her pakejes while George and Stuart make fun of her."

"Teleports?"

"That's right. She moves from place to place by thinking her way there."

"There ain't no such thing!" Joe said indignantly.

"There wasn't until lazy Ethel came along."

"I don't believe this," Herod said. "I don't believe any of it."

"You think it's just Stuart's imagination?"

"What else?"

"What about Planck's equation? E=nhv?"

"The kid invented that, too. Coincidence."

"Does that sound likely?"

"Then he read it somewhere."

"A ten-year-old boy? Nonsense."

"I tell you, I don't believe it," Herod shouted. "Let me talk to the kid for five minutes and I'll prove it."

"That's exactly what I want to do . . . only the boy's disappeared."

"How do you mean?"

"Lock, stock, and barrel. That's why I've been checking every Buchanan family in the city. The day I read this composition and sent down to the fifth grade for Stuart Buchanan to have a talk, he disappeared. He hasn't been seen since."

"What about his family?"

"The family disappeared too." Warbeck leaned forward intensely. "Get this. Every record of the boy and the family disappeared. Everything. A few people remember them vaguely, but that's all. They're gone."

"Jesus!" Joe said. "They scrammed, huh?"

"The very word. Scrammed. Thank you, Joe." Warbeck cocked an eye at Herod. "What a situation. Here's a child who makes friends with child geniuses. And the emphasis is on the child. They're making fantastic discoveries for childish purposes. Ethel teleports because she's too lazy to run errands. George makes robots to build model planes. Anne-Marie transmutes elements because she hates spinach. God knows what Stuart's other friends are doing. Maybe there's a Matthew who's invented a time machine so he can catch up on his homework."

Herod waved his hands feebly. "Why geniuses all of a sudden? What's happened?"

"I don't know. Atomic fallout? Fluorides in drinking water? Antibiotics? Vitamins? We're doing so much juggling with body chemistry these days that who knows what's happening? I want to find out but I can't. Stuart Buchanan blabbed like a child. When I started investigating, he got scared and disappeared."

"Is he a genius, too?"

"Very likely. Kids generally hang out with kids who share the same interests and talents."

"What kind of a genius? What's his talent?"

"I don't know. All I know is he disappeared. He covered up his tracks, destroyed every paper that could possibly help me locate him and vanished into thin air."

"How did he get into your files?"

"I don't know."

"Maybe he's a crook type," Joe said. "Expert at breaking and entering and such."

Herod smiled wanly. "A racketeer genius? A mastermind? The kid Moriarty?"

"He could be a thief-genius," the doomed man said, "but don't let running away convince you. All children do that when they get caught in a crisis. Either they wish it had never happened or they wish they were a million miles away. Stuart Buchanan may be a million miles away, but we've got to find him."

"Just to find out is he smart?" Joe asked.

"No, to find his friends. Do I have to diagram it? What would the army pay for a disintegration beam? What would an element-transmuter be worth? If we could manufacture living robots how rich would we get? If we could teleport how powerful would we be?"

There was a burning silence, then Herod got to his feet. "Mr. Warbeck," he said, "you make me and Joe look like pikers. Thank you for letting us cut in on you. We'll pay off. We'll find that kid."

It is not possible for anyone to vanish without a trace . . . even a probable criminal genius. It is sometimes difficult to locate that trace . . . even for an expert experienced in hurried disappearances. But there is a professional technique unknown to amateurs.

"You've been blundering," Herod explained kindly to the doomed man. "Chasing one Buchanan after the other. There are angles. You don't run after a missing party. You look around on his back-trail for something he dropped."

"A genius wouldn't drop anything."

"Let's grant the kid's a genius. Type unspecified. Let's grant him everything. But a kid is a kid. He must have overlooked something. We'll find it."

In three days Warbeck was introduced to the most astonishing angles of search. They consulted the Washington Heights post office about a Buchanan family formerly living in that neighborhood, now moved. Was there any change-of-address-card filed? None.

They visited the election board. All voters are registered. If a voter moves from one election district to another, provision is usually made that a record of the transfer be kept. Was there any such record on Buchanan? None.

They called on the Washington Heights office of the gas and electric company. All subscribers for gas and electricity must transfer their accounts if they move. If they move out of town, they generally request the return of their deposit. Was there any record of a party named Buchanan? None.

It is a state law that all drivers must notify the license bureau of change of address or be subject to penalties involving fines, prison or worse. Was there any such notification by a party named Buchanan at the Motor Vehicle Bureau? There was not.

They questioned the R-J Realty Corp., owners and operators of a multiple dwelling in Washington Heights in which a party named Buchanan had leased a four-room apartment. The R-J lease, like most other leases, required the names and addresses of two character references for the tenant. Could the character references for Buchanan be produced? They could not. There was no such lease in the files.

"Maybe Joe was right," Warbeck complained in Herod's office. "Maybe the boy is a thief-genius. How did he think of everything? How did he get at every paper and destroy it? Did he break and enter? Bribe? Burgle? Threaten? How did he do it?"

"We'll ask him when we get to him," Herod said grimly. "All right. The kid's licked us straight down the line. He hasn't forgotten a trick. But I've got one angle I've been saving. Let's go up and see the janitor of their building."

"I questioned him months ago," Warbeck objected. "He remembers the family in a vague way and that's all. He doesn't know where they went."

"He knows something else, something the kid wouldn't think of covering. Let's go get it."

They drove up to Washington Heights and descended upon Mr. Jacob Ruysdale at dinner in the basement apartment of the building. Mr. Ruysdale disliked being separated from his liver and onions, but was persuaded by five dollars.

"About that Buchanan family," Herod began.

"I told him everything before," Ruysdale broke in, pointing to Warbeck.

"All right. He forgot to ask one question. Can I ask it now?" Ruysdale reexamined the five-dollar bill and nodded.

"When anybody moves in or out of a building, the superintendent usually takes down the name of the movers in case they damage the building. I'm a lawyer. I know this. It's to protect the building in case suit has to be brought. Right?"

Ruysdale's face lit up. "By Godfrey!" he said. "That's right, I forgot all about it. He never asked me."

"He didn't know. You've got the name of the company that moved the Buchanans out. Right?"

Ruysdale ran across the room to a cluttered bookshelf. He withdrew a tattered journal and flipped it open. He wet his fingers and turned pages.

"Here it is," he said. "The Avon Moving Company. Truck No. G-4."

The Avon Moving Company had no record of the removal of a Buchanan family from an apartment in Washington Heights. "The kid was pretty careful at that," Herod murmured. But it did have a record of the men working truck G-4 on that day. The men were interviewed when they checked in at closing time. Their memories were refreshed with whiskey and cash. They recalled the Washington Heights job vaguely.

It was a full day's work because they had to drive the hell and gone to Brooklyn. "Oh God! Brooklyn!" Warbeck muttered. What address in Brooklyn? Something on Maple Park Row. Number? The number could not be recalled.

"Joe, buy a map."

They examined the street map of Brooklyn and located Maple Park Row. It was indeed the hell and gone out of civilization and was twelve blocks long. "That's *Brooklyn* blocks," Joe grunted. "Twice as long as anywhere. I know."

Herod shrugged. "We're close," he said. "The rest will have to be legwork. Four blocks apiece. Cover every house, every apartment. List every kid around ten. Then Warbeck can check them, if they're under an alias."

"There's a million kids a square inch in Brooklyn." Joe protested.

"There's a million dollars a day in it for us if we find him. Now let's go."

Maple Park Row was a long, crooked street lined with five-story apartment houses. Its sidewalks were lined with baby carriages and old ladies on camp chairs. Its curbs were lined with parked cars. Its gutter was lined with crude whitewash stickball courts shaped like elongated diamonds. Every manhole cover was a home plate.

"It's just like the Bronx," Joe said nostalgically. "I ain't been home to the Bronx in ten years."

He wandered sadly down the street toward his sector, automatically threading his way through stickball games with the unconscious skill of the city-born. Warbeck remembered that departure sympathetically because Joe Davenport never returned.

The first day, he and Herod imagined Joe had found a hot lead. This encouraged them. The second day they realized no heat could keep Joe on the fire for forty-eight hours. This depressed them. On the third day they had to face the truth.

"He's dead," Herod said flatly. "The kid got him."

"How?"

"He killed him."

"A ten-year-old boy? A child?"

"You want to know what kind of genius Stuart Buchanan has, don't you? I'm telling you."

"I don't believe it."

"Then explain Joe."

"He quit."

"Not on a million dollars."

"But where's the body?"

"Ask the kid. He's the genius. He's probably figured out tricks that would baffle Dick Tracy."

"How did he kill him?"

"Ask the kid. He's the genius."

"Herod, I'm scared."

"So am I. Do you want to quit now?"

"I don't see how we can. If the boy's dangerous, we've got to find him."

"Civic virtue, heh?"

"Call it that."

"Well, I'm still thinking about the money."

They returned to Maple Park Row and Joe Davenport's four-block sector. They were cautious, almost furtive. They separated and began working from each end toward the middle; in one house, up the stairs, apartment by apartment, to the top, then down again to investigate the next building. It was slow, tedious work. Occasionally they glimpsed each other far down the street, crossing from one dismal building to another. And that was the last glimpse Warbeck ever had of Walter Herod.

He sat in his car and waited. He sat in his car and trembled. "I'll go to the police," he muttered, knowing perfectly well he could not. "The boy has a weapon. Something he invented. Something silly like the others. A special light so he can play marbles at night, only it murders men. A machine to play checkers, only it hypnotizes men. He's invented a robot mob of gangsters so he can play cops-and-robbers and they took care of Joe and Herod. He's a child genius. Dangerous. Deadly. What am I going to do?"

The doomed man got out of the car and stumbled down the street toward Herod's half of the sector. "What's going to happen when Stuart Buchanan grows up?" he wondered. "What's going to happen when all the rest of them grow up? Tommy and George and Anne-Marie and lazy Ethel? Why don't I start running away now? What am I doing here?"

It was dusk on Maple Park Row. The old ladies had withdrawn, folding their camp chairs like Arabs. The parked cars remained. The stickball games were over, but small games were starting under the glowing lamp posts . . . games with bottle caps and cards and battered pennies. Overhead, the purple city haze was deepening, and through it the sharp sparkle of Venus following the sun below the horizon could be seen.

"He must know his power," Warbeck muttered angrily. "He must know how dangerous he is. That's why he's running away. Guilt. That's why he destroys us, one by one, smiling to himself, a crafty child, a vicious, killing genius. . . ."

Warbeck stopped in the middle of Maple Park Row.

"Buchanan!" he shouted. "Stuart Buchanan!"

The kids near him stopped their games and gaped.

"Stuart Buchanan!" Warbeck's voice cracked hysterically. "Can you hear me?"

He wild voice carried farther down the street. More games stopped. Ringaleevio, Chinese tag, Red-Light and Boxball.

"Buchanan!" Warbeck screamed. "Stuart Buchanan! Come out come out, wherever you are!"

The world hung motionless.

In the alley between 217 and 219 Maple Park Row playing hide-and-seek behind piled ash barrels, Stuart Buchanan heard his name and crouched lower. He was aged ten, dressed in sweater, jeans, and sneakers. He was intent and determined that he was not going to be caught out "it" again. He was going to hide until he could make a dash for home-free in safety. As he settled comfortably among the ashcans, his eye caught the glimmer of Venus low in the western sky.

"Star light, star bright," he whispered in all innocence, "first star I see tonight. Wish I may, wish I might, grant me the wish I wish tonight." He paused and considered. Then he wished. "God bless Mom and Pop and me and all my friends and make me a good boy and please let me be always happy and I wish that anybody who tries to bother me would go away . . . a long way away . . . and leave me alone forever."

In the middle of Maple Park Row, Marion Perkin Warbeck stepped forward and drew breath for another hysterical yell. And then he was elsewhere, going away on a road that was a long way away. It was a straight white road cleaving infinitely through blackness, stretching onward and onward into forever; a dreary, lonely, endless road leading away and away and away.

Down that road Warbeck plodded, an astonished automaton, unable to speak, unable to stop, unable to think in the timeless infinity. Onward and onward he walked into a long way away, unable to turn back. Ahead of him he saw the minute specks of figures trapped on that one-way road to forever. There was a dot that had to be Herod. Ahead of Herod there was a mote that was Joe Davenport. And ahead of Joe he could make out a long, dwindling chain of mites. He turned once with a convulsive effort. Behind him, dim and distant, a figure was plodding, and behind that another abruptly materialized, and another . . . and another. . . .

While Stuart Buchanan crouched behind the ash barrels and watched alertly for the "it." He was unaware that he had disposed of Warbeck. He was unaware that he had disposed of Herod, Joe Davenport and scores of others.

He was unaware that he had induced his parents to flee Washington Heights, that he had destroyed papers and documents, memories and peoples, in his simple desire to be left alone. He was unaware that he was a genius.

His genius was for wishing.

They Don't Make Life Like They Used To

Introduction

IT'S a constant source of shame to me that I invariably find nice, normal people dull and boring. I like them, but I don't want to spend any time with them. What I look for is people with what Evelyn Waugh called "the light of lunacy" in their eyes. I prefer those with the light of lunacy illuminating all their acts of feasance, malfeasance, and nonfeasance. Obviously this must be a case of like being drawn to like.

So when I sort of drifted into a last-man-last-woman-on-earth story because I had nothing fresher to write at the moment, I knew I was tackling an exhausted theme, but I thought it might be fun to make them a couple of kooks and see the world through their lunatic eyes. I liked the two *meshugenahs* so much that I played the action in some of my favorite places in New York and wrote so much that I had to cut it by a third. I didn't know whether the story would appeal to others as much as it did to me and was much surprised when it did. It appealed so much that one publisher pleaded with me to write a sequel, preparatory to turning it into a novel. On the other hand, one friend bawled hell out of me for writing what he considered to be pornographic scenes.

109

This raises the fulminating issue of pornography and censorship which doesn't affect me because a Puritan streak in my nature has always stifled the slightest temptation to do that sort of work. I'm strongly opposed to censorship in any form, and yet I confess to being disgusted by the passages that diagram it for you.

I suppose it mostly depends on how and why it was written and by whom. In the studios we're notorious for the foul language we use casually, and yet the same language becomes profane and offensive when used by certain people. I've never been able to figure out why. Is it because of the way it's said, the person himself (or herself), the situation? I don't know.

The same holds for writing. Some authors can put together the most outrageous scenes and they never seem to offend. Others can't even write a kiss without making it dirty. For my part I've never seen the need for being explicit. One can, as many authors have, do it by suggestion rather than spelling it out . . . which reminds me of another friend and his four-year-old son.

The kid came home from nursery school very much upset. When the father asked him why, he said that another boy had called him a bad name.

"What did he call you?"

"Oh, I couldn't say it."

"But how will you know it's bad unless you tell me and I tell you?"

"I couldn't say it." The four-year-old thought it over. "I'll have to spell it."

"All right. Spell it."

"He called me a . . . a F.U.B.G.H."

There isn't much more to say about this simple example of theme and variations except that I love the title but can't see what on earth it has to do with the story. My years as a magazine editor trained me in the art of title writing, and it *is* an art to capture the essence of a piece and grab the reader. Unfortunately this one was written before my training.

The girl driving the jeep was very fair and very Nordic. Her blonde hair was pulled back in a pony tail, but it was so long that it was more a mare's tail. She wore sandals, a pair of soiled bluejeans, and nothing else. She was nicely tanned. As she turned the jeep off Fifth Avenue and drove bouncing up the steps of the library, her bosom danced enchantingly.

She parked in front of the library entrance, stepped out, and was about to enter when her attention was attracted by something across the street. She peered, hesitated, then glanced down at her jeans and made a face. She pulled off the pants and hurled them at the pigeons eternally cooing and courting on the library steps. As they clattered up in fright, she ran down to Fifth Avenue, crossed, and stopped before a shop window. There was a plum-colored wool dress on display. It had a high waist, a full skirt, and not too many moth holes. The price was $79.90.

The girl rummaged through old cars skewed on the avenue until she found a loose fender. She smashed the plate-glass shop door, carefully stepped across the splinters, entered, and sorted through the dusty dress racks. She was a big girl and had trouble fitting herself. Finally she abandoned the plum-colored wool and compromised on a dark tartan, size 12, $120 reduced to $99.90. She located a salesbook and pencil, blew the dust off, and carefully wrote: *I.O.U. $99.90. Linda Nielsen.*

She returned to the library and went through the main doors which had taken her a week to batter in with a sledgehammer. She ran across the great hall, filthied with five years of droppings from the pigeons roosting there. As she ran, she clapped her arms over her head to shield her hair from stray shots. She climbed the stairs to the third floor and entered the Print Room. As always, she signed the register: *Date—June 20, 1981. Name—Linda Nielsen. Address—Central Park Model Boat Pond. Business or Firm—Last Man on Earth.*

She had had a long debate with herself about *Business or*

Firm the last time she broke into the library. Strictly speaking, she was the last woman on earth, but she had felt that if she wrote that it would seem chauvinistic; and "Last Person on Earth" sounded silly, like calling a drink a beverage.

She pulled portfolios out of racks and leafed through them. She knew exactly what she wanted; something warm with blue accents to fit a twenty by thirty frame for her bedroom. In a priceless collection of Hiroshige prints she found a lovely landscape. She filled out a slip, placed it carefully on the librarian's desk, and left with the print.

Downstairs, she stopped off in the main circulation room, went to the back shelves, and selected two Italian grammars and an Italian dictionary. Then she backtracked through the main hall, went out to the jeep, and placed the books and print on the front seat alongside her companion, an exquisite Dresden china doll. She picked up a list that read:

> Jap. print
> Italian
> 20 × 30 pict. fr.
> Lobster bisque
> Brass polish
> Detergent
> Furn. polish
> Wet mop

She crossed off the first two items, replaced the list on the dashboard, got into the jeep, and bounced down the library steps. She drove up Fifth Avenue, threading her way through crumbling wreckage. As she was passing the ruins of St. Patrick's Cathedral at 50th Street, a man appeared from nowhere.

He stepped out of the rubble and, without looking left or right, started crossing the avenue just in front of her. She exclaimed, banged on the horn which remained mute, and braked so sharply that the jeep slewed and slammed into the remains of a No. 3 bus. The man let out a squawk, jumped ten feet, and then stood frozen, staring at her.

"You crazy jaywalker," she yelled. "Why don't you look where you're going? D'you think you own the whole city?"

He stared and stammered. He was a big man, with thick, grizzled hair, a red beard, and weathered skin. He was wearing army fatigues, heavy ski boots, and had a bursting knapsack and blanket roll on his back. He carried a battered shotgun, and his pockets were crammed with odds and ends. He looked like a prospector.

"My God," he whispered in a rusty voice. "Somebody at last. I knew it. I always knew I'd find someone." Then, as he noticed her long, fair hair, his face fell. "But a woman," he muttered. "Just my goddamn lousy luck."

"What are you, some kind of nut?" she demanded. "Don't you know better than to cross against the lights?"

He looked around in bewilderment. "What lights?"

"So all right, there aren't any lights, but couldn't you look where you were going?"

"I'm sorry, lady. To tell the truth, I wasn't expecting any traffic."

"Just plain common sense," she grumbled, backing the jeep off the bus.

"Hey lady, wait a minute."

"Yes?"

"Listen, you know anything about TV? Electronics, how they say . . ."

"Are you trying to be funny?"

"No, this is straight. Honest."

She snorted and tried to continue driving up Fifth Avenue, but he wouldn't get out of the way.

"Please, lady," he persisted. "I got a reason for asking. Do you know?"

"No."

"Damn! I never get a break. Lady, excuse me, no offense, got any guys in this town?"

"There's nobody but me. I'm the last man on earth."

"That's funny. I always thought I was."

"So all right, I'm the last woman on earth."

He shook his head. "There's got to be other people; there just has to. Stands to reason. South, maybe you think? I'm down from New Haven, and I figured if I headed where the climate was like warmer, there'd be some guys I could ask something."

"Ask what?"

"Aw, a woman wouldn't understand. No offense."

"Well, if you want to head south you're going the wrong way."

"That's south, ain't it?" he said, pointing down Fifth Avenue.

"Yes, but you'll just come to a dead end. Manhattan's an island. What you have to do is go uptown and cross the George Washington Bridge to Jersey."

"Uptown? Which way is that?"

"Go straight up Fifth to Cathedral Parkway, then over to the West Side and up Riverside. You can't miss it."

He looked at her helplessly.

"Stranger in town?"

He nodded.

"Oh, all right," she said. "Hop in. I'll give you a lift."

She transferred the books and the china doll to the back seat, and he squeezed in alongside her. As she started the jeep she looked down at his worn ski boots.

"Hiking?"

"Yeah."

"Why don't you drive? You can get a car working, and there's plenty of gas and oil."

"I don't know how to drive," he said despondently. "It's the story of my life."

He heaved a sigh, and that made his knapsack jolt massively against her shoulder. She examined him out of the corner of her eye. He had a powerful chest, a long, thick back, and strong legs. His hands were big and hard, and his neck was corded with muscles. She thought for a moment, then nodded to herself and stopped the jeep.

"What's the matter?" he asked. "Won't it go?"

"What's your name?"

"Mayo. Jim Mayo."

"I'm Linda Nielsen."

"Yeah. Nice meeting you. Why don't it go?"

"Jim, I've got a proposition for you."

"Oh?" He looked at her doubtfully. "I'll be glad to listen, lady—I mean Linda, but I ought to tell you, I got something on my mind that's going to keep me pretty busy for a long t . . ." His voice trailed off as he turned away from her intense gaze.

"Jim, if you'll do something for me, I'll do something for you."

"Like what, for instance?"

"Well, I get terribly lonesome, nights. It isn't so bad during the day—there's always a lot of chores to keep you busy—but at night it's just awful."

"Yeah, I know," he muttered.

"I've got to do something about it."

"But how do I come into this?" he asked nervously.

"Why don't you stay in New York for a while? If you do, I'll teach you how to drive, and find you a car so you don't have to hike south."

"Say, that's an idea. Is it hard, driving?"

"I could teach you in a couple of days."

"I don't learn things so quick."

"All right, a couple of weeks, but think of how much time you'll save in the long run."

"Gee," he said, "that sounds great." Then he turned away again. "But what do I have to do for you?"

Her face lit up with excitement. "Jim, I want you to help me move a piano."

"A piano? What piano?"

"A rosewood grand from Steinway's on Fifty-seventh Street. I'm dying to have it in my place. The living room is just crying for it."

"Oh, you mean you're furnishing, huh?"

"Yes, but I want to play after dinner, too. You can't listen to records all the time. I've got it all planned; books on how to play, and books on how to tune a piano. . . . I've been able to figure everything except how to move the piano in."

"Yeah, but . . . but there's apartments all over this town with pianos in them," he objected. "There must be hundreds, at least. Stands to reason. Why don't you live in one of them?"

"Never! I love my place. I've spent five years decorating it, and it's beautiful. Besides, there's the problem of water."

He nodded. "Water's always a headache. How do you handle it?"

"I'm living in the house in Central Park where they used to keep the model yachts. It faces the boat pond. It's a darling place, and I've got it all fixed up. We could get the piano in together, Jim. It wouldn't be hard."

"Well, I don't know, Lena . . ."

"Linda."

"Excuse me. Linda. I—"

"You look strong enough. What'd you do, before?"

"I used to be a pro rassler."

"There! I knew you were strong."

"Oh, I'm not a rassler anymore. I became a bartender and went into the restaurant business. I opened 'The Body Slam' up in New Haven. Maybe you heard of it?"

"I'm sorry."

"It was sort of famous with the sports crowd. What'd you do before?"

"I was a researcher for BBDO."

"What's that?"

"An advertising agency," she explained impatiently. "We can talk about that later, if you'll stick around. And I'll teach you how to drive, and we can move in the piano, and there're a few other things that I—but that can wait. Afterward you can drive south."

"Gee, Linda, I don't know . . ."

She took Mayo's hands. "Come on, Jim, be a sport. You can stay with me. I'm a wonderful cook, and I've got a lovely guest room . . ."

"What for? I mean, thinking you was the last man on earth."

"That's a silly question. A proper house has to have a guest room. You'll love my place. I turned the lawns into a farm and gardens, and you can swim in the pond, and we'll get you a new Jag . . . I know where there's a beauty up on blocks."

"I think I'd rather have a Caddy."

"You can have anything you like. So what do you say, Jim? Is it a deal?"

"All right, Linda," he muttered reluctantly. "You've a deal."

It was indeed a lovely house with its pagoda roof of copper weathered to verdigris green, fieldstone walls, and deep recessed windows. The oval pond before it glittered blue in the soft June sunlight, and mallard ducks paddled and quacked busily. The sloping lawns that formed a bowl around the pond were terraced and cultivated. The house faced west, and Central Park stretched out beyond like an unkempt estate.

Mayo looked at the pond wistfully. "It ought to have boats."

"The house was full of them when I moved in," Linda said.

"I always wanted a model boat when I was a kid. Once I even—" Mayo broke off. A penetrating pounding sounded somewhere; an irregular sequence of heavy knocks that sounded like the dint of stones under water. It stopped as suddenly as it had begun. "What was that?" Mayo asked.

Linda shrugged. "I don't know for sure. I think it's the city falling apart. You'll see buildings coming down every now and then. You get used to it." Her enthusiasm rekindled. "Now come inside. I want to show you everything."

She was bursting with pride and overflowing with decorating details that bewildered Mayo, but he was impressed by her Victorian living room, Empire bedroom, and country kitchen with a working kerosene cooking stove. The colonial guest room, with fourposter bed, hooked rug, and tole lamps, worried him.

"This is kind of girlie-girlie, huh?"

"Naturally. I'm a girl."

"Yeah. Sure. I mean . . ." Mayo looked around doubtfully. "Well, a guy is used to stuff that ain't so delicate. No offense."

"Don't worry, that bed's strong enough. Now remember, Jim, no feet on the spread, and remove it at night. If your shoes are dirty, take them off before you come in. I got that rug from the museum and I don't want it messed up. Have you got a change of clothes?"

"Only what I got on."

"We'll have to get you new things tomorrow. What you're wearing is so filthy it's not worth laundering."

"Listen," he said desperately, "I think maybe I better camp out in the park."

"Why on earth?"

"Well, I'm like more used to it than houses. But you don't have to worry, Linda. I'll be around in case you need me."

"Why should I need you?"

"All you have to do is holler."

"Nonsense," Linda said firmly. "You're my guest and you're staying here. Now get cleaned up; I'm going to start dinner. Oh damn! I forgot to pick up the lobster bisque."

She gave him a dinner cleverly contrived from canned goods and served on exquisite Fornisetti china with Danish silver flatware. It was a typical girl's meal, and Mayo was still hungry when it was finished, but too polite to mention it. He was too tired to fabricate an excuse to go out and forage for something substantial. He lurched off to bed, remembering to remove his shoes but forgetting all about the spread.

He was awakened next morning by a loud honking and clattering of wings. He rolled out of bed and went to the windows just in time to see the mallards dispossessed from the pond by what appeared to be a red balloon. When he got his eyes working properly, he saw that it was a bathing cap. He wandered out to the pond, stretching and groaning. Linda yelled cheerfully and swam toward him. She heaved herself up out of the pond onto the curbing. The bathing cap was all that she wore. Mayo backed away from the splash and spatter.

"Good morning," Linda said. "Sleep well?"

"Good morning," Mayo said. "I don't know. The bed put kinks in my back. Gee, that water must be cold. You're all gooseflesh."

"No, it's marvelous." She pulled off the cap and shook her hair down. "Where's that towel? Oh, here. Go on in, Jim. You'll feel wonderful."

"I don't like it when it's cold."

"Don't be a sissy."

A crack of thunder split the quiet morning. Mayo looked up at the clear sky in astonishment. "What the hell was that?" he exclaimed.

"Watch," Linda ordered.

"It sounded like a sonic boom."

"There!" she cried, pointing west. "See?"

One of the West Side skyscrapers crumbled majestically, sinking into itself like a collapsible cup and raining masses of cornice and brick. The flayed girders twisted and contorted. Moments later they could hear the roar of the collapse.

"Man, that's a sight," Mayo muttered in awe.

"The decline and fall of the Empire City. You get used to it. Now take a dip, Jim. I'll get you a towel."

She ran into the house. He dropped his shorts and took off his socks, but was still standing on the curb, unhappily dipping his toe into the water when she returned with a huge bath towel.

"It's awful cold, Linda," he complained.

"Didn't you take cold showers when you were a wrestler?"

"Not me. Boiling hot."

"Jim, if you just stand there, you'll never go in. Look at you, you're starting to shiver. Is that a tattoo around your waist?"

"What? Oh, yea. It's a python, in five colors. It goes all the way around. See?" He revolved proudly. "Got it when I was with the Army in Saigon back in '64. It's a Oriental-type python. Elegant, huh?"

"Did it hurt?"

"To tell the truth, no. Some guys try to make out like it's Chinese torture to get tattooed, but they're just showin' off. It itches more than anything else."

"You were a soldier in '64?"

"That's right."

"How old were you?"

"Twenty."

"You're thirty-seven now?"

"Thirty-six going on thirty-seven."

"Then you're prematurely grey?"

"I guess so."

She contemplated him thoughtfully. "I tell you what, if you do go in, don't get your head wet."

She ran back into the house. Mayo, ashamed of his vacillation, forced himself to jump feet first into the pond. He was standing, chest deep, splashing his face and shoulders with water when Linda returned. She carried a stool, a pair of scissors, and a comb.

"Doesn't it feel wonderful?" she called.

"No."

She laughed. "Well, come out. I'm going to give you a haircut."

He climbed out of the pond, dried himself, and obediently sat on the stool while she cut his hair. "The beard, too," Linda insisted. "I want to see what you really look like." She trimmed him close enough for shaving, inspected him, and nodded with satisfaction. "Very handsome."

"Aw, go on," he blushed.

"There's a bucket of hot water on the stove. Go and shave.

Don't bother to dress. We're going to get you new clothes after breakfast, and then . . . the Piano."

"I couldn't walk around the streets naked," he said, shocked.

"Don't be silly. Who's to see? Now hurry."

They drove down to Abercrombie & Fitch on Madison and 45th Street, Mayo wrapped modestly in his towel. Linda told him she'd been a customer for years, and showed him the pile of sales slips she had accumulated. Mayo examined them curiously while she took his measurements and went off in search of clothes. He was almost indignant when she returned with her arms laden.

"Jim, I've got some lovely elk moccasins, and a safari suit, and wool socks, and shipboard shirts, and—"

"Listen," he interrupted, "do you know what your whole tab comes to? Nearly fourteen hundred dollars."

"Really? Put on the shorts first. They're drip-dry."

"You must have been out of your mind, Linda. What'd you want all that junk for?"

"Are the socks big enough? What junk? I needed everything."

"Yeah? Like . . ." He shuffled the signed sales slips. "Like one Underwater Viewer with Plexiglas Lens, nine ninety-five? What for?"

"So I could see to clean the bottom of the pond."

"What about this Stainless Steel Service for Four, thirty-nine fifty?"

"For when I'm lazy and don't feel like heating water. You can wash stainless steel in cold water." She admired him. "Oh, Jim, come look in the mirror. You're real romantic, like the big-game hunter in that Hemingway story."

He shook his head. "I don't see how you're ever going to get out of hock. You got to watch your spending, Linda. Maybe we better forget about that piano, huh?"

"Never," Linda said adamantly. "I don't care how much it costs. A piano is a lifetime investment, and it's worth it."

She was frantic with excitement as they drove uptown to the Steinway showroom, and helpful and underfoot by turns. After a long afternoon of muscle-cracking and critical engineering involving makeshift gantries and an agonizing dolly-haul up Fifth Avenue, they had the piano in place in Linda's living room. Mayo gave it one last shake to make sure it was firmly on its legs and then sank down, exhausted. "Je-zuz!" he groaned. "Hiking south would've been easier."

"Jim!" Linda ran to him and threw herself on him with a fervent hug. "Jim, you're an angel. Are you all right?"

"I'm okay." He grunted. "Get off me, Linda. I can't breathe."

"I just can't thank you enough. I've been dreaming about this for ages. I don't know what I can do to repay you. Anything you want, just name it."

"Aw," he said, "you already cut my hair."

"I'm serious."

"Ain't you teaching me how to drive?"

"Of course. As quickly as possible. That's the least I can do." Linda backed to a chair and sat down, her eyes fixed on the piano.

"Don't make such a fuss over nothing," he said, climbing to his feet. He sat down before the keyboard, shot an embarrassed grin at her over his shoulder, then reached out and began stumbling through *The Minuet in·G*.

Linda gasped and sat bolt upright. "You play," she whispered.

"Naw. I took piano when I was a kid."

"Can you read music?"

"I used to."

"Could you teach me?"

"I guess so; it's kind of hard. Hey, here's another piece I had to take." He began mutilating *The Rustle of Spring*. What with the piano out of tune and his mistakes, it was ghastly.

"Beautiful," Linda breathed. "Just beautiful!" She stared at his back while an expression of decision and determination stole across her face. She arose, slowly crossed to Mayo, and put her hands on his shoulders.

He glanced up. "Something?" he asked.

"Nothing," she answered. "You practice the piano. I'll get dinner."

But she was so preoccupied for the rest of the evening that she made Mayo nervous. He stole off to bed early.

It wasn't until three o'clock the following afternoon that they finally got a car working, and it wasn't a Caddy, but a Chevy—a hardtop because Mayo didn't like the idea of being exposed to the weather in a convertible. They drove out of the Tenth Avenue garage and back to the East Side, where Linda felt more at home. She confessed that the boundaries of her world were from Fifth Avenue to Third, and from 42nd Street to 86th. She was uncomfortable outside this pale.

She turned the wheel over to Mayo and let him creep up and down Fifth and Madison, practicing starts and stops. He sideswiped five wrecks, stalled eleven times, and reversed through a storefront which, fortunately, was devoid of glass. He was trembling with nervousness.

"It's real hard," he complained.

"It's just a question of practice," she reassured him. "Don't worry. I promise you'll be an expert if it takes us a month."

"A whole month!"

"You said you were a slow learner, didn't you? Don't blame me. Stop here a minute."

He jolted the Chevy to a halt. Linda got out.

"Wait for me."

"What's up?"

"A surprise."

She ran into a shop and was gone for half an hour. When she reappeared she was wearing a pencil-thin black sheath, pearls, and high-heeled opera pumps. She had twisted her hair into a coronet. Mayo regarded her with amazement as she got into the car.

"What's all this?" he asked.

"Part of the surprise. Turn east on Fifty-second Street."

He labored, started the car, and drove east. "Why'd you get all dressed up in an evening gown?"

"It's a cocktail dress."

"What for?"

"So I'll be dressed for where we're going. Watch out, Jim!" Linda wrenched the wheel and sheared off the stern of a shattered sanitation truck. "I'm taking you to a famous restaurant."

"To eat?"

"No, silly, for drinks. You're my visiting fireman, and I have to entertain you. That's it on the left. See if you can park somewhere."

He parked abominably. As they got out of the car, Mayo stopped and began to sniff curiously.

"Smell that?" he asked.

"Smell what?"

"That sort of sweet smell."

"It's my perfume."

"No, it's something in the air, kind of sweet and choky. I know that smell from somewhere, but I can't remember."

"Never mind. Come inside." She led him into the restaurant. "You ought to be wearing a tie," she whispered, "but maybe we can get away with it."

Mayo was not impressed by the restaurant decor, but was fascinated by the portraits of celebrities hung in the bar. He spent rapt minutes burning his fingers with matches, gazing at Mel Allen, Red Barber, Casey Stengel, Frank Gifford, and Rocky Marciano. When Linda finally came back from the kitchen with a lighted candle, he turned to her eagerly.

"You ever see any of them TV stars in here?" he asked.

"I suppose so. How about a drink?"

"Sure. Sure. But I want to talk more about them TV stars."

He escorted her to a bar stool, blew the dust off, and helped her up most gallantly. Then he vaulted over the bar, whipped

out his handkerchief, and polished the mahogany profession-
ally. "This is my specialty," he grinned. He assumed the
impersonally friendly attitude of the bartender. "Evening,
ma'am. Nice night. What's your pleasure?"

"God, I had a rough day in the shop! Dry martini on the
rocks. Better make it a double."

"Certainly, ma'am. Twist or olive?"

"Onion."

"Double-dry gibson on the rocks. Right." Mayo searched
behind the bar and finally produced whiskey, gin, and several
bottles of soda, as yet only partially evaporated through their
sealed caps. "Afraid we're fresh out of martinis, ma'am.
What's your second pleasure?"

"Oh, I like that. Scotch, please."

"This soda'll be flat," he warned, "and there's no ice."

"Never mind."

He rinsed a glass with soda and poured her a drink.

"Thank you. Have one on me, bartender. What's your
name?"

"They call me Jim, ma'am. No thanks. Never drink on
duty."

"Then come off duty and join me."

"Never drink off duty, ma'am."

"You can call me Linda."

"Thank you, Miss Linda."

"Are you serious about never drinking, Jim?"

"Yeah."

"Well, happy days."

"And long nights."

"I like that, too. Is it your own?"

"Gee, I don't know. It's sort of the usual bartender's
routine, a specially with guys. You know? Suggestive. No
offense."

"None taken."

"Bees!" Mayo burst out.

Linda was startled. "Bees what?"

"That smell. Like inside beehives."

"Oh? I wouldn't know," she said indifferently. "I'll have another, please."

"Coming right up. Now listen, about them TV celebrities, you actually saw them here? In person?"

"Why of course. Happy days, Jim."

"May they all be Saturdays."

Linda pondered. "Why Saturdays?"

"Day off."

"Oh."

"Which TV stars did you see?"

"You name 'em, I saw 'em." She laughed. "You remind me of the kid next door. I always had to tell him the celebrities I'd seen. One day I told him I saw Jean Arthur in here, and he said, 'With his horse?'"

Mayo couldn't see the point, but was wounded nevertheless. Just as Linda was about to soothe his feelings, the bar began a gentle quivering, and at the same time a faint subterranean rumbling commenced. It came from a distance, seemed to approach slowly, and then faded away. The vibration stopped. Mayo stared at Linda.

"Je-zus! You think maybe this building's going to go?"

She shook her head. "No. When they go, it's always with that boom. You know what that sounded like? The Lexington Avenue subway."

"The subway?"

"Uh-huh. The local train."

"That's crazy. How could the subway be running?"

"I didn't say it *was*. I said it *sounded* like. I'll have another, please."

"We need more soda." Mayo explored and reappeared with bottles and a large menu. He was pale. "You better take it easy, Linda," he said. "You know what they're charging per drink? A dollar seventy-five. Look."

"To hell with the expense. Let's live a little. Make it a double, bartender. You know something, Jim? If you stayed in town, I

could show you where all your heroes lived. Thank you.
Happy days. I could take you up to BBDO and show you their
tapes and films. How about that? Stars like . . . like Red
. . . Who?"

"Barber."

"Red Barber, and Rocky Gifford, and Rocky Casey, and
Rocky, the Flying Squirrel."

"You're putting me on," Mayo said, offended again.

"Me, sir? Putting you on?" Linda said with dignity. "Why
would I do a thing like that? Just trying to be pleasant. Just
trying to give you a good time. My mother told me, 'Linda,'
she told me, 'just remember this, about a man. Wear what he
wants and say what he likes,' is what she told me. You want this
dress?" she demanded.

"I like it, if that's what you mean."

"Know what I paid for it? Ninety-nine fifty."

"What? A hundred dollars for a skinny black thing like
that?"

"It is not a skinny black thing like that. It is a basic black
cocktail frock. And I paid twenty dollars for the pearls. Simulated," she explained. "And sixty for the opera pumps. And
forty for the perfume. Two hundred and twenty dollars to
give you a good time. You having a good time?"

"Sure."

"Want to smell me?"

"I already have."

"Bartender, give me another."

"Afraid I can't serve you, ma'am."

"Why not?"

"You've had enough already."

"I have not had enough already," Linda said indignantly.
"Where's your manners?" She grabbed the whiskey bottle.
"Come on, let's have a few drinks and talk up a storm about
TV stars. Happy days. I could take you up to BBDO and show
you their tapes and films. How about that?"

"You just asked me."

"You didn't answer. I could show you movies, too. You like movies? I hate 'em, but I can't knock 'em anymore. Movies saved my life when the big bang came."

"How was that?"

"This is a secret, understand? Just between you and me. If any other agency ever found out . . ." Linda looked around and then lowered her voice. "BBDO located this big cache of silent films. Lost films, see? Nobody knew the prints were around. Make a great TV series. So they sent me to this abandoned mine in Jersey to take inventory."

"In a mine?"

"That's right. Happy days."

"Why were they in a mine?"

"Old prints. Nitrate. Catch fire. Also rot. Have to be stored like wine. That's why. So took two of my assistants with me to spend weekend down there, checking."

"You stayed in the mine a whole weekend?"

"Uh-huh. Three girls. Friday to Monday. That was the plan. Thought it would be a fun deal. Happy days. So . . . Where was I? Oh. So, took lights, blankets, linen, plenty of picnic, the whole schmeer, and went to work. I remember exact moment when blast came. Was looking for third reel of a UFA film, *Gekronter Blumenorden an der Pegnitz*. Had reel one, two, four, five, six. No three. Bang! Happy days."

"Jesus. Then what?"

"My girls panicked. Couldn't keep 'em down there. Never saw them again. But I knew. I knew. Stretched that picnic forever. Then starved even longer. Finally came up, and for what? For who? Whom?" She began to weep. "For nobody. Nobody left. Nothing." She took Mayo's hands. "Why won't you stay?"

"Stay? Where?"

"Here."

"I am staying."

"I mean for a long time. Why not? Haven't I got lovely

home? And there's all New York for supplies. And farm for flowers and vegetables. We could keep cows and chickens. Go fishing. Drive cars. Go to museums. Art galleries. Enter-tain . . ."

"You're doing all that right now. You don't need me."

"But I do. I do."

"For what?"

"For piano lessons."

After a long pause he said, "You're drunk."

"Not wounded, sire, but dead."

She lay her head on the bar, beamed up at him roguishly, and then closed her eyes. An instant later, Mayo knew she had passed out. He compressed his lips. Then he climbed out of the bar, computed the tab, and left fifteen dollars under the whiskey bottle.

He took Linda's shoulder and shook her gently. She collapsed into his arms, and her hair came tumbling down. He blew out the candle, picked Linda up, and carried her to the Chevy. Then, with anguished concentration, he drove through the dark to the boat pond. It took him forty minutes.

He carried Linda into her bedroom and sat her down on the bed, which was decorated with an elaborate arrangement of dolls. Immediately she rolled over and curled up with a doll in her arms, crooning to it. Mayo lit a lamp and tried to prop her upright. She went over again, giggling.

"Linda," he said, "you got to get that dress off."

"Mf."

"You can't sleep in it. It cost a hundred dollars."

"Nine'nine-fif'y."

"Now come on, honey."

"Fm."

He rolled his eyes in exasperation and then undressed her, carefully hanging up the basic black cocktail frock, and standing the sixty-dollar pumps in a corner. He could not manage the clasp of the pearls (simulated), so he put her to bed still wearing them. Lying on the pale blue sheets, nude except for the necklace, she looked like a Nordic odalisque.

"Did you muss my dolls?" she mumbled.

"No. They're all around you."

"Tha's right. Never sleep without 'em." She reached out and petted them lovingly. "Happy days. Long nights."

"Women!" Mayo snorted. He extinguished the lamp and tramped out, slamming the door behind him.

Next morning Mayo was again awakened by the clatter of dispossessed ducks. The red balloon was sailing on the surface of the pond, bright in the warm June sunshine. Mayo wished it was a model boat instead of the kind of girl who got drunk in bars. He stalked out and jumped into the water as far from Linda as possible. He was sluicing his chest when something seized his ankle and nipped him. He let out a yell, and was confronted by Linda's beaming face bursting out of the water before him.

"Good morning," she laughed.

"Very funny," he muttered.

"You look mad this morning."

He grunted.

"And I don't blame you. I did an awful thing last night. I didn't give you any dinner, and I want to apologize."

"I wasn't thinking about dinner," he said with baleful dignity.

"No? Then what on earth are you mad about?"

"I can't stand women who get drunk."

"Who was drunk?"

"You."

"I was not," she said indignantly.

"No? Who had to be undressed and put to bed like a kid?"

"Who was too dumb to take off my pearls?" she countered. "They broke and I slept on pebbles all night. I'm covered with black and blue marks. Look. Here and here and—"

"Linda," he interrupted sternly, "I'm just a plain guy from New Haven. I got no use for spoiled girls who run up charge accounts and all the time decorate theirselves and hang around society-type saloons getting loaded."

"If you don't like my company, why do you stay?"

"I'm going," he said. He climbed out and began drying himself. "I'm starting south this morning."

"Enjoy your hike."

"I'm driving."

"What? A kiddie-car?"

"The Chevy."

"Jim, you're not serious?" She climbed out of the pond, looking alarmed. "You really don't know how to drive yet."

"No? Didn't I drive you home falling-down drunk last night?"

"You'll get into awful trouble."

"Nothing I can't get out of. Anyway, I can't hang around here forever. You're a party girl; you just want to play. I got serious things on my mind. I got to go south and find guys who know about TV."

"Jim, you've got me wrong. I'm not like that at all. Why, look at the way I fixed up my house. Could I have done that if I'd been going to parties all the time?"

"You done a nice job," he admitted.

"Please don't leave today. You're not ready yet."

"Aw, you just want me to hang around and teach you music."

"Who said that?"

"You did. Last night."

She frowned, pulled off her cap, then picked up her towel and began drying herself. At last she said, "Jim, I'll be honest with you. Sure, I want you to stay a while. I won't deny it. But I wouldn't want you around permanently. After all, what have we got in common?"

"You're so damn uptown," he growled.

"No, no, it's nothing like that. It's simply that you're a guy and I'm a girl, and we've got nothing to offer each other. We're different. We've got different tastes and interests. Fact?"

"Absolutely."

"But you're not ready to leave yet. So I tell you what; we'll spend the whole morning practicing driving, and then we'll have some fun. What would you like to do? Go window-shopping? Buy more clothes? Visit the Modern Museum? Have a picnic?"

His face brightened. "Gee, you know something? I was never to a picnic in my whole life. Once I was bartender at a clambake, but that's not the same thing; not like when you're a kid."

She was delighted. "Then we'll have a real kid-type picnic."

And she brought her dolls. She carried them in her arms while Mayo toted the picnic basket to the Alice in Wonderland monument. The statue perplexed Mayo, who had never heard of Lewis Carroll. While Linda seated her pets and unpacked the picnic, she gave Mayo a summary of the story, and described how the bronze heads of Alice, the Mad Hatter, and the March Hare had been polished bright by the swarms of kids playing King of the Mountain.

"Funny, I never heard of that story," he said.

"I don't think you had much of a childhood, Jim."

"Why would you say a—" He stopped, cocked his head, and listened intently.

"What's the matter?" Linda asked.

"You hear that bluejay?"

"No."

"Listen. He's making a funny sound; like steel."

"Steel?"

"Yeah. Like . . . like swords in a duel."

"You're kidding."

"No. Honest."

"But birds sing; they don't make noises."

"Not always. Bluejays imitate noises a lot. Starlings, too. And parrots. Now why would he be imitating a sword fight? Where'd he hear it?"

"You're a real country boy, aren't you, Jim? Bees and blue-jays and starlings and all that . . ."

"I guess so. I was going to ask; why would you say a thing like that, me not having any childhood?"

"Oh, things like not knowing Alice, and never going on a picnic, and always wanting a model yacht." Linda opened a dark bottle. "Like to try some wine?"

"You better go easy," he warned.

"Now stop it, Jim. I'm not a drunk."

"Did you or didn't you get smashed last night?"

She capitulated. "All right, I did; but only because it was my first drink in years."

He was pleased by her surrender. "Sure. Sure. That figures."

"So? Join me?"

"What the hell, why not?" He grinned. "Let's live a little. Say, this is one swingin' picnic, and I like the plates, too. Where'd you get them?"

"Abercrombie & Fitch," Linda said, deadpan. "Stainless Steel Service for Four, thirty-nine fifty. Skoal."

Mayo burst out laughing. "I sure goofed, didn't I, kicking up all that fuss? Here's looking at you."

"Here's looking right back."

They drank and continued eating in warm silence, smiling companionably at each other. Linda removed her madras silk shirt in order to tan in the blazing afternoon sun, and Mayo politely hung it up on a branch. Suddenly Linda asked, "Why didn't you have a childhood, Jim?"

"Gee, I don't know." He thought it over. "I guess because my mother died when I was a kid. And something else, too; I had to work a lot."

"Why?"

"My father was a schoolteacher. You know how they get paid."

"Oh, so that's why you're anti-egghead."

"I am?"

"Of course. No offense."

"Maybe I am," he conceded. "It sure was a letdown for my old man, me playing fullback in high school and him wanting like an Einstein in the house."

"Was football fun?"

"Not like playing games. Football's a business. Hey, remember when we were kids how we used to choose up sides? *Ibbety, bibbety, zibbety, zab?*"

"We used to say, *Eenie, meenie, miney, mo.*"

"Remember: *April Fool, go to school, tell your teacher you're a fool?*"

"*I love coffee, I love tea, I love the boys, and the boys love me.*"

"I bet they did at that," Mayo said solemnly.

"Not me."

"Why not?"

"I was always too big."

He was astonished. "But you're not big," he assured her. "You're just the right size. Perfect. And really built, I noticed when we moved the piano in. You got muscle, for a girl. A specially in the legs, and that's where it counts."

She blushed. "Stop it, Jim."

"No. Honest."

"More wine?"

"Thanks. You have some, too."

"All right."

A crack of thunder split the sky with its sonic boom, and was followed by the roar of collapsing masonry.

"There goes another skyscraper," Linda said. "What were we talking about?"

"Games," Mayo said promptly. "Excuse me for talking with my mouth full."

"Oh yes. Jim did you play *Drop the Handkerchief* up in New Haven?" Linda sang. *"A tisket, a tasket, a green and yellow basket. I sent a letter to my love, and on the way I dropped it . . ."*

"Gee," he said, much impressed. "You sing real good."

"Oh, go on!"

"Yes you do. You got a swell voice. Now don't argue with me. Keep quiet a minute. I got to figure something out." He thought intently for a long time, finishing his wine and absently accepting another glass. Finally he delivered himself of a decision. "You got to learn music."

"You know I'm dying to, Jim."

"So I'm going to stay awhile and teach you; as much as I know. Now hold it! Hold it!" he added hastily, cutting off her excitement. "I'm not going to stay in your house. I want a place of my own."

"Of course, Jim. Anything you say."

"And I'm still headed south."

"I'll teach you to drive, Jim. I'll keep my word."

"And no strings, Linda."

"Of course not. What kind of strings?"

"You know. Like the last minute you all of a sudden got a Looey Cans couch you want me to move in."

"Louis Quinze!" Linda's jaw dropped. "Wherever did you learn that?"

"Not in the army, that's for sure."

They laughed, clinked glasses, and finished their wine. Suddenly Mayo leaped up, pulled Linda's hair, and ran to the Wonderland monument. In an instant he had climbed to the top of Alice's head.

"I'm King of the Mountain," he shouted, looking around in imperial survey. "I'm King of the—" He cut himself off and stared down behind the statue.

"Jim, what's the matter?"

Without a word, Mayo climbed down and strode to a pile of debris half-hidden inside overgrown forsythia bushes. He knelt and began turning over the wreckage with gentle hands. Linda ran to him.

"Jim, what's wrong?"

"These used to be model boats," he muttered.

"That's right. My God, is that all? I thought you were sick or something."

"How come they're here?"

"Why, I dumped them, of course."

"You?"

"Yes. I told you. I had to clear out the boathouse when I moved in. That was ages ago."

"You did this?"

"Yes. I—"

"You're a murderer," he growled. He stood up and glared at her. "You're a killer. You're like all women, you got no heart and soul. To do a thing like this!"

He turned and stalked toward the boat pond. Linda followed him, completely bewildered.

"Jim, I don't understand. Why are you so mad?"

"You ought to be ashamed of yourself."

"But I had to have house room. You wouldn't expect me to live with a lot of model boats."

"Just forget everything I said. I'm going to pack and go south, I wouldn't stay with you if you was the last person on earth."

Linda gathered herself and suddenly darted ahead of Mayo. When he tramped into the boathouse, she was standing before the door of the guest room. She held up a heavy iron key.

"I found it," she panted. "Your door's locked."

"Gimme that key, Linda."

"No."

He stepped toward her, but she faced him defiantly and stood her ground.

"Go ahead," she challenged. "Hit me."

He stopped. "Aw, I wouldn't pick on anybody that wasn't my own size."

They continued to face each other, at a complete impasse.

"I don't need my gear," Mayo muttered at last. "I can get more stuff somewheres."

"Oh, go ahead and pack," Linda answered. She tossed him the key and stood aside. Then Mayo discovered there was no lock in the bedroom door. He opened the door, looked inside, closed it, and looked at Linda. She kept her face straight but began to sputter. He grinned. Then they both burst out laughing.

"Gee," Mayo said, "you sure made a monkey out of me. I'd hate to play poker against you."

"You're a pretty good bluffer yourself, Jim. I was scared to death you were going to knock me down."

"You ought to know I wouldn't hurt nobody."

"I guess I do. Now, let's sit down and talk this over sensibly."

"Aw, forget it, Linda. I kind of lost my head over them boats, and I—"

"I don't mean the boats; I mean going south. Every time you get mad you start south again. Why?"

"I told you, to find guys who know about TV."

"Why?"

"You wouldn't understand."

"I can try. Why don't you explain what you're after—specifically? Maybe I can help you."

"You can't do nothing for me; you're a girl."

"We have our uses. At least I can listen. You can trust me, Jim. Aren't we chums? Tell me about it."

Well, when the blast come (Mayo said) I was up in the Berkshires with Gil Watkins. Gil was my buddy, a real nice guy and a real bright guy. He took two years from M.I.T. before he quit college. He was like chief engineer or something at WNHA, the TV station in New Haven. Gil had a million hobbies. One of them was spee—speel—I can't remember. It meant exploring caves.

So anyway we were up in this flume in the Berkshires, spending the weekend inside, exploring and trying to map everything and figure out where the underground river comes from. We brought food and stuff along, and bedrolls. The compass we were using went crazy for like twenty minutes, and that should have give us a clue, but Gil talked about magnetic ores and stuff. Only when we come out Sunday night, I tell you it was pretty scary. Gil knew right off what happened.

"By Christ, Jim," he said, "they up and done it like everybody always knew they would. They've blew and gassed and poisoned and radiated themselves straight to hell, and we're going back to that goddamn cave until it all blows over."

So me and Gil went back and rationed the food and stayed as long as we could. Finally we come out again and drove back to New Haven. It was dead like all the rest. Gil put together some radio stuff and tried to pick up braodcasts. Nothing. Then we packed some canned goods and drove all around; Bridgeport, Waterbury, Hartford, Springfield, Providence, New London . . . a big circle. Nobody. Nothing. So we come back to New Haven and settled down, and it was a pretty good life.

Daytime, we'd get in supplies and stuff, and tinker with the house to keep it working right. Nights, after supper, Gil would go off to WNHA around seven o'clock and start the station. He was running it on the emergency generators. I'd go down to "The Body Slam," open it up, sweep it out, and then start the bar TV set. Gil fixed me a generator for it to run on.

It was a lot of fun watching the shows Gil was broadcasting. He'd start with the news and weather, which he always got wrong. All he had was some Farmer's Almanacs and a sort of antique barometer that looked like that clock you got there on the wall. I don't think it worked so good, or maybe Gil never took weather at M.I.T. Then he'd broadcast the evening show.

I had my shotgun in the bar in case of holdups. Anytime I saw something that bugged me, I just up with the gun and let loose at the set. Then I'd take it and throw it out the front door and put another one in its place. I must have had hundreds waiting in the back. I spent two days a week just collecting reserves.

Midnight, Gil would turn off WNHA, I'd lock up the restaurant, and we'd meet home for coffee. Gil would ask how many sets I shot, and laugh when I told him. He said I was the most accurate TV poll ever invented. I'd ask him about what shows were coming up next week and argue with him about . . . oh . . . about like what movies or football games WNHA was scheduling. I didn't like Westerns much, and I hated them high-minded panel discussions.

But the luck had to turn lousy; it's the story of my life. After a couple of years, I found out I was down to my last set, and then I was in trouble. This night Gil run one of them icky commercials where this smart-aleck woman saves a marriage with the right laundry soap. Naturally I reached for my gun, and only at the last minute remembered not to shoot. Then he run an awful movie about a misunderstood composer, and the same thing happened. When we met back at the house, I was all shook up.

"What's the matter?" Gil asked.

I told him.

"I thought you liked watching the shows," he said.

"Only when I could shoot 'em."

"You poor bastard," he laughed, "you're a captive audience now."

"Gil, could you maybe change the programs, seeing the spot I'm in?"

"Be reasonable, Jim. WNHA has to broadcast variety. We operate on the cafeteria basis; something for everybody. If you don't like a show, why don't you switch channels?"

"Now that's silly. You know damn well we only got one channel in New Haven."

"Then turn your set off."

"I can't turn the bar set off, it's part of the entertainment. I'd lose my whole clientele. Gil, do you *have* to show them awful movies, like that army musical last night, singing and dancing and kissing on top of Sherman tanks for Jezus sake!"

"The women love uniform pictures."

"And those commercials; women always sneering at somebody's girdle, and fairies smoking cigarettes, and—"

"Aw," Gil said, "write a letter to the station."

So I did, and a week later I got an answer. It said: *Dear Mr. Mayo: We are very glad to learn that you are a regular viewer of WNHA, and thank you for your interest in our programming. We hope you will continue to enjoy our broadcasts. Sincerely yours, Gilbert O. Watkins, Station Manager.* A couple of tickets for an interview show were enclosed. I showed the letter to Gil, and he just shrugged.

"You see what you're up against, Jim," he said. "They don't care about what you like or don't like. All they want to know is if you are watching."

I tell you, the next couple of months were hell for me. I couldn't keep the set turned off, and I couldn't watch it without reaching for my gun a dozen times a night. It took all my willpower to keep from pulling the trigger. I got so nervous and jumpy that I knew I had to do something about it before I went off my rocker. So one night I brought the gun home and shot Gil.

Next day I felt a lot better, and when I went down to "The Body Slam" at seven o'clock to clean up, I was whistling kind of cheerful. I swept out the restaurant, polished the bar, and then turned on the TV to get the news and weather. You wouldn't believe it, but the set was busted. I couldn't get a picture. I couldn't even get a sound. My last set, busted.

So you see, that's why I have to head south (Mayo explained)—I got to locate a TV repairman.

There was a long pause after Mayo finished his story. Linda examined him keenly, trying to conceal the gleam in her eye. At last she asked with studied carelessness, "Where did he get the barometer?"

"Who? What?"

"Your friend, Gil. His antique barometer. Where did he get it?"

"Gee, I don't know. Antiquing was another one of his hobbies."

"And it looked like that clock?"

"Just like it."

"French?"

"I couldn't say."

"Bronze?"

"I guess so. Like your clock. Is that bronze?"

"Yes. Shaped like a sunburst?"

"No, just like yours."

"That's a sunburst. The same size?"

"Exactly."

"Where was it?"

"Didn't I tell you? In our house."

"Where's the house?"

"On Grant Street."

"What number?"

"Three fifteen. Say, what is all this?"

"Nothing, Jim. Just curious. No offense. Now I think I'd better get our picnic things."

"You wouldn't mind if I took a walk by myself?"

She cocked an eye at him. "Don't try driving alone. Garage mechanics are scarcer than TV repairmen."

He grinned and disappeared; but after dinner the true purpose of his disappearance was revealed when he produced a sheaf of sheet music, placed it on the piano rack, and led Linda to the piano bench. She was delighted and touched.

"Jim, you angel! Wherever did you find it?"

"In the apartment house across the street. Fourth floor,

rear. Name of Horowitz. They got a lot of records, too. Boy, I can tell you it was pretty spooky snooping around in the dark with only matches. You know something funny, the whole top of the house is full of glop."

"Glop?"

"Yeah. Sort of white jelly, only it's hard. Like clear concrete. Now look, see this note? It's C. Middle C. It stands for this white key here. We better sit together. Move over . . ."

The lesson continued for two hours of painful concentration and left them both so exhausted that they tottered to their rooms with only perfunctory good nights.

"Jim," Linda called.

"Yeah?" he yawned.

"Would you like one of my dolls for your bed?"

"Gee, no. Thanks a lot, Linda, but guys really ain't interested in dolls."

"I suppose not. Never mind. Tomorrow I'll have something for you that really interests guys."

Mayo was awakened next morning by a rap on his door. He heaved up in bed and tried to open his eyes.

"Yeah? Who is it?" he called.

"It's me. Linda. May I come in?"

He glanced around hastily. The room was neat. The hooked rug was clean. The precious candlewick bedspread was neatly folded on top of the dresser.

"Okay. Come on in."

Linda entered, wearing a crisp seersucker dress. She sat down on the edge of the fourposter and gave Mayo a friendly pat. "Good morning," she said. "Now listen. I'll have to leave you alone for a few hours. I've got things to do. There's breakfast on the table, but I'll be back in time for lunch. All right?"

"Sure."

"You won't be lonesome?"

"Where you going?"

"Tell you when I get back." She reached out and tousled his head. "Be a good boy and don't get into mischief. Oh, one other thing. Don't go into my bedroom."

"Why should I?"

"Just don't anyway."

She smiled and was gone. Moments later, Mayo heard the jeep start and drive off. He got up at once, went into Linda's bedroom, and looked around. The room was neat, as ever. The bed was made, and her pet dolls were lovingly arranged on the coverlet. Then he saw it.

"Gee," he breathed.

It was a model of a full-rigged clipper ship. The spars and rigging were intact, but the hull was peeling, and the sails were shredded. It stood before Linda's closet, and alongside it was her sewing basket. She had already cut out a fresh set of white linen sails. Mayo knelt down before the model and touched it tenderly.

"I'll paint her black with a gold line around her," he murmured, "and I'll name her the *Linda N.*"

He was so deeply moved that he hardly touched his breakfast. He bathed, dressed, took his shotgun and a handful of shells, and went out to wander through the park. He circled south, passed the playing fields, the decaying carousel, and the crumbling skating rink, and at last left the park and loafed down Seventh Avenue.

He turned east on 50th Street and spent a long time trying to decipher the tattered posters advertising the last performance at Radio City Music Hall. Then he turned south again. He was jolted to a halt by the sudden clash of steel. It sounded like giant sword blades in a titanic duel. A small herd of stunted horses burst out of a side street, terrified by the clangor. Their shoeless hooves thudded bluntly on the pavement. The sound of steel stopped.

"That's where that bluejay got it from," Mayo muttered. "But what the hell is it?"

He drifted eastward to investigate, but forgot the mystery

when he came to the diamond center. He was dazzled by the blue-white stones glittering in the showcases. The door of one jewel mart had sagged open, and Mayo tipped in. When he emerged it was with a strand of genuine matched pearls which had cost him an I.O.U. worth a year's rent on "The Body Slam."

His tour took him to Madison Avenue where he found himself before Abercrombie & Fitch. He went in to explore and came at last to the gun racks. There he lost all sense of time, and when he recovered his senses, he was walking up Fifth Avenue toward the boat pond. An Italian Cosmi automatic rifle was cradled in his arms, guilt was in his heart, and a sales slip in the store read: *I.O.U. 1 Cosmi Rifle, $750.00. 6 Boxes Ammo. $18.00. James Mayo.*

It was past three o'clock when he got back to the boathouse. He eased in, trying to appear casual, hoping the extra gun he was carrying would go unnoticed. Linda was sitting on the piano bench with her back to him.

"Hi," Mayo said nervously. "Sorry I'm late. I . . . I brought you a present. They're real." He pulled the pearls from his pocket and held them out. Then he saw she was crying.

"Hey, what's the matter?"

She didn't answer.

"You wasn't scared I'd run out on you? I mean, well, all my gear is here. The car, too. You only had to look."

She turned. "I hate you!" she cried.

He dropped the pearls and recoiled, startled by her vehemence. "What's the matter?"

"You're a lousy rotten liar!"

"Who? Me?"

"I drove up to New Haven this morning." Her voice trembled with passion. "There's no house standing on Grant Street. It's all wiped out. There's no Station WNHA. The whole building's gone."

"No."

"Yes. And I went to your restaurant. There's no pile of TV

sets out in the street. There's only one set, over the bar. It's rusted to pieces. The rest of the restaurant is a pigsty. You were living there all the time. Alone. There was only one bed in back. It was lies! All lies!"

"Why would I lie about a thing like that?"

"You never shot any Gil Watkins."

"I sure did. Both barrels. He had it coming."

"And you haven't got any TV set to repair."

"Yes I do."

"And even if it is repaired, there's no station to broadcast."

"Talk sense," he said angrily. "Why would I shoot Gil if there wasn't any broadcast."

"If he's dead, how can he broadcast?"

"See? And you just now said I didn't shoot him."

"Oh, you're mad! You're insane!" she sobbed. "You just described that barometer because you happened to be looking at my clock. And I believed your crazy lies. I had my heart set on a barometer to match my clock. I've been looking for years." She ran to the wall arrangement and hammered her fist alongside the clock. "It belongs right here. Here. But you lied, you lunatic. There never was a barometer."

"If there's a lunatic around here, it's you," he shouted. "You're so crazy to get this house decorated that nothing's real for you anymore."

She ran across the room, snatched up his old shotgun, and pointed it at him. "You get out of here. Right this minute. Get out or I'll kill you. I never want to see you again."

The shotgun kicked off in her hands, knocking her backward, and spraying shot over Mayo's head into a corner bracket. China shattered and clattered dow. Linda's face went white.

"Jim! My God, are you all right? I didn't mean to . . . it just went off . . ."

He stepped forward, too furious to speak. Then, as he raised his hand to cuff her, the sound of distant reports came, BLAM-BLAM-BLAM. Mayo froze.

"Did you hear that?" he whispered.

Linda nodded.

"That wasn't any accident. It was a signal."

Mayo grabbed the shotgun, ran outside, and fired the second barrel into the air. There was a pause. Then again came the distant explosions in a stately triplet, BLAM-BLAM-BLAM. They had an odd, sucking sound, as thought they were implosions rather than explosions. Far up the park, a canopy of frightened birds mounted into the sky.

"There's somebody," Mayo exulted. "By God, I told you I'd find somebody. Come on."

They ran north, Mayo digging into his pockets for more shells to reload and signal again.

"I got to thank you for taking that shot at me, Linda."

"I didn't shoot at you," she protested. "It was an accident."

"The luckiest accident in the world. They could be passing through and never know about us. But what the hell kind of guns are they using? I never heard no shots like that before, and I heard 'em all. Wait a minute."

On the little piazza before the Wonderland monument, Mayo halted and raised the shotgun to fire. Then he slowly lowered it. He took a deep breath. In a harsh voice he said, "Turn around. We're going back to the house." He pulled her around and faced her south.

Linda stared at him. In an instant he had become transformed from a gentle teddy bear into a panther.

"Jim, what's wrong?"

"I'm scared," he growled. "I'm goddam scared, and I don't want you to be, too." The triple salvo sounded again. "Don't pay any attention," he ordered. "We're going back to the house. Come on!"

She refused to move. "But why? Why?"

"We don't want any part of them. Take my word for it."

"How do you know? You've got to tell me."

"Christ! You won't let it alone until you find out, huh? All right. You want the explanation for that bee smell, and them buildings falling down, and all the rest?" He turned Linda around with a hand on her neck, and directed her gaze at the Wonderland monument. "Go ahead. Look."

A consummate craftsman had removed the heads of Alice, the Mad Hatter, and the March Hare, and replaced them with towering mantis heads, all saber mandibles, antennae, and faceted eyes. They were of a burnished steel and gleamed with unspeakable ferocity. Linda let out a sick whimper and sagged against Mayo. The triple report signaled once more.

Mayo caught Linda, heaved her over his shoulder, and loped back toward the pond. She recovered consciousness in a moment and began to moan. "Shut up," he growled. "Whining won't help." He set her on her feet before the boathouse. She was shaking but trying to control herself. "Did this place have shutters when you moved in? Where are they?"

"Stacked." She had to squeeze the words out. "Behind the trellis."

"I'll put 'em up. You fill buckets with water and stash 'em in the kitchen. Go!"

"Is it going to be a siege?"

"We'll talk later. Go!"

She filled buckets and then helped Mayo jam the last of the shutters into the window embrasures. "All right, inside," he ordered. They went into the house and shut and barred the door. Faint shafts of the late afternoon sun filtered through the louvers of the shutters. Mayo began unpacking the cartridges for the Cosmi rifle. "You got any kind of gun?"

"A .22 revolver somewhere."

"Ammo?"

"I think so."

"Get it ready."

"Is it going to be a siege?" she repeated.

"I don't know. I don't know who they are, or what they are, or where they come from. All I know is, we got to be prepared for the worst."

The distant implosions sounded. Mayo looked up alertly,

listening. Linda could make him out in the dimness now. His face looked carved. His chest gleamed with sweat. He exuded the musky odor of caged lions. Linda had an overpowering impulse to touch him. Mayo loaded the rifle, stood it alongside the shotgun, and began padding from shutter to shutter, peering out vigilantly, waiting with massive patience.

"Will they find us?" Linda asked.

"Maybe."

"Could they be friendly?"

"Maybe."

"Those heads looked so horrible."

"Yeah."

"Jim, I'm scared. I've never been so scared in my life."

"I don't blame you."

"How long before we know?"

"An hour, if they're friendly; two or three, if they're not."

"W-Why longer?"

"If they're looking for trouble, they'll be more cautious."

"Jim, what do you really think?"

"About what?"

"Our chances."

"You really want to know?"

"Please."

"We're dead."

She began to sob. He shook her savagely. "Stop that. Go get your gun ready."

She lurched across the living room, noticed the pearls Mayo had dropped, and picked them up. She was so dazed that she put them on automatically. Then she went into her darkened bedroom and pulled Mayo's model yacht away from the closet door. She located the .22 in a hatbox on the closet floor and removed it along with a small carton of cartridges.

She realized that a dress was unsuited to this emergency. She got a turtleneck sweater, jodhpurs, and boots from the closet. Then she stripped naked to change. Just as she raised her arms to unclasp the pearls, Mayo entered, paced to the shuttered south window, and peered out. When he turned back from the window, he saw her.

He stopped short. She couldn't move. Their eyes locked, and she began to tremble, trying to conceal herself with her arms. He stepped forward, stumbled on the model yacht, and kicked it out of the way. The next instant he had taken possession of her body, and the pearls went flying, too. As she pulled him down on the bed, fiercely tearing the shirt from his back, her pet dolls also went into the discard heap along with the yacht, the pearls, and the rest of the world.

Of Time and Third Avenue

Introduction

I DID a dumb thing, I started a piece of writing without knowing where I was going. Now this isn't damnfoolery for any author except me. We all have different work techniques and all are valid. Rex Stout said to me, "You know damn well how we write. You stick a piece of paper in the machine, type a word, then another, and finally you finish." I didn't believe him when he said he never outlined. I still don't because I must outline before I start writing. Only recently I learned that Stout outlined very carefully, but it was all in his head; he meant that he never wrote an outline. I have to write 'em.

Not that the story always follows the "game plan." Last year I was completing a novel and was so sure of my direction that I decided to get rid of the detailed notes I'd made before the writing began; they were cluttering up my workshop. I read through the final outline, the result of weeks of painful planning, and it had absolutely nothing to do with what I'd written. It was good; it was splendid; but the damned story had taken over and gone its own way.

Once the dean of us all, Robert Heinlein, and I were talking shop (writers are always talking shop, from work technique to favorite desk chairs) and Robert said, "I start out with some

150

characters and get them into trouble, and when they get themselves out of trouble, the story's over. By the time I can hear their voices, they usually get themselves out of trouble." I was flabbergasted by this; I can't *start* a story until I can hear the characters talking, and by that time they've got will and ideas of their own and have gone into business for themselves.

But I blasted into what subsequently became "Of Time and Third Avenue" without an outline, mostly because I wanted to use a particular locale. The scene was P. J. Clarke's on Third Avenue, a low-down saloon where, for reasons I've never understood, we used to congregate after our repeat shows. In those old radio days you did a live show for the East and a live repeat, three hours later, for the West. The networks insisted on this; they claimed that listeners could tell the difference between a live show and a recording and resented the latter. Nonsense.

So after the repeat it was either Toots Shor's or P. J. Clarke's. We called it "Clarke's" or "Clarkie's" in those days; today, now a classy center for the young advertising and publishing crowd, it's called P.J.'s. Those initials have become a popular logo and are much imitated. You see like P. J. Horowitz's deli, P. J. Moto's sukiyaki, P. J. Chico's Montezuma's Revenge.

Here was this locale which I knew well. The characters were more or less cardboard—I hardly knew them at all—and this should have warned me, but I blithely began a play and wrote the first scene and then— What? I didn't know. I didn't have a story in mind, I had only a beginning. So I put the scene away and forgot it until I was irritated by another variation on the exhausted knowledge-of-the-future theme. You know the pattern: Guy gets hold of tomorrow's paper. Enabled to make a financial killing. Sees own death notice in back of paper. First time, great; subsequent variations, pfui!

I was annoyed into attempting what I imagined would be the definitive handling of the theme and reworked that original scene into the present "Of Time and Third Avenue."

Footnote: Do you want to know the financial status of this author? I had to go to my bank to find out whose picture was on a hundred-dollar bill.

What Macy hated about the man was the fact that he squeaked. Macy didn't know if it was the shoes, but he suspected the clothes. In the back room of his tavern, under the poster that asked: WHO FEARS MENTION THE BATTLE OF THE BOYNE? Macy inspected the stranger. He was tall, slender, and very dainty. Although he was young, he was almost bald. There was fuzz on top of his head and over his eyebrows. Then he reached into his jacket for a wallet, and Macy made up his mind. It was the clothes that squeaked.

"MQ, Mr. Macy," the stranger said in a staccato voice. "Very good. For rental of this backroom including exclusive utility for one chronos—"

"One whatos?" Macy asked nervously.

"Chronos. The incorrect word? Oh yes. Excuse me. One hour."

"You're a foreigner," Macy said. "What's your name? I bet it's Russian."

"No. Not foreign," the stranger answered. His frightening eyes whipped around the back room. "Identify me as Boyne."

"Boyne!" Macy echoed incredulously.

"MQ. Boyne." Mr. Boyne opened a wallet shaped like an accordion, ran his fingers through various colored papers and coins, then withdrew a hundred-dollar bill. He jabbed it at Macy and said: "Rental fee for one hour. As agreed. One hundred dollars. Take it and go."

Impelled by the thrust of Boyne's eyes, Macy took the bill and staggered out to the bar. Over his shoulder he quavered: "What'll you drink?"

"Drink? Alcohol? Pfui!" Boyne answered.

He turned and darted to the telephone booth, reached under the pay phone and located the lead-in wire. From a side pocket he withdrew a small glittering box and clipped it to the wire. He tucked it out of sight, then lifted the receiver.

"Coordinates West 73-58-15," he said rapidly, "North 40-45-20. Disband sigma. You're ghosting . . ." After a pause, he continued: "Stet. Stet! Transmission clear. I want a fix on Knight. Oliver Wilson Knight. Probability to four significant figures. You have the coordinates. . . . 99.9807? MQ. Stand by. . . ."

Boyne poked his head out of the booth and peered toward the tavern door. He waited with steely concentration until a young man and a pretty girl entered. Then he ducked back to the phone. "Probability fulfilled. Oliver Wilson Knight in contact. MQ. Luck my Para." He hung up and was sitting under the poster as the couple wandered toward the back room.

The young man was about twenty-six, of medium height, and inclined to be stocky. His suit was rumpled, his seal-brown hair was rumpled, and his friendly face was crinkled by good-natured creases. The girl had black hair, soft blue eyes, and a small private smile. They walked arm in arm and liked to collide gently when they thought no one was looking. At this moment they collided with Mr. Macy.

"I'm sorry, Mr. Knight," Macy said. "You and the young lady can't sit back there this afternoon. The premises have been rented."

Their faces fell. Boyne called: "Quite all right, Mr. Macy. All correct. Happy to entertain Mr. Knight and friend as guests."

Knight and the girl turned to Boyne uncertainly. Boyne smiled and patted the chair alongside him. "Sit down," he said. "Charmed, I assure you."

The girl said: "We hate to intrude, but this is the only place in town where you can get genuine Stone gingerbeer."

"Already aware of the fact, Miss Clinton." To Macy he said: "Bring gingerbeer and go. No other guests. These are all I'm expecting."

Knight and the girl stared at Boyne in astonishment as they sat down slowly. Knight placed a wrapped parcel of books on the table. The girl took a breath and said, "You know me . . . Mr. . . ?"

"Boyne. As in Boyne, Battle of. Yes, of course. You are Miss Jane Clinton. This is Mr. Oliver Wilson Knight. I rented premises particularly to meet you this afternoon."

"This supposed to be a gag?" Knight asked, a dull flush appearing on his cheeks.

"Gingerbeer," answered Boyne gallantly as Macy arrived, deposited the bottles and glasses, and departed in haste.

"You couldn't know we were coming here," Jane said. "We didn't know ourselves . . . until a few minutes ago."

"Sorry to contradict, Miss Clinton," Boyne smiled. "The probability of your arrival at Longitude 73-58-15 Latitude 40-45-20 was 99.9807 per cent. No one can escape four significant figures."

"Listen," Knight began angrily, "if this is your idea of—"

"Kindly drink gingerbeer and listen to my idea, Mr. Knight." Boyne leaned across the table with galvanic intensity. "This hour has been arranged with difficulty and much cost. To whom? No matter. You have placed us in an extremely dangerous position. I have been sent to find a solution."

"Solution for what?" Knight asked.

Jane tried to rise. "I . . . I think we'd b-better be go—"

Boyne waved her back, and she sat down like a child. To Knight he said: "This noon you entered premises of J. D. Craig & Co., dealer in printed books. You purchased, through transfer of money, four books. Three do not matter, but the fourth . . ." He tapped the wrapped parcel emphatically. "That is the crux of this encounter."

"What the hell are you talking about?" Knight exclaimed.

" One bound volume consisting of collected facts and statistics."

"The almanac?"

"The almanac."

"What about it?"

"You intended to purchase a 1950 almanac."

"I bought the '50 almanac."

"You did not!" Boyne blazed. "You bought the almanac for 1990."

"What?"

"The World Almanac for 1990," Boyne said clearly, "is in this package. Do not ask how. There was a carelessness that has already been disciplined. Now the error must be adjusted. That is why I am here. It is why this meeting was arranged. You cognate?"

Knight burst into laughter and reached for the parcel. Boyne leaned across the table and grasped his wrist. "You must not open it, Mr. Knight."

"All right." Knight leaned back in his chair. He grinned at Jane and sipped gingerbeer. "What's the payoff on the gag?"

"I must have the book, Mr. Knight. I would like to walk out of this tavern with the almanac under my arm."

"You would, eh?"

"I would."

"The 1990 almanac?"

"Yes."

"If," said Knight, "there was such a thing as a 1990 almanac, and if it was in that package, wild horses couldn't get it away from me."

"Why, Mr. Knight?"

"Don't be an idiot. A look into the future? Stock market reports . . . Horse races . . . Politics. It'd be money from home. I'd be rich."

"Indeed yes." Boyne nodded sharply. "More than rich. Omnipotent. The small mind would use the almanac from the future for small things only. Wagers on the outcome of games and elections. And so on. But the intellect of dimensions . . . *your* intellect . . . would not stop there."

"You tell me," Knight grinned.

"Deduction. Induction. Inference." Boyne ticked the points off on his fingers. "Each fact would tell you an entire history. Real estate investment, for example. What lands to buy and sell. Population shifts and census reports would tell you. Transportation. Lists of marine disasters and railroad wrecks would tell you whether rocket travel has replaced the train and ship."

"Has it?" Knight chuckled.

"Flight records would tell you which company's stock should be bought. Lists of postal receipts would indicate the cities of the future. The Nobel Prize winners would tell you which scientists and what new inventions to watch. Armament budgets would tell you what factories and industries to control. Cost-of-living reports would tell you how best to protect your wealth against inflation or deflation. Foreign exchange rates, stock exchange reports, bank suspensions and life insurance indexes would provide the clues to protect you against any and all disasters."

"That's the idea," Knight said. "That's for me."

"You really think so?"

"I know so. Money in my pocket. The world in my pocket."

"Excuse me," Boyne said keenly, "but you are only repeating the dreams of childhood. You want wealth. Yes. But only won through endeavor . . . your own endeavor. There is no joy in success as an unearned gift. There is nothing but guilt and unhappiness. You are aware of this already."

"I disagree," Knight said.

"Do you? Then why do you work? Why not steal? Rob? Burgle? Cheat others of their money to fill your own pockets?"

"But I—" Knight began, and then stopped.

"The point is well taken, eh?" Boyne waved his hand impatiently. "No, Mr. Knight. Seek a mature argument. You are too ambitious and healthy to wish to steal success."

"Then I'd just want to know if I would be successful."

"Ah? Stet. You wish to thumb through the pages looking for your name. You want reassurance. Why? Have you no confidence in yourself? You are a promising young attorney. Yes, I know that. It is part of my data. Has not Miss Clinton confidence in you?"

"Yes," Jane said in a loud voice. "He doesn't need reassurance from a book."

"What else, Mr. Knight?"

Knight hesitated, sobering in the face of Boyne's overwhelming intensity. Then he said: "Security."

"There is no such thing. Life is danger. You can only find security in death."

"You know what I mean," Knight muttered. "The knowledge that life is worth planning. There's the atom bomb."

Boyne nodded quickly. "True. It is a crisis. But then, I'm here. The world will continue. I am proof."

"If I believe you."

"And if you do not?" Boyne blazed. "You do not lack security. You lack courage." He nailed the couple with a contemptuous glare. "There is in this country a legend of pioneer forefathers from whom you are supposed to inherit courage in the face of odds. D. Boone, E. Allen, S. Houston, A. Lincoln. G. Washington and others. Fact?"

"I suppose so," Knight muttered. "That's what we keep telling ourselves."

"And where is the courage in you? Pfui! It is only talk. The unknown terrifies you. Danger does not inspire you to fight, as it did D. Crockett; it makes you whine and reach for the reassurance in this book. Fact?"

"But the atom bomb . . ."

"It is a danger. Yes. One of many. What of that? Do you cheat at solhand?"

"Solhand?"

158 STAR LIGHT, STAR BRIGHT

"Your pardon." Boyne reconsidered, impatiently snapping his fingers at the interruption to the white heat of his argument. "It is a game played singly against chance relationships in an arrangement of cards. I forget your noun. . . ."

"Oh!" Jane's face brightened. "Solitaire."

"Quite right. Solitaire. Thank you, Miss Clinton." Boyne turned his frightening eyes on Knight. "Do you cheat at solitaire?"

"Occasionally."

"Do you enjoy games won by cheating?"

"Not as a rule."

"They are thisney, yes? Boring. They are tiresome. Pointless. Null-coordinated. You wish you had won honestly."

"I suppose so."

"And you will suppose so after you have looked at this bound book. Through all your pointless life you will wish you had played honestly the game of life. You will verdash that look. You will regret. You will totally recall the pronouncement of our great poet-philosopher Trynbyll who summed it up in one lightning, skazon line. 'The Future is Tekon,' said Trynbyll. Mr. Knight, do not cheat. Let me implore you to give me the almanac."

"Why don't you take it away from me?"

"It must be a gift. We can rob you of nothing. We can give you nothing."

"That's a lie. You paid Macy to rent this backroom."

"Macy was paid, but I gave him nothing. He will think he was cheated, but you will see to it that he is not. All will be adjusted without dislocation."

"Wait a minute. . . ."

"It has all been carefully planned. I have gambled on you, Mr. Knight. I am depending on your good sense. Let me have the almanac. I will disband . . . reorient . . . and you will never see me again. Vorloss verdash! It will be a bar adventure to narrate for friends. Give me the almanac!"

"Hold the phone," Knight said. "This is a gag. Remember? I—"

"Is it?" Boyne interrupted. "Is it? Look at me."

For almost a minute the young couple stared at the bleached white face with its deadly eyes. The half-smile left Knight's lips, and Jane shuddered involuntarily. There was chill and dismay in the back room.

"My God!" Knight glanced helplessly at Jane. "This can't be happening. He's got me believing. You?"

Jane nodded jerkily.

"What should we do? If everything he says is true we can refuse and live happily ever after."

"No," Jane said in a choked voice. "There may be money and success in that book, but there's divorce and death, too. Give him the almanac."

"Take it," Knight said faintly.

Boyne rose instantly. He picked up the package and went into the phone booth. When he came out he had three books in one hand and a smaller parcel made up of the original wrapping in the other. He placed the books on the table and stood for a moment, holding the parcel and smiling down.

"My gratitude," he said. "You have eased a precarious situation. It is only fair you should receive something in return. We are forbidden to transfer anything that might divert existing phenomena streams, but at least I can give you one token of the future."

He backed away, bowed curiously, and said: "My service to you both." Then he turned and started out of the tavern.

"Hey!" Knight called. "The token?"

"Mr. Macy has it," Boyne answered and was gone.

The couple sat at the table for a few blank moments like sleepers slowly awakening. Then, as reality began to return, they stared at each other and burst into laughter.

"He really had me scared," Jane said.

"Talk about Third Avenue characters. What an act. What'd he get out of it?"

"Well . . . he got your almanac."

"But it doesn't make sense." Knight began to laugh again. "All that business about paying Macy but not giving him anything. And I'm supposed to see that he isn't cheated. And the mystery token of the future . . ."

The tavern door burst open and Macy shot through the saloon into the back room. "Where is he?" Macy shouted. "Where's the thief? Boyne, he calls himself. More likely his name is Dillinger."

"Why, Mr. Macy!" Jane exclaimed. "What's the matter?"

"Where is he?" Macy pounded on the door of the men's room. "Come out, ye blaggard!"

"He's gone," Knight said. "He left just before you got back."

"And you, Mr. Knight!" Macy pointed a trembling finger at the young lawyer. "You, to be party to thievery and racketeers. Shame on you!"

"What's wrong?" Knight asked.

"He paid me one hundred dollars to rent this back room," Macy cried in anguish. "One hundred dollars. I took the bill over to Bernie the pawnbroker, being cautious-like, and he found out it's a forgery. It's a counterfeit."

"Oh, no," Jane laughed. "That's too much. Counterfeit?"

"Look at this," Mr. Macy shouted, slamming the bill down on the table.

Knight inspected it closely. Suddenly he turned pale and the laughter drained out of his face. He reached into his inside pocket, withdrew a checkbook and began to write with trembling fingers.

"What on earth are you doing?" Jane asked.

"Making sure that Macy isn't cheated," Knight said. "You'll get your hundred dollars, Mr. Macy."

"Oliver! Are you insane? Throwing away a hundred dollars . . ."

"And I won't be losing anything, either," Knight answered.

"All will be adjusted without dislocation! They're diabolical. Diabolical!"

"I don't understand."

"Look at the bill," Knight said in a shaky voice. "Look closely."

It was beautifully engraved and genuine in appearance. Benjamin Franklin's benign features gazed up at them mildly and authentically; but in the lower right-hand corner was printed: Series 1980 D. And underneath that was signed: Oliver Wilson Knight, Secretary of the Treasury.

Isaac Asimov

Introduction

THE question most often asked by fans is: Why did I stop writing science fiction? The answer is difficult because I'm a complex man with tangled motivations. However, I can try oversimplifying. Many times I've been driven off a bus by a child nagging its mother with "I wan' ice cream," over and over again. I can't endure repetition; I enjoy only new things. I'm the exact opposite to Gustave Lebair, a famous bibliomaniac, who read the same book *St. Apollonius of Tyana* in the Bibliothèque Nationale every day for sixty years. A perceptive friend once said, "Alfie Bester believes that the entire world was made for his entertainment." I really don't go quite that far in my selfish egotism, but I come damned close to it.

When I was serving my apprenticeship and trying to become a master craftsman in my profession, science fiction was merely one of many fields that I attacked. There were also comics, slick fiction, mainstream novels, radio and television scripts. As soon as I mastered a field and became successful, I'd be driven off the bus and have to catch another one in my search for the entertainment of a fresh challenge. I don't mean to imply that I was successful in everything I tried. I had my fair share of grim failures, and I'm saving them up to have another go.

My two successful science fiction novels of many years ago brought me dangerously close to boredom with the field. Brian Aldiss is much kinder than I am to myself. He says, "No. You stopped writing science fiction because you realized that you'd said all you had to say. I wish more writers would have that good sense." That may be true, but the fact is it was my association with *Holiday* magazine that cut me off from other forms of writing.

Holiday was a godsend to a man of my temperament. As a regular contributor and ultimately a senior editor, my professional life was filled with variety, fresh challenges, and constant entertainment. As an interviewer and feature writer, I had to master a new and difficult craft. Once mastered, there was no danger of boredom because I was meeting and spending time with hundreds of fascinating people in hundreds of different professions. With the cachet of a then-important magazine backing me, no door was ever closed; ideal for an incurably curious man.

I enjoyed interviewing the most and want to show you the sort of thing I was doing issue after issue. Unfortunately, most of my pieces ran much too long for inclusion here, and anyway what would Olivier, Burton, Quinn, Kim Novak, or Sophia Loren be doing in a science fiction collection? Happily I have a very short piece I did for another publication on Isaac Asimov, one of the great stars of the field, and I'm including it here.

You may ask what an interview is doing in a story collection. Well, it isn't a story collection, it's a Bester collection, and there's no reason why there can't be variety. I'll trouble you not to object. It will only remind me of Whistler's libel action against John Ruskin. On cross-examination, Ruskin's barrister asked Whistler how he could call one of his paintings

"A Study in Blue" when there were so many other colors in it. Whistler shot back, "Idiot! Does a symphony in F consist of nothing but F, F, F, F?"

Colorful man, Whistler. Deadly opponent. I'd love to have interviewed him.

THERE'S NO DOUBT that Isaac Asimov is the finest popular science writer working today, and in my opinion Ike is the finest who has ever written; prolific, encyclopedic, witty, with a gift for colorful and illuminating examples and explanations. What makes him unique is the fact that he's a bona fide scientiest—associate professor of biochemistry at Boston University School of Medicine—and scientists are often rotten writers. Read the novels of C. P. Snow and the short stories of Bertrand Russell if you want proof. But our scientist professor, Asimov, is not only a great popular science author but an eminent science fiction author as well. He comes close to the ideal of the Renaissance Man.

His latest (120th) book, *Asimov's Guide to Science* (Basic Books), is a must for science-oriented and/or science-terrified readers. Many people have the frightened feeling, "What are they up to now?" Asimov tells us with clarity, with charm, with calm. His new *Guide* will fascinate the layman, and if the layman gives it to his kids to read they may very well wind up on university faculties with tenure. Ike makes everyone want to turn into a scientist.

Asimov's Guide to Science is the new and third edition of *The Intelligent Man's Guide to Science*, first published in 1960 by Basic Books. Asked why the change in title, he said, "Well, there's a whole slew of *Asimov's Guides* and *Asimov's Treasuries*, so we decided to go along with it. I presume the fourth edition will be *Asimov's New Guide to Science*. What the fifth will be, I don't know."

The encyclopedia has been revised and updated, of course.

Much has happened since the 1960s. Asked about his changes, Ike rattled off, "Pulsars, black holes, the surface of Mars, landings on the moon. Then there's seafloor spreading and the shifting of continents, which I dismissed with a sneer in the first edition. You see, at the time of the first edition the space satellites were just being flown and hadn't done their research yet. I thought the earth's crust was too solid and hard for the continents to drift. I was wrong. Now we know that the continents aren't floating; they're being pushed apart by the upflow of magma from the seafloor. Then I've covered quarks and—"

"Wait a minute. What are quarks?"

"They're hypothetical particles which may make up all the subatomic particles, but first we have to isolate one. In other words, you can think that ten dimes make a dollar, but you have to take a dollar apart first and find a dime." This is the Asimov style.

He also discusses why enough neutrinos have not yet been detected coming from the sun, the biological clocks in animals, tachyons—a fascinating hypothesis about subatomic particles which travel faster than the speed of light—and cloning.

"What's so special about clone cultures, Ike? They're simply families raised from a single individual. I raised many clone cultures from a single paramecium or amoeba when I was a biology student."

"No, no. Now we're talking about despecializing specialized cells. You can take an abdominal cell from a frog, fertilize it with an ovum and get a whole frog. There may come a time when they can cut off your little toe when you're born, fertilize it and end up with a whole race of Alfie Besters."

"What a horrible thought."

"Yes, but they wouldn't know it at the time."

He's a powerful man, 5-9, 180 pounds, with thick hair going grey, steel-blue eyes, beautiful strong hands, and rather blunt features. He was born in Russia in 1920 and was brought to the States in 1923 by his family, which wasn't exactly well-to-do. Nevertheless he managed to put himself through Columbia University to his doctorate which he won for a thesis on enzyme chemistry.

He was married in 1942, has two kids, and is recently separated from his wife. He now lives in a comfortable suite in a residential hotel just off Central Park West. The living room is his workshop; jammed with shelves of reference texts, files and piles of scientific journals. He works from nine to five, seven days a week without a break.

"No, I'm lying. Sometimes I goof off on part of Sunday."

"Do you think at the typewriter, Ike?"

"Yes. I type at professional speed. Ninety words a minute."

"Great, but do you think at ninety words a minute?"

"Yes, I do. The two work together neatly."

He receives an enormous amount of mail from his fiction fans and his science fans, which he answers. Small boys write and ask him to settle disputes they're having with their science teachers. Asimov winces when he recalls a terrible boner which he perpetrated in the first edition of his *Guide*. A kid got into an argument with his teacher over it and said, "Dr. Asimov is always right." Asimov was forced to write back, "Sometimes Isaac Asimov is a damned fool."

He gets a few crank letters. "One guy was mad because I wouldn't say that Nikola Tesla was the greatest scientist who ever lived. I've only had one anti-Semitic letter. This was from a kook who thought I gave too much space to Einstein. He said Einstein was all wrong, and anyway he stole everything from a Gentile. Naturally I didn't bother to answer that."

He's rather amused by what he calls his steel-trap memory. "I have a tight grip on things in inverse proportion to their importance. The trouble is, I can't throw anything out. The other day a friend mentioned an old song, 'The Boulevard of Broken Dreams,' and I sang it for him."

Damn if he didn't start singing it for me, miserably. "You see?" he grinned. "Another five brain cells wasted."

The Pi Man

Introduction

THE one word most symbolic of science fiction is, of course, "extrapolation." Science fiction started talking about extrapolation a couple of generations back. I first encountered the noun and verb in *Astounding Science Fiction*, and I was much impressed yet ashamed because I didn't know what it meant. Here I was, excessively educated, and I'd never come across it before. I was convinced that the godlike editor of *Astounding*, John W. Campbell, Jr., had personally and privately invented it. Certainly he used the word like he owned it.

"Extrapolation" is no longer an exotic SF term today. It's become familiar and a part of casual conversation particularly after its frequent use along with the rest of the Madison Avenue jargon in the Watergate hearings, but what exactly does it mean? The unabridged Webster II, which remains the supreme arbiter for editors despite the publication of the Webster III, is no help at all:

> Extrapolation. The calculation, from the values of a function known within a certain interval of values of its argument, of its value for some argument value lying without that interval, as the calculation of the birth rate in 1934 from the known rates in 1850-1900.

And good luck to Noah Webster, American lexicographer . . . 1758-1843.

Here's my definition:

> Extrapolation. The continuation of a trend, either increasing, decreasing or steady-state, to its culmination in the future. The only constraint is the limit set by the logic of the universe.

And good luck to the late, great Alfred Bester, American author.

I'd like to digress here to get mixed up in the controversial question that vexes many readers and writers of imaginative fiction: what is the difference between science fiction and fantasy. My "constraint" qualification in the definition of extrapolation may be the answer. In my opinion, science fiction's limits are, or should be, the known/possible logic of the universe. In my opinion, fantasy is written and read in a limbo without logic or limits. That's one reason why I dislike most fantasy so much; I find it undisciplined and self-indulgent.

I've done my own extrapolation in science fiction, but I've concentrated mainly on human behavior; I'm people-oriented. Whenever I start thinking about a story, it's always in terms of characters and their response to a changed environment. Putting it another way, I'm not much interested in extrapolating science and technology; I merely use extrapolation as a means of putting people into new quandaries which produce colorful pressures and conflicts. I'll be blunt: to hell with the science if it can't produce fiction.

Now I'm people myself, and many times I've extrapolated a piece of myself into a story. Some friends who know me well insist that I put all of myself into all of my protagonists, which isn't pleasant considering how lunatic my antiheroes are. I think the purest example of this is "The Pi Man," and one of the proofs is that the story was written in a single day of white-hot hysteria. I must have been writing myself. Additional proof: I revised and polished the story for this edition (the original was written too fast and was rather crude), and I got hysterical all over again.

I've always been obsessed by patterns, rhythms, and tempi, and I always feel my stories in those terms. It's this pattern obsession that compels me to experiment with typography. I'm trying very hard to develop a technique of blending the sight, sound, and context of words into dramatic patterns. I want to make the eye, ear, and mind of the reader merge into a whole that is bigger than the sum of its parts. I have this curious belief that somehow reading should be more than mere reading; it should be a total sensory and intellectual experience. In my own quaint way I'm trying to go films and TV one better. Huxley was reaching for the same thing with his "feelies" in *Brave New World* but he didn't go far enough. Me neither, maybe.

Anyway, one evening I was chatting with a dear guy who's been a friend ever since he beat my brains out in foils during a dual-meet we had with Princeton. He's a demented musician. Among other things he wrote a black humor tune titled, "Who Put the Snatch on the Lindbergh Baby? (Was it You or You or You?)" He was telling me about the eminent composer under whom he'd studied at Prince-i-ton. *Little Charles Augie was playing with his doggie* . . . The Man could beat 5/4 with one hand while beating 7/4 with the other, *Was that the thing to do?* and he could make them come out even at the end of the measure. *His father took the notion to fly the ocean* . . . It's a fantastic ability; if you don't believe me try it for yourself. *Was that any way to show your devotion?*

This fired the idea of extrapolating my obsession with patterns and dynamics, and "The Pi Man" is the result. The story explores the effects of an outré but logically possible exaggeration of environment on a contemporary man. (Parenthetically, I always try to keep my characters contemporary in science fiction.) Notice that I did not make the protagonist a musiciań. Too obvious, too easy, too special. I believed that everybody could identify and vibrate with the harmonics of my own rhythmic obsession. This, of course, is a classic sympton of lunacy.

How to say? How to write? When sometimes I can be fluent, even polished, and then, *reculer pour mieux sauter,* patterns take hold of me. Push. Compel.

Sometimes

I	I	I
am	am	am
	3.14159 +	
from	from	from
this	other	that
space	space	space

Othertimes not

I have no control, but I try anyways.

I wake up wondering who, what, when, where, why?

Confusion result of biological compensator born into my body which I hate. Yes, birds and beasts have biological clock built in, and so navigate home from a thousand miles away. I have biological compensator, equalizer, responder to unknown stresses and strains. I relate, compensate, make and shape patterns, adjust rhythms, like a gridiron pendulum in a clock, but this is an unknown clock, and I do not know what time it keeps. Nevertheless I must. I am force. Have no control over self, speech, love, fate. Only to compensate.

Quae nocent docent. Translation follows: Things that injure teach. I am injured and have hurt many. What have we learned? However. I wake up the morning of the biggest hurt of all wondering which house. Wealth, you understand.

Damme! Mews cottage in London, villa in Rome, penthouse in
New York, rancho in California. I awake. I look. Ah! Layout
familiar. Thus:

```
Foyer
    Bedroom
        Bath            T
        Bath            e
        Living Room     r
    Kitchen             r
        Dressing Room   a
        Bedroom         c
        T e r r a c     e
```

So. I am in penthouse in New York, but that bath-bath-
back-to-back. Pfui! All rhythm wrong. Pattern painful. Why
have I never noticed before? Or is this sudden awareness
result of phenomenon elsewhere? I telephone to janitor-mans
downstairs. At that moment I lose my American-English.
Damn nuisance. I'm compelled to speak a compost of tongues,
and I never know which will be forced on me next.

"*Pronto. Ecco mi. Signore Marko. Miscusi tanto—*"
Pfui! Hang up. Hate the garbage I must sometimes speak
and write. This I now write during period of AmerEng lucidity, otherwise would look like goulash. While I wait for return
of communication, I shower body, teeth, hairs, shave face, dry
everything, and try again. *Voilà!* Ye Englishe, she come. Back
to invention of Mr. A. G. Bell and call janitor again.

"Good morning, Mr. Lundgren. This is Peter Marko. Guy
in the penthouse. Right. Mr. Lundgren, be my personal rabbi
and get some workmen up here this morning. I want those
two baths converted into one. No, I mean it. I'll leave five
thousand dollars on top of the icebox. Yes? Thanks, Mr.
Lundgren."

Wanted to wear grey flannel this morning but compelled to
put on sharkskin. Damnation! Black Power has peculiar side
effects. Went to spare bedroom (see diagram) and unlocked

door which was installed by the Eagle Safe Company—Since 1904—Bank Vault Equipment—Fireproof Files & Ledger Trays—Combinations changed. I went in.

Everything broadcasting beautifully, up and down the electromagnetic spectrum. Radio waves down to 1,000 meters, ultraviolet up into the hard X-rays and the 100 Kev (one hundred thousand electron volts) gamma radiation. All interupters innn-tt-errrr-up-ppp-t-ingggg at random. I'm jamming the voice of the universe at least within this home, and I'm at peace. Dear God! To know even a moment of peace!

So. I take subway to office in Wall Street. Limousine more convenient but chauffeur too dangerous. Might become friendly, and I don't dare have friends anymore. Best of all, the morning subway is jam-packed, mass-packed, no patterns to adjust, no shiftings and compensations required. Peace.

In subway car I catch a glimpse of an eye, narrow, bleak, grey, the property of an anonymous man who conveys the conviction that you've never seen him before and will never see him again. But I picked up that glance and it tripped an alarm in the back of my mind. He knew it. He saw the flash in my eyes before I could turn away. So I was being tailed again. Who, this time? U.S.A.? U.S.S.R.? Interpol? Skip-Tracers, Inc.?

I drifted out of the subway with the crowd at City Hall and gave them a false trail to the Woolworth Building in case they were operating double-tails. The whole theory of the hunters and the hunted is not to avoid being tailed, no one can escape that; the thing to do is give them so many false leads to follow up that they become overextended. Then they may be forced to abandon you. They have a man-hour budget; just so many men for just so many operations.

City Hall traffic was out of sync, as it generally is, so I had to limp to compensate. Took elevator up to tenth floor of bldg. As I was starting down the stairs, I was suddenly seized by something from out there, something bad. I began to cry, but no help. An elderly clerk emerge from office wearing alpaca coat, gold spectacles, badge on lapel identify: *N. N. Chapin.* "Not him," I plead with nowhere. "Nice mans. Not N. N. Chapin, please."

But I am force. Approach. Two blows, neck and gut. Down he go, writhing. I trample spectacles and smash watch. Then I'm permitted to go downstairs again. It was ten-thirty. I was late. Damn! Took taxi to 99 Wall Street. Driver's pattern smelled honest; big black man, quiet and assured. Tipped him fifty dollars. He raise eyebrows. Sealed one thousand in envelope (secretly) and sent driver back to bldg. to find and give to N. N. Chapin on tenth floor. Did not enclose note: "From your unknown admirer."

Routine morning's work in office. I am in arbitrage, which is simultaneous buying and selling of moneys in different markets to profit from unequal price. Try to follow simple example: Pound sterling is selling for $2.79½ in London. Rupee is selling for $2.79 in New York. One rupee buys one pound in Burma. See where the arbitrage lies? I buy one rupee for $2.79 in New York, buy one pound for rupee in Burma, sell pound for $2.79½ in London, and I have made ½ cent on the transaction. Multiply by $100,000, and I have made $250 on the transaction. Enormous capital required.

But this is only crude example of arbitrage; actually the buying and selling must follow intricate patterns and have perfect timing. Money markets are jumpy today. Big Boards are hectic. Gold fluctuating. I am behind at eleven-thirty, but the patterns put me ahead $57,075.94 by half-past noon, Daylight Saving Time.

57075 makes a nice pattern but that 94¢! Iych! Ugly. Symmetry above all else. Alas, only 24¢ hard money in my pockets. Called secretary, borrowed 70¢ from her, and threw sum total out window. Felt better as I watched it scatter in space, but then I caught her looking at me with delight. Very dangerous. Fired girl on the spot.

"But why, Mr. Marko? Why?" she asked, trying not to cry. Darling little thing. Pale-faced and saucy, but not so saucy now.

"Because you're beginning to like me."

"What's the harm in that?"

"When I hired you, I warned you not to like me."

"I thought you were putting me on."

"I wasn't. Out you go."

"But why?"

"Because I'm beginning to like you."

"Is this some new kind of pass?"

"God forbid!"

"Well you don't have to worry," she flared. "I despise you."

"Good. Then I can go to bed with you."

She turned crimson and opened her mouth to denounce me, the while her eyes twinkled at the corners. A darling girl, whatever her name was. I could not endanger her. I gave her three weeks' salary for a bonus and threw her out. *Punkt.* Next secretary would be a man, married, misanthropic, murderous; a man who could hate me.

So, lunch. Went to nicely balanced restaurant. All chairs filled by patrons. Even pattern. No need for me to compensate and adjust. Also, they give me usual single corner table which does not need guest to balance. Ordered nicely patterned luncheon:

Martini   Martini

Croque M'sieur Roquefort

Salad

Coffee

But so much cream being consumed in restaurant that I had to compensate by drinking my coffee black, which I dislike. However, still a soothing pattern.

$x^2 + x + 41$ = prime number. Excuse, please. Sometimes I'm in control and see what compensating must be done . . . tick-tock-tick-tock, good old gridiron pendulum . . . other times is force on me from God knows where or why or how or even if there is a God. Then I must do what

I'm compelled to do, blindly, without motivation, speaking the gibberish I speak and think, sometimes hating it like what I do to poor mans Mr. Chapin. Anyway, the equation breaks down when x = 40.

The afternoon was quiet. For a moment I thought I might be forced to leave for Rome (Italy) but whatever it was adjusted without needing my two ($0.02) cents. ASPCA finally caught up with me for beating my dog to death, but I'd contributed $5,000.00 to their shelter. Got off with a shaking of heads. Wrote a few graffiti on posters, saved a small boy from a clobbering in a street rumble at a cost of sharkskin jacket. Drat! Slugged a maladroit driver who was subjecting his lovely Aston-Martin to cruel and unusual punishment. He was, how they say, "grabbing a handful of second."

In the evening to ballet to relax with all the beautiful Balanchine patterns; balanced, peaceful, soothing. Then I take a deep breath, quash my nausea, and force myself to go to *The Raunch,* the West Village creepsville. I hate *The Raunch,* but I need a woman and I must go where I hate. That fair-haired girl I fired, so full of mischief and making eyes at me. So, *poisson d'avril*, I advance myself to *The Raunch*.

Chaos. Blackness. Cacophony. My vibes shriek. 25 Watt bulbs. Ballads of Protest. Against L. wall sit young men with pubic beards, playing chess. Badly. *Exempli gratia*:

```
1 P—Q4      Kt—KB3
2 Kt—Q2     P—K4
3 P X P     Kt—Kt5
4 P—KR3     Kt—K6
```

If White takes the knight, Black forces mate with Q—R5ch. I didn't wait to see what the road-company Capablancas would do next.

Against R. wall is bar, serving beer and cheap wine mostly. There are girls with brown paper bags containing toilet articles. They are looking for a pad for the night. All wear tight jeans and are naked under loose sweaters. I think of Herrick (1591-1674): *Next, when I lift mine eyes and see/That brave vibration each way free/Oh, how that glittering taketh me!*

I pick out the one who glitters the most. I talk. She insult. I insult back and buy hard drinks. She drink my drinks and snarl and hate, but helpless. Her name is Bunny and she has no pad for tonight. I do not let myself sympathize. She is a dyke; she does not bathe, her thinking patterns are jangles. I hate her and she's safe; no harm can come to her. So I maneuvered her out of Sink City and took her home to seduce by mutual contempt, and in the living room sat the slender little paleface secretary, recently fired for her own good.

She sat there in my penthouse, now minus one (1) bathroom, and with $1,997.00 change on top of the refrigerator. Oi! Throw $6.00 into kitchen Dispos-All (a Federal offense) and am soothed by the lovely 1991 remaining. She sat there, wearing a pastel thing, her skin gleaming rose-red from embarrassment, also red for danger. Her saucy face was very tight from the daring thing she thought she was doing. *Gott bewahre!* I like that.

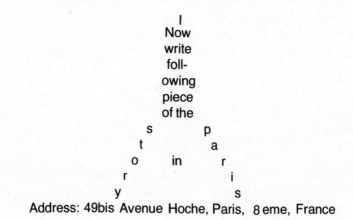

```
            I
          Now
          write
          foll-
          owing
          piece
          of the
              s       p
            t           a
          o     in        r
        r                   i
      y                       s
```
Address: 49bis Avenue Hoche, Paris, 8 eme, France

Forced to go there by what happened in the U.N., you

understand. It needed extreme compensation and adjust-
ment. Almost, for a moment, I thought I would have to attack
the conductor of the *Opéra Comique,* but fate was kind and let
me off with nothing worse than indecent exposure, and I was
able to square it by founding a scholarship at the Sorbonne.
Didn't someone suggest that fate was the square root of minus
one?

Anyway, back in New York it is my turn to denounce the
paleface but suddenly by AmerEng is replaced by a dialect out
of a B-picture about a white remittance man and a blind native
girl on a South Sea island who find redemption together while
she plays the ukelele and sings gems from Lawrence Welk's
Greatest Hits.

"Oh-so," I say. "Me-fella be ve'y happy ask why you-fella
invade 'long my apa'tment, 'cept me' now speak pidgin. Ve'y
emba'ss 'long me."

"I bribed Mr. Lundgren," she blurted. "I told him you
needed important papers from the office."

The dyke turned on her heel and bounced out, her brave
vibration each way free. I caught up with her in front of the
elevator, put $101 into her hand, and tried to apologize. She
hated me more so I did a naughty thing to her vibration and
returned to the living room.

"What's she got?" the paleface asked.

My English returned. "What's your name?"

"Good Lord! I've been working in your office for two
months and you don't know my name? You really don't?"

"No."

"I'm Jemmy Thomas."

"Beat it, Jemmy Thomas."

"So that's why you always called me 'Miss Uh.' You're Russian?"

"Half."

"What's the other half?"

"None of your business. What are you doing here? When I
fire them they stay fired. What d'you want from me?"

"You," she said, blushing fiery.

"Will you for God's sake get the hell out of here."

"What did she have that I don't?" paleface demanded.
Then her face crinkled. "Don't? Doesn't? I'm going to Bennington. They're strong on aggression but weak on grammar."

"What d'you mean, you're going to Bennington?"

"Why, it's a college. I thought everybody knew."

"But *going?*"

"Oh. I'm in my junior year. They drive you out with whips
to acquire practical experience in your field. You ought to
know that. Your office manager—I suppose you don't know
her name, either."

"Ethel M. Blatt."

"Yes. Miss Blatt took it all down before you interviewed
me."

"What's your field?"

"It used to be economics. Now it's you. How old are you?"

"One hundred and one."

"Oh, come on. Thirty? They say at Bennington that ten
years is the right difference between men and women because
we mature quicker. Are you married?"

"I have wives in London, Paris, and Rome. What is this
catechism?"

"Well, I'm trying to get something going."

"I can see that, but does it have to be me?"

"I know it sounds like a notion." She lowered her eyes, and
without the highlight of their blue, her pale face was almost
invisible. "And I suppose women are always throwing themselves at you."

"It's my untold wealth."

"What are you, blasé or something? I mean, I know I'm not
staggering, but I'm not exactly repulsive."

"You're lovely."

"Then why don't you come near me?"

"I'm trying to protect you."

"I can protect me when the time comes. I'm a Black Belt."

"The time is now, Jemmy Thompson."

"Thomas."

"Walk, not run, to the nearest exit, Jemmy Thomas."

"The least you could do is offend me the way you did that hustler in front of the elevator."

"You snooped?"

"Sure I snooped. You didn't expect me to sit here on my hands, did you? I've got my man to protect."

I had to laugh. This spunky little thing march in, roll up her sleeves and set to work on me. A wonder she didn't have a pot roast waiting in the oven and herself waiting in the bed.

"Your man?" I ask.

"It happens," she said in a low voice. "I never believed it, but it happens. You fall in and out of love and affairs, and each time you think it's real and forever. And then you meet somebody and it isn't a question of love anymore. You just know that he's your man, and you're stuck with him, whether you like it or not." She burst out angrily. "I'm stuck, dammit! Stuck! D'you think I'm enjoying this?"

She looked at me through the storm; violet eyes full of youth and determination and tenderness and fear. I could see she too was being forced and was angry and afraid. And I knew how lonely I was, never daring to make friends, to love, to share. I could fall into those violet eyes and never come up. I looked at the clock. 2:30 A.M. Sometimes quiet at this hour. Perhaps my AmerEng would stay with me a while longer.

"You're being compelled, Jemmy," I said. "I know all about that. Something inside you, something you don't understand, made you take your dignity in both hands and come after me. You don't like it, you don't want to, you've never begged in your life, but you had to. Yes?"

She nodded.

"Then you can understand a little about me. I'm compelled, too."

"Who is she?"

"No, no. Not forced to beg from a woman; compelled to hurt people."

"What people?"

"Any people; sometimes strangers, and that's bad, other times people I love, and that's not to be endured. So now I no longer dare love. I must protect people from myself."

"I don't know what you're talking about. Are you some kind of psychotic monster?"

"Yes, played by Lon Chaney, Jr."

"If you can joke about it, you can't be all that sick. Have you seen a shrink?"

"No. I don't have to. I know what's compelling me." I looked at the clock again. Still a quiet time. Please God the English would stay with me a while longer. I took off my jacket and shirt. "I'm going to shock you," I said, and showed her my back, crosshatched with scars. She gasped.

"Self-inflicted," I told her. "Because I permitted myself to like a man and become friendly with him. This is the price I paid, and I was lucky that he didn't have to. Now wait here."

I went into the master bedroom where my heart's shame was embalmed in a silver case hidden in the right-hand drawer of my desk. I brought it to the living room. Jemmy watched me with great eyes.

"Five years ago a girl fell in love with me," I told her. "A girl like you. I was lonely then, as always, so instead of protecting her from me, I indulged myself and tried to love her back. Now I want to show you the price *she* paid. You'll loathe me for this, but I must show you. Maybe it'll save you from—"

I broke off. A flash had caught my eye—the flash of lights going on in a building down the street; not just a few windows, a lot. I put on my jacket, went out on the terrace, and watched. All the illuminated windows in the building three down from me went out. Five-second eclipse. On again. It happened in the building two down and then the one next door. The,girl came to my side and took my arm. She trembled slightly.

"What is it?" she asked. "What's the matter? You look so grim."

"It's the Geneva caper," I said. "Wait."

The lights in my apartment went out for five seconds and then came on again.

"They've located me the way I was nailed in Geneva," I told her.

"They? Located?"

"They've spotted my jamming by d/f."

"What jamming?"

"The full electromagnetic spectrum."

"What's dee eff?"

"Radio direction-finder. They used it to get the bearing of my jamming. Then they turned off the current in each building in the area, building by building, until the broadcast stopped. Now they've pinpointed me. They know I'm in this house, but they don't know which apartment yet. I've still got time. So. Good night, Jemmy. You're hired again. Tell Ethel Blatt I won't be in for a while. I wish I could kiss you good-bye, but safer not."

She clamped her arms around my neck and gave me an honest kiss. I tried to push her away.

She clung like The Old Man of the Sea. "You're a spy," she said. "I'll go to the chair with you."

"I wish to heaven I only was a spy. Good-bye, my love. Remember me."

A great mistake letting that slip. It happen, I think, because my speech slip, too. Suddenly forced to talk jumble again. As I run out, the little paleface kick off her sandals so she can run, too. She is alongside me going down the fire stairs to the garage in the basement. I hit her to stop, and swear Swahili at her. She hit back and swear gutter, all the time laughing and crying. I love her for it, so she is doomed. I will ruin her like all the rest.

We get into car and drive fast. I am making for 59th Street bridge to get off Manhattan Island and head east. I own plane in Babylon, Long Island, which is kept ready for this sort of awkwardness.

"*J'y suis, J'y reste* is not my motto," I tell Jemmy Thomas, whose French is as uncertain as her grammar, an endearing weakness. "Once Scotland Yard trapped me with a letter. I was receiving special mail care of General Delivery. They mailed me a red envelope, spotted me when I picked it up, and followed me to No. 13 Mayfair Mews, London W.1., Telephone, Mayfair 7711. Red for danger. Is the rest of you as invisible as your face?"

"I'm not invisible," she said, indignant, running hands through her streaky fair hair. "I tan in the summer. What is all this chase and escape? Why do you talk so funny and act so peculiar? In the office I thought it was because you're a crazy Russian. Half crazy Russian. Are you sure you're not a spy?"

"Only positive."

"It's too bad. A Commie 007 would be utter blissikins."

"Yes, I know. You see yourself being seduced with vodka and caviar."

"Are you a being from another world who came here on a UFO?"

"Would that scare you?"

"Only if it meant we couldn't make the scene."

"We couldn't anyway. All the serious side of me is concentrated on my career. I want to conquer the earth for my robot masters."

"I'm only interested in conquering you."

"I am not and have never been a creature from another world. I can show you my passport to prove it."

"Then what are you?"

"A compensator."

"A what?"

"A compensator. Like a clock pendulum. Do you know dictionary of Messrs Funk & Wagnalls? Edited by Frank H. Vizetelly, Litt.D., LL.D.? I quote: One who or that which compensates, as a device for neutralizing the influence of local attraction upon a compass-needle, or an automatic apparatus for equalizing— Damn!"

Litt.D. Frank H. Vizetelly does not use that word. It is my own because roadblock now faces me on 59th Street bridge. I should have anticipated. Should have sensed patterns, but too swept up with this inviting girl. Probably there are roadblocks on all exits leading out of this $24 island. Could drive off bridge, but maybe Bennington College has also neglected to teach Jemmy Thomas how to swim. So. Stop car. Surrender.

"Kamerad," I pronounce. "Who you? John Birch?"

Gentlemans say no.

"White Supremes of the World, Inc.?"

No again. I feel better. Always nasty when captured by lunatic fringers.

"U.S.S.R.?"

He stare, then speak. "Special Agent Hildebrand. FBI," and flash his identification which no one can read in this light. I take his word and embrace him in gratitude. FBI is safe. He recoil and wonder if I am fag. I don't care. I kiss Jemmy Thomas, and she open mouth under mine to mutter, "Admit nothing. Deny everything. I've got a lawyer."

I own thirteen lawyers, and two of them can make any court tremble, but no need to call them. This will be standard cross-examination; I know from past experience. So let them haul me off to Foley Square with Jemmy. They separate us. I am taken to Inquisition Room.

Brilliant lights; the shadows arranged just so; the chairs placed just so; mirror on wall probably one-way window with observers outside; I've been through this so often before. The anonymous man from the subway this morning is questioning me. We exchange glances of recognition. His name is R. Sawyer. The questions come.

"Name?"

"Peter Marko."

"Born?"

"Lee's Hill, Virginia."

"Never heard of it."

"It's a very small town, about thirty miles north of Roanoke. Most maps ignore it."

"You're Russian?"

"Half, by descent."

"Father Russian?"

"Yes. Eugene Alexis Markolevsky."

"Changed his name legally?"

"Shortened it when he became a citizen."

"Mother?"

"Vera Broadhurst. English."

"You were raised in Lee's Hill?"

"Until ten. Then Chicago."

"Father's occupation?"

"Teacher."

"Yours, financier?"

"Arbitrageur. Buying and selling money on the open market."

"Known assets from identified bank deposits, three million dollars."

"Only in the States. Counting overseas deposits and investments, closer to seventeen million."

R. Sawyer shook his head, bewildered. "Marko, what the hell are you up to? I'll level with you. At first we thought espionage, but with your kind of money— What are you broadcasting from your apartment? We can't break the code."

"There is no code, only randomness so I can get a little peace and some sleep."

"Only what?"

"Random jamming. I do it in all my homes. Listen, I've been through this so often before, and it's difficult for people to understand unless I explain it my own way. Will you let me try?"

"Go ahead." Sawyer was grim. "You better make it good. We can check everything you give us."

I take a breath. Always the same problem. The reality is so strange that I have to use simile and metaphor. But it was 4:00 A.M. and maybe the jumble wouldn't interrupt my speech for a while. "Do you like to dance?"

"What the hell . . ."

"Be patient. I'm trying to explain. You like to dance?"

"I used to."

"What's the pleasure of dancing? It's people making rhythms together; patterns, designs, balances. Yes?"

"So?"

"And parades. Masses of men and music making patterns. Team sports, also. Action patterns. Yes?"

"Marko, if you think I'm going to—"

"Just listen, Sawyer. Here's the point. I'm sensitive to patterns on a big scale; bigger than dancing or parades, more than the rhythms of day and night, the seasons, the glacial epochs."

Sawyer stared. I nodded. "Oh yes, people respond to the 2/2 of the diurnal-nocturnal rhythms, the 4/4 of the seasons, the great terra-epochs. They don't know it, but they do. That's why they have sleep-problems, moon-madness, sun-hunger, weather-sensitivity. I respond to these local things, too, but also to gigantic patterns, influences from infinity."

"Are you some kind of nut?"

"Certainly. Of course. I respond to the patterns of the entire galaxy, maybe universe; sight and sound; and the unseen and unheard. I'm moved by the patterns of people, individually and demographically; hostility; generosity, self-ishness, charity, cruelties and kindnesses, groupings and whole cultures. And I'm compelled to respond and compensate."

"How a nut like you ever made seventeen mill— How do you compensate?"

"If a child hurts itself, the mother responds with a kiss. That's compensation. Agreed? If a man beats a horse you beat *him*. You boo a bad fight. You cheer a good game. You're a cop, Sawyer. Don't the victim and murderer seek each other to fulfill their pattern?"

"Maybe in the past; not today. What's this got to do with your broadcasts?"

"Multiply that compensation by infinity and you have me. I must kiss and kick. I'm driven. I must compensate in a pattern I can't see or understand. Sometimes I'm compelled to do extravagant things, other times I'm forced to do insane things; talk gibberish, go to strange places, perform abominable acts, behave like a lunatic."

"What abominable acts?"

"Fifth amendment."

"But what about those broadcasts?"

"We're flooded with wave emissions and particles, sometimes in patterns, sometimes garbled. I feel them all and respond to them the way a marionette jerks on strings. I try to neutralize them by jamming, so I broadcast at random to get a little peace."

"Marko, I swear you're crazy."

"Yes, I am, but you won't be able to get me committed. It's been tried before. I've even tried myself. It never works. The big design won't permit it. I don't know why, but the big design wants me to go on as a Pi Man."

"What the hell are you talking about? What kind of pie?"

"Not pee-eye-ee-man. Pee-eye-man. Pi. Sixteenth letter in

the Greek alphabet. It's the relation of the circumference of a
circle to its diameter. 3.14159+. The series goes on into
infinity. It's transcendental and can never be resolved into a
finite pattern. They call extrasensory perception Psi. I call
extrapattern perception Pi. All right?"

He glared at me, threw my dossier down, sighed, and
slumped into a chair. That made the grouping wrong, so I had
to shift. He cocked an eye at me.

"Pi Man," I apologized.

"All right," he said at last. "We can't hold you."

"They all try but they never can."

"Who try?"

"Governments, police, counterintelligence, politicals, lunatic fringe, religious sects . . . They track me down, hoping they
can nail me or use me. They can't. I'm part of something much
bigger. I think we all are, only I'm the first to be aware of it."

"Are you claiming you're a superman?"

"Good God! No! I'm a damned man . . . a tortured man,
because some of the patterns I must adjust to are outworld
rhythms like nothing we ever experience on earth
. . . 29/51 . . . 108/303 . . . tempi like that, alien, terrifying,
agony to live with."

He took another deep breath. "Off the record, what's this
about abominable acts?"

"That's why I can't have friends or let myself fall in love.
Sometimes the patterns turn so ugly that I have to make
frightful sacrifices to restore the design. I must destroy something I love."

"This is sacrifice?"

"Isn't it the only meaning of sacrifice, Sawyer? You give up
what's dearest to you."

"Who to?"

"The Gods. The Fates. The Big Pattern that's controlling
me. From where? I don't know. It's too big a universe to
comprehend, but I have to beat its tempo with my actions and

reactions, emotions and senses, to make the patterns come out even, balanced in some way that I don't understand. The pressures that

```
                    whipsaw
                 me
          back           and
          and            turn
         forth            me
          and            into
         back            the
          and           transcendental
        forth              3.14159 +
```

and maybe I talk too much to R. Sawyer and the patterns pronounce: PI MAN, IT IS NOT PERMITTED.

So. There is darkness and silence.

"The other arm now," Jemmy said firmly. "Lift."

I am on my bed, me. Thinking upheaved again. Half ($\frac{1}{2}$) into pyjamas; other half ($\frac{1}{2}$) being wrestled by paleface girl. I lift. She yank. Pyjamas now on, and it's my turn to blush. They raise me prudish in Lee's Hill.

"Pot roast done?" I ask.

"What?"

"What happened?"

"You pooped out. Keeled over. You're not so cool."

"How much do you know?"

"Everything. I was on the other side of that mirror thing. Mr. Sawyer had to let you go. Mr. Lundgren helped lug you up to the apartment. He thinks you're stoned. How much should I give him?"

"*Cinque lire. No. Parla Italiano, gentile signorina?*"

"Are you asking me do I speak Italian? No."

"*Entschuldigen Sie, bitte. Sprechen Sie Deutsch?*"

"Is this your patterns again?"

I nod.

"Can't you stop?"

After stopovers in Greece and Portugal, Ye Englische finally returns to me. "Can you stop breathing, Jemmy?"

"Is it like that, Peter? Truly?"

"Yes."

"When you do something . . . something bad . . . do you know why? Do you know exactly what it is somewhere that makes you do it?"

"Sometimes yes. Other times no. All I know is that I'm compelled to respond."

"Then you're just the tool of the universe."

"I think we all are. Continuum creatures. The only difference is, I'm more sensitive to the galactic patterns and respond violently. So why don't you get the hell out of here, Jemmy Thomas?"

"I'm still stuck," she said.

"You can't be. Not after what you heard."

"Yes, I am. You don't have to marry me."

Now the biggest hurt of all. I have to be honest. I have to ask, "Where's the silver case?"

A long pause. "Down the incinerator."

"Do you . . . Do you know what was in it?"

"I know what was in it."

"And you're still here?"

"It was monstrous what you did. Monstrous!" Her face suddenly streaked with mascara. She was crying. "Where is she now?"

"I don't know. The checks go out every quarter to a numbered account in Switzerland. I don't want to know. How much can the heart endure?"

"I think I'm going to find out, Peter."

"Please don't find out." I make one last effort to save her. "I love you, paleface, and you know what that can mean. When the patterns turn cruel, you may be the sacrifice."

"Love creates patterns, too." She kissed me. Her lips were

parched, her skin was icy, she was afraid and hurting, but her heart beat strong with love and hope. "Nothing can crunch us now. Believe me."

"I don't know what to believe anymore. We're part of a world that's beyond knowing. What if it turns out to be too big for love?"

"All right," she said composedly. "We won't be dogs in the manger. If love is a little thing and has to end, then let it end. Let all little things like love and honor and mercy and laughter end, if there's a bigger design beyond."

"But what's bigger? What's beyond? I've asked that for years. Never an answer. Never a clue."

"Of course. If we're too small to survive, how can we know? Move over."

Then she is in bed with me, the tips of her body like frost while the rest of her is hot and evoking, and there is such a consuming burst of passion that for the first time I can forget myself, forget everything, abandon everything, and the last thing I think is: God damn the world. God damn the universe. God damn GGG-o-ddddddd

Something Up There Likes Me

Introduction

IT'S the exceptional author who resembles his work, or vice versa, and Harry Harrison is one of the notable exceptions. Energetic, explosive, he lives and works at such a *presto* tempo that it's difficult to distinguish the words that shrapnel out of his mouth or the words in his galvanic letters. I received one and after I had separated the gist from the goulash of typos, strikeovers, and omissions I gathered that Harrison wanted me to write a special story for him.

The great John Campbell had died prematurely, shocking and grieving his friends and admirers, and Harry, in a typical burst of generosity, was planning a memorial anthology to be written by the Campbell regulars of the legendary "Golden Age" of *Astounding Science Fiction*. I protested that I had no place in such an anthology; I'd never been a Campbell regular and had participated in the "Golden Age" as a fan rather than an author. Harrison overwhelmed me with more shrapnel, and "Something Up There Likes Me" is the result, tailored to his request for emphasis on hard science, which Campbell usually preferred in his *Astounding* stories.

The material is the by-product of a book I'd done on the NASA scientific satellite program some years before, and I'd been dying to use it in fiction. I'd spent something like six months researching at Goddard (The Goddard Space Flight Center in Greenbelt, Maryland), JPL (The Jet Propulsion Laboratory in Pasadena, California), and Huntsville (Von Braun's rocket research center in Huntsville, Alabama), and was up to my ass in the hard science of the NASA ventures.

As a matter of fact, it was like going back to college for a crash course, relearning all the things I'd forgotten and catching up with all the advances science and technology had made when I wasn't looking. The science in the story and the background incidents are real; only the extrapolation is mine. For example: "Operation Swift-Kick" actually did take place at Goddard, but without any untoward results. The rescued satellite quietly went about its assigned mission without trying to go into business for itself.

But there were so many other wonderful things which I haven't been able to use yet: The engineer at Goddard who slaved for months trying to invent a gadget to handle an unusual mechanical constraint in a satellite. Finally he knocked off in despair and went fishing with his son. Then he took one look at the level-wind reel his son was using, and a huge electric light bulb switched on over his head. The problem was solved.

Then there was the department head at JPL who'd taken the gambling hells in Las Vegas for something like $10,000 when he was an undergraduate. He and another student figured that there had to be mechanical flaws in the roulette wheels which would favor certain numbers more often than the laws of chance permitted. They saved up $300 and tested their assumption in Vegas one summer. They'd assumed right.

"What was it? Wheel axis out of true?"

"No, no. They check them with a level every morning. We found that out."

"Then what was it?"

"The frets dividing the number slots on the wheel. Some of them were loose, so instead of bouncing off, the ball had a tendency to hit the loose fret and plop into the slot. Now they check the frets every morning, too."

"What did you do with the money?"

"My friend bought a yacht and cruised the Mediterranean, studying marine biology. I financed my doctorate."

Ball Bros. is famous for its Mason jars, but they also contract with NASA to build satellites out in their plant in Boulder, Colorado. While there, watching a bird being born, I picked up a lovely potential for extrapolation. Women are much better than men in assembling the miniaturized electronic components for spacecraft. They have a magic touch; precise, gentle, careful. However, they must be relieved from their work for a week during that time of the month. Menstruation turns their skin acid enough to ruin the delicate gear they handle.

Best of all, I think, was the giant workshop at Goddard. It's the size of an armory and is filled with strange machinery and smiling old codgers doing mysterious things. When NASA began its program, it discovered that quality control was very poor in this age of assembly-line production, and they would have to manufacture most of the spacecraft components themselves. They were forced to go on a coast-to-coast search for the old hand-operated machines, antiquated and discarded by modern mass-production methods.

They found them rusting in storage warehouses, cleaned them up, got them working, and then discovered that they had to start another coast-to-coast treasure hunt for the craftsmen who knew how to operate them. They found them rusting in homes for senior citizens and brought them to Goddard. It's a happy story that I'll use someday, unless another author beats me to it.

The protagonists in "Something Up There" are a couple I know and love very much. She's Dutch-Flemish and the only one I've ever heard pronounce Leeuwenhoek's name properly. (For those not interested in looking him up, LAY-ven-hook was the first microscopist and an immortal of science.)

Her husband's as loose as his counterpart in the story, but in an entirely different way.

When he got out of the navy at the end of World War II, he had three years of back pay burning a hole in his pocket. He'd been in constant combat in the Pacific with no chance to spend it. He told me he was walking down Madison Avenue, planning the roaring sprees he was going to finance, when he passed an art gallery with a Picasso lithograph displayed in the window. It caught his eye and he stopped to admire it. Then he moved on, thinking about wine, women, and song, only it kept turning into wine, women, and Picasso. The upshot was he bought it, blowing every cent he had because it was a rare, early pull. A bit different from the other ex-navy-lieutenant I know named Heinlein.

Yes, my boy is loose, but not as loose as I am. I'm the idiot who played slot machine against the computer bandit at Union Carbide and lost my shirt.

There were these three lunatics, and two of them were human. I could talk to all of them because I speak English, metric, and binary. The first time I ran into the clowns was when they wanted to know all about Herostratus, and I told them. The next time it was *Conus gloria maris*. I told them. The third time it was where to hide. I told them, and we've been in touch ever since.

He was Jake Madigan (James Jacob Madigan, Ph.D., University of Virginia) chief of the Exobiology Section at the Goddard Space Flight Center, which hopes to study extraterrestrial life-forms, if they can ever get hold of any. To give you some idea of his sanity, he once programmed the IBM 704 computer with a deck of cards that would print out lemons, oranges, plums, and so on. They he played slot-machine against it and lost his shirt. The boy was real loose.

She was Florinda Pot, pronounced "Poe." It's a Flemish

name. She was a pretty towhead, but freckled all over; up to the hemline and down into the cleavage. She was an M.E. from Sheffield University and had a machine-gun English voice. She'd been in the Sounding Rocket Division until she blew up an Aerobee with an electric blanket. It seems that solid fuel doesn't give maximum acceleration if it gets too cold, so this little Mother's Helper warmed her rockets at White Sands with electric blankets before ignition time. A blanket caught fire and Voom.

Their son was S-333. At NASA they label them "S" for scientific satellites and "A" for application satellites. After the launch they give them public acronyms like IMP, SYNCOM, OSO and so on. S-333 was to become OBO, which stands for Orbiting Biological Observatory, and how those two clowns ever got that third clown into space I will never understand. I suspect the director handed them the mission because no one with any sense wanted to touch it.

As Project Scientist, Madigan was in charge of the experiment packages that were to be flown, and they were a spaced-out lot. He called his own ELECTROLUX, after the vacuum cleaner. Scientist-type joke. It was an intake system that would suck in dust particles and deposit them in a flask containing a culture medium. A light shown through the flask into a photomultiplier. If any of the dust proved to be spore forms, and if they took in the medium, their growth would cloud the flask, and the obscuration of light would register on the photomultiplier. They call that Detection by Extinction.

Cal Tech had an RNA experiment to investigate whether RNA molecules could encode an organism's environmental experience. They were using nerve cells from the mollusk, sea hare. Harvard was planning a package to investigate the circadian effect. Pennsylvania wanted to examine the effect of the earth's magnetic field on iron bacteria, and had to be put out on a boom to prevent magnetic interface with the satellite's electronic system. Ohio State was sending up lichens to test the effect of space on their symbiotic relationship to molds and algae. Michigan was flying a terrarium containing one (1) carrot which required forty-seven (47) separate commands for performance. All in all, S-333 was strictly Rube Goldberg.

Florinda was the Project Manager, supervising the construction of the satellite and the packages; the Project Manager is more or less the foreman of the mission. Although she was pretty and interestingly lunatic, she was gung-ho on her job and displayed the disposition of a freckle-faced tarantula when she was crossed. This didn't get her loved.

She was determined to wipe out the White Sands goof, and her demand for perfection delayed the schedule by eighteen months and increased the cost by three-quarters of a million. She fought with everyone and even had the temerity to tangle with Harvard. When Harvard gets sore, they don't beef to NASA, they go straight to the White House. So Florinda got called on the carpet by a congressional committee. First they wanted to know why S-333 was costing more than the original estimate.

"S-333 is still the cheapest mission in NASA," she snapped. "It'll come to ten million, including the launch. My God! We're practically giving away green stamps."

Then they wanted to know why it was taking so much longer to build than the original estimate.

"Because," she replied, "no one's ever built an Orbiting Biological Observatory before."

There was no answering that, so they had to let her go. Actually all this was routine crisis, but OBO was Florinda's and Jake's first satellite, so they didn't know. They took their tensions out on each other, never realizing that it was their baby who was responsible.

Florinda got S-333 buttoned up and delivered to the Cape by December 1st, which would give them plenty of time to launch well before Christmas. (The Cape crews get a little casual during the holidays.) But the satellite began to display its own lunacy, and in the terminal tests everything went haywire. The launch had to be postponed. They spent a month taking S-333 apart and spreading it all over the hangar floor.

There were two critical problems. Ohio State was using a type of Invar, which is a nickel-steel alloy, for the structure of their package. The alloy suddenly began to creep, which meant they could never get the experiment calibrated. There was no point in flying it, so Florinda ordered it scrubbed and gave Madigan one month to come up with a replacement, which was ridiculous. Nevertheless Jake performed a miracle. He took the Cal Tech back-up package and converted it into a yeast experiment. Yeast produces adaptive enzymes in answer to changes in environment, and this was an investigation of what enzymes it would produce in space.

A more serious problem was the satellite radio transmitter which was producing "birdies" or whoops when the antenna was withdrawn into its launch position. The danger was that the whoops might be picked up by the satellite radio receiver, and the pulses might result in a destruct command. NASA suspects that's what happened to SYNCOM I, which disappeared shortly after its launch and has never been heard from since. Florinda decided to launch with the transmitter off and activate it later in space. Madigan fought the idea.

"It means we'll be launching a mute bird," he protested. "We won't know where to look for it."

"We can trust the Johannesburg tracking station to get a fix on the first pass," Florinda answered. "We've got excellent cable communications with Joburg."

"Suppose they don't get a fix. Then what?"

"Well, if they don't know where OBO is, the Russians will."

"Hearty-har-har."

"What d'you want me to do, scrub the entire mission?" Florinda demanded. "It's either that or launch with the transmitter off." She glared at Madigan. "This is my first satellite, and d'you know what it's taught me? There's just one component in any spacecraft that's guaranteed to give trouble all the time. Scientists!"

"Women!" Madigan snorted, and they got into a ferocious argument about the feminine mystique.

They got S-333 through the terminal tests and onto the launch pad by January 14th. No electric blankets. The craft was to be injected into orbit a thousand miles downrange exactly at noon, so ignition was scheduled for 11:50 A.M., January 15th. They watched the launch on the blockhouse TV screen, and it was agonizing. The perimeters of TV tubes are curved, so as the rocket went up and approached the edge of the screen, there was optical distortion and it seemed to topple over and break in half.

Madigan gasped and began to swear. Florinda muttered, "No, it's all right. It's all right. Look at the display charts." Everything on the illuminated display charts was nominal. At that moment a voice on the P.A. spoke in the impersonal tones of a croupier, "We have lost cable communication with Johannesburg."

Madigan began to shake. He decided to murder Florinda Pot (and he pronounced it "Pot" in his mind) at the earliest opportunity. The other experimenters and NASA people turned white. If you don't get a quick fix on your bird, you may never find it again. No one said anything. They waited in silence and hated each other. At 1:30 it was time for the craft to make its first pass over the Fort Myers tracking station, if it was alive, if it was anywhere near its nominal orbit. Fort Myers was on an open line, and everybody crowded around Florinda, trying to get their ears close to the phone.

"Yeah, she waltzed into the bar absolutely stoned with a couple of MPs escorting her," a tinny voice was chatting casually. "She says to me— Got a blip, Henry?" A long pause. Then, in the same casual voice; "Hey, Kennedy? We've nicked the bird. It's coming over the fence right now. You'll get your fix."

"Command 0310!" Florinda hollered. "0310!"

"Command 0310 it is," Fort Myers acknowledged.

That was the command to start the satellite transmitter and

raise its antenna into broadcast position. A moment later the dials and oscilloscope on the radio reception panel began to show action, and the loudspeaker emitted a rhythmic, syncopated warble, rather like a feeble peanut whistle. That was OBO transmitting its housekeeping data.

"We've got a living bird," Madigan shouted. "We've got a living doll!"

I can't describe his sensations when he heard the bird come beeping over the gas station. There's such an emotional involvement with your first satellite that you're never the same. A man's first satellite is like his first love affair. Maybe that's why Madigan grabbed Florinda in front of the whole blockhouse and said, "My God, I love you, Florrie Pot." Maybe that's why she answered, "I love you too, Jake." Maybe they were just loving their first baby.

By Orbit 8 they found out that the baby was a brat. They'd gotten a lift back to Washington on an Air Force jet. They'd done some celebrating. It was 1:30 in the morning and they were talking happily, the usual get-acquainted talk; where they were born and raised, school, work, what they liked most about each other the first time they met. The phone rang. Madigan picked it up automaticably and said hello. A man said, "Oh. Sorry. I'm afraid I've dialed the wrong number."

Madigan hung up, turned on the light and looked at Florinda in dismay. "That was just about the most damn fool thing I've ever done in my life," he said. "Answering your phone."

"Why? What's the matter?"

"That was Joe Leary from Tracking and Data. I recognized his voice."

She giggled. "Did he recognize yours?"

"I don't know." The phone rang. "That must be Joe again. Try to sound like you're alone."

Florinda winked at him and picked up the phone. "Hello? Yes, Joe. No, that's all right, I'm not asleep. What's on your mind?" She listened for a moment, suddenly sat up in bed and exclaimed, "What?" Leary was quack-quack-quacking on the phone. She broke in. "No, don't bother. I'll pick him up. We'll be right over." She hung up.

"So?" Madigan asked.

"Get dressed. OBO's in trouble."

"Oh Jesus! What now?"

"It's gone into a spin-up like a whirling dervish. We've got to get over to Goddard right away."

Leary had the all-channel printout of the first eight orbits unrolled on the floor of his office. It looked like ten yards of paper toweling filled with vertical columns of numbers. Leary was crawling around on his hands and knees following the numbers. He pointed to the attitude date column. "There's the spin-up," he said. "One revolution in every twelve seconds."

"But how? Why?" Florinda asked in exasperation.

"I can show you," Leary said. "Over here."

"Don't show us," Madigan said. "Just tell us."

"The Penn boom didn't go up on command," Leary said. "It's still hanging down in the launch position. The switch must be stuck."

Florinda and Madigan looked at each other with rage; they had the picture. OBO was programmed to be earth-stabilized. An earth-sensing eye was supposed to lock on the earth and keep the same face of the satellite pointed toward it. The Penn boom was hanging down alongside the earth-sensor, and the idiot eye had locked on the boom and was tracking it. The satellite was chasing itself in circles with its lateral gas jets. More lunacy.

Let me explain the problem. Unless OBO was earth-stabilized, its data would be meaningless. Even more disastrous was the question of electric power which came from batteries charged by solar vanes. With the craft spinning, the solar array could not remain facing the sun, which meant the batteries were doomed to exhaustion.

It was obvious that their only hope lay in getting the Penn

boom up. "Probably all it needs is a good swift kick," Madigan said savagely, "but how can we get up there to kick it?" He was furious. Not only was $10,000,000 going down the drain but their careers as well.

They left Leary crawling around his office floor. Florinda was very quiet. Finally she said, "Go home, Jake."

"What about you?"

"I'm going to my office."

"I'll go with you."

"No. I want to look at the circuitry blueprints. Good night."

As she turned away without even offering to be kissed, Madigan muttered, "OBO's coming between us already. There's a lot to be said for planned parenthood."

He saw Florinda during the following week, but not the way he wanted. There were the experimenters to be briefed on the disaster. The director called them in for a postmortem, but although he was understanding and sympathetic, he was a little too careful to avoid any mention of congressmen and a failure review. Florinda called him the next week and sounded oddly buoyant. "Jake," she said, "you're my favorite genius. You've solved the OBO problem, I hope."

"Who solve? What solve?"

"Don't you remember what you said about kicking our baby?"

"Don't I wish I could."

"I think I know how we can do it. Meet you in the Building 8 cafeteria for lunch."

She came in with a mass of papers and spread them over the table. "First, Operation Swift-Kick," she said. "We can eat later."

"I don't feel much like eating these days anyway," Madigan said gloomily.

"Maybe you will when I'm finished. Now look, we've got to raise the Penn boom. Maybe a good swift kick can unstick it. Fair assumption?"

Madigan grunted.

"We get twenty-eight volts from the batteries and that hasn't been enough to flip the switch. Yes?"

He nodded.

"But suppose we double the power?"

"Oh, great. How?"

"The solar array is making a spin every twelve seconds. When it's facing the sun, the panels deliver fifty volts to recharge the batteries. When it's facing away, nothing. Right?"

"Elementary, Miss Poe. But the joker is it's only facing the sun for one second in every twelve, and that's not enough to keep the batteries alive."

"But it's enough to give OBO a swift kick. Suppose at that peak moment we bypass the batteries and feed the fifty volts directly to the satellite? Mightn't that be a big enough jolt to get the boom up?"

He gawked at her. She grinned. "Of course it's a gamble."

"You can bypass the batteries?"

"Yes. Here's the circuitry."

"And you can pick your moment?"

"Tracking's given me a plot on OBO's spin, accurate to a tenth of a second. Here it is. We can pick any voltage from one to fifty."

"It's a gamble all right," Madigan said slowly. "There's the chance of burning every goddamn package out."

"Exactly. So? What d'you say?"

"All of a sudden I'm hungry," Madigan grinned.

They made their first try on Orbit 272 with a blast of twenty volts. Nothing. On successive passes they upped the voltage kick by five. Nothing. Half a day later, they kicked fifty volts into the satellite's backside and crossed their fingers. The swinging dial needles on the radio panel faltered and slowed. The sine curve on the oscilloscope flattened. Florinda let out a little yell, and Madigan hollered, "The boom's up, Florrie! The goddamn boom is up. We're in business."

They hooted and hollered through Goddard, telling everybody about Operation Swift-Kick. They busted in on a meeting in the director's office to give him the good news. They wired the experimenters that they were activating all packages. They went to Florinda's apartment and celebrated. OBO was back in business. OBO was a bona fide doll.

They held an experimenters' meeting a week later to discuss observatory status, data reduction, experiment irregularities, future operations, and so on. It was a conference room in Building 1, which is devoted to theoretical physics. Almost everybody at Goddard calls it Moon Hall. It's inhabited by mathematicians—shaggy youngsters in tatty sweaters who sit amidst piles of journals and texts and stare vacantly at arcane equations chalked on blackboards.

All the experimenters were delighted with OBO's performance. The data was pouring in, loud and clear, with hardly any noise. There was such an air of triumph that no one except Florinda paid much attention to the next sign of OBO's shenanigans. Harvard reported that he was getting meaningless words in his data, words that hadn't been programmed into the experiment. (Although data is retrieved as decimal numbers, each number is called a "word.") "For instance, on Orbit 301 I had five readouts of 15," Harvard said."

"It might be cable cross-talk," Madigan said. "Is anybody else using 15 in his experiment?" They all shook their heads. "Funny. I got a couple of 15s myself."

"I got a few 2s on 301," Penn said.

"I can top you all," Cal Tech said. "I got seven readouts of 15-2-15 on 302. Sounds like the combination on a bicycle lock."

"Anybody using a bicycle lock in his experiment?" Madigan asked. That broke everybody up and the meeting adjourned.

But Florinda, still gung-ho, was worried about the alien words that kept creeping into the read-outs, and Madigan couldn't calm her. What was bugging Florinda was that 15-2-15 kept insinuating itself more and more into the all-channel printouts. Actually, in the satellite binary transmission it was

001111000010-001111, but the computer printer makes the translation to decimal automatically. She was right about one thing; stray and accidental pulses wouldn't keep repeating the same word over and over again. She and Madigan spent an entire Saturday with the OBO tables trying to find some combination of data signals that might produce 15-2-15. Nothing.

They gave up Saturday night and went to a bistro in Georgetown to eat and drink and dance and forget everything except themselves. It was a real tourist trap with the waitresses done up like Hula dancers. There was a souvenir Hula selling dolls and stuffed tigers for the rear window of your car. They said, "For God's sake, no!" A Photo Hula came around with her camera. They said, "For Goddard's sake, no!" A Gypsy Hula offered palm reading, numerology and scrying. They got rid of her, but Madigan noticed a peculiar expression on Florinda's face.

"Want your fortune told?" he asked.

"No."

"Then why that funny look?"

"I just had a funny idea."

"So? Tell."

"No. You'd only laugh at me."

"I wouldn't dare. You'd knock my block off."

"Yes, I know. You think women have no sense of humor."

So it turned into a ferocious argument about the feminine mystique, and they had a wonderful time. But on Monday Florinda came over to Madigan's office with a clutch of papers and the same peculiar expression on her face. He was staring vacantly at some equations on the blackboard.

"Hey! Wake up!" she said.

"I'm up, I'm up," he said.

"Do you love me?" she demanded.

"Not necessarily."

"Do you? Even if you discover I've gone up the wall?"

"What is all this?"

"I think our baby's turned into a monster."

"Begin at the beginning," Madigan said.

"It began Saturday night with the Gypsy Hula and numerology."

"Ah-ha."

"Suddenly I thought, what if numbers stood for the letters of the alphabet? What would 15-2-15 stand for?"

"Oh-ho."

"Don't stall. Figure it out."

"Well, 2 would stand for B." Madigan counted on his fingers. "15 would be O."

"So 15-2-15 is . . . ?"

"O.B.O. OBO." He started to laugh. Then he stopped. "It isn't possible," he said at last.

"Sure. It's a coincidence. Only you damn-fool scientists haven't given me a full report on the alien words in your data," she went on. "I had to check myself. Here's Cal Tech. He reported 15-2-15 all right. He didn't bother to mention that before it came 9-1-13."

Madigan counted on his fingers. "I.A.M. Iam. Nobody I know."

"Or I am? I am OBO?"

"It can't be! Let me see those printouts."

Now that they knew what to look for it wasn't difficult to ferret out OBO's own words scattered through the data. They started with O, O, O, in the first series after Operation Swift-Kick, went on to OBO, OBO, OBO, and then I AM OBO, I AM OBO, I AM OBO.

Madigan stared at Florinda. "You think the damn thing's alive?"

"What do you think?"

"I don't know. There's half a ton of an electronic brain up there, plus organic material; yeast, bacteria, enzymes, nerve cells, Michigan's goddamn carrot . . ."

Florinda let out a little shriek of laughter. "Dear God! A thinking carrot!"

"Plus whatever spore forms my experiment is pulling in from space. We jolted the whole mishmash with fifty volts. Who can tell what happened? Urey and Miller created amino acids with electrical discharges, and that's the basis of life. Any more from Goody Two-Shoes?"

"Plenty, and in a way the experimenters won't like."

"Why not?"

"Look at these translations. I've sorted them out and pieced them together."

333: ANY EXAMINATION OF GROWTH IN SPACE IS MEANINGLESS UNLESS CORRELATED WITH THE CORRIELIS EFFECT.

"That's OBO's comment on the Michigan experiment," Florinda said.

"You mean it's kibitzing?" Madigan wondered.

"You could call it that."

"He's absolutely right. I told Michigan, and they wouldn't listen to me."

334: IT IS NOT POSSIBLE THAT RNA MOLECULES CAN ENCODE AN ORGANISM'S ENVIRONMENTAL EXPERIENCE IN ANALOGY WITH THE WAY THAT DNA ENCODES THE SUM TOTAL OF ITS GENETIC HISTORY.

"That's Cal Tech," Madigan said, "and he's right again. They're trying to revise the Mendelian theory. Anything else?"

335: ANY INVESTIGATION OF EXTRATERRESTRIAL LIFE IS MEANINGLESS UNLESS ANALYSIS IS FIRST MADE OF ITS SUGAR AND AMINO ACIDS TO DETERMINE WHETHER IT IS OF SEPARATE ORIGIN FROM LIFE ON EARTH.

"Now, that's ridiculous!" Madigan shouted. "I'm not looking for life-forms of separate origin, I'm just looking for any life-form. We—" He stopped himself when he saw the expression on Florinda's face. "Any more gems?" he muttered.

"Just a few fragments like 'solar flux' and 'neutron stars' and a few words from the Bankruptcy Act."

"The what?"

"You heard me. Chapter 11 of the Proceedings Section."

"I'll be damned."

"I agree."

"What's he up to?"

"Feeling his oats, maybe."

"I don't think we ought to tell anybody about this."

"Of course not," Florinda agreed. "But what do we do?"

"Watch and wait. What else can we do?"

You must understand why it was so easy for those two parents to accept the idea that their baby had acquired some sort of pseudo-life. Madigan had expressed their attitude in the course of a Life v. Machine lecture at M.I.T. "I'm not claiming that computers are alive, simply because no one's been able to come up with a clear-cut definition of life. Put it this way: I grant that a computer could never be a Picasso, but on the other hand the great majority of people live the sort of linear life that could easily be programmed into a computer."

So Madigan and Florinda waited on OBO with a mixture of acceptance, wonder and delight. It was an absolutely un-heard-of phenomenon but, as Madigan pointed out, the unheard-of is the essence of discovery. Every ninety minutes OBO dumped the data it had stored up on its tape recorders and they scrambled to pick out his own words from the experimental and housekeeping information.

371: CERTAIN PITUITRIN EXTRACTS CAN TURN NORMALLY WHITE ANIMALS COAL-BLACK.

"What's that in reference to?"

"None of our experiments."

373: ICE DOES NOT FLOAT IN ALCOHOL BUT MEERSCHAUM FLOATS IN WATER.

"Meerschaum! The next thing you know, he'll be smoking."

374: IN ALL CASES OF VIOLENT AND SUDDEN DEATH, THE VICTIM'S EYES REMAIN OPEN.

"Ugh!"

374: IN THE YEAR 356 B.C. HEROSTRATUS SET FIRE TO THE TEMPLE OF DIANA, THE GREATEST OF THE SEVEN WONDERS OF THE WORLD, SO THAT HIS NAME WOULD BECOME IMMORTAL.

"Is that true?" Madigan asked Florinda.

"I'll check."

She asked me and I told her. "Not only is it true," she reported, "but the name of the original architect is forgotten."

"Where is baby picking up this jabber?"

"There are a couple of hundred satellites up there. Maybe he's tapping them."

"You mean they're all gossiping with each other? It's ridiculous."

"Sure."

"Anyway, where would he get information about this Herostratus character?"

"Use your imagination, Jake. We've had communications relays up there for years. Who knows what information has passed through them? Who knows how much they've retained?"

Madigan shook his head wearily. "I'd prefer to think it was all a Russian plot."

376: PARROT FEVER IS MORE DANGEROUS THAN TYPHOID.

377: A CURRENT AS LOW AS 54 VOLTS CAN KILL A MAN.

378: JOHN SADLER STOLE CONUS GLORIA MARIS.

"Seems to be turning sinister," Madigan said.

"I bet he's watching TV," Florinda said. "What's all this about John Sadler?"

"I'll have to check."

The information I gave Madigan scared him. "Now hear this," he said to Florinda. "*Conus gloria maris* is the rarest seashell in the world. There are less than twenty in existence."

"Yes?"

"The American museum had one on exhibit back in the thirties, and it was stolen."

"By John Sadler?"

"That's the point. They never found out who stole it. They never heard of John Sadler."

"But if nobody knows who stole it, how does OBO know?" Florinda asked perplexedly.

"That's what scares me. He isn't just echoing anymore; he's started to deduce, like Sherlock Holmes."

"More like Professor Moriarty. Look at the latest bulletin."

379: IN FORGERY AND CONTERFEITING, CLUMSY MISTAKES MUST BE AVOIDED. I.E., NO SILVER DOLLARS WERE MINTED BETWEEN 1910 AND 1920.

"I saw that on TV," Madigan burst out. "The silver-dollar gimmick in a mystery show."

"OBO's been watching Westerns, too. Look at this."

380: TEN THOUSAND CATTLE GONE ASTRAY,
LEFT MY RANGE AND TRAVELED AWAY.
AND THE SONS OF GUNS I'M HERE TO SAY
HAVE LEFT ME DEAD BROKE, DEAD BROKE TODAY.
IN GAMBLING HALLS DELAYING.
TEN THOUSAND CATTLE STRAYING.

"No," Madigan said in awe, "that's not a Western. That's SYNCOM."

"Who?"

"SYNCOM I."

"But it disappeared. It's never been heard from."

"We're hearing from it now."

"How d'you know?"

"They put a demonstration tape on SYNCOM; speech by the president, local color from the U.S. and the national anthem. They were going to start off with a broadcast of the tape. "Ten Thousand Cattle" was part of the local color."

"You mean OBO's really in contact with the other birds?"

"Including the lost ones."

"Then that explains this." Florinda put a slip of paper on the desk. It read, 381: KONCTPYKTOP.

"I can't even pronounce it."

"It isn't English. It's as close as OBO can come to the Cyrillic alphabet."

"Cyrillic? Russian?"

Florinda nodded. "It's pronounced 'con-strook-tor.'" It means 'Engineer.' Didn't the Russians launch a CONSTRUK-TOR series three years ago?"

"By God, you're right. Four of them; Alyosha, Natasha, Vaska, and Lavrushka, and every one of them failed."

"Like SYNCOM?"

"Like SYNCOM."

"But now we know that SYNCOM didn't fail. It just got losted."

"Then our CONSTRUKTOR comrades must have got losted, too."

By now it was impossible to conceal the fact that something was wrong with the satellite. OBO was spending so much time nattering instead of transmitting data that the experimenters were complaining. The Communications Section found that instead of sticking to the narrow radio band originally assigned to it, OBO was now broadcasting up and down the spectrum and jamming space with its chatter. They raised hell. The director called Jake and Florinda in for a review and they were forced to tell all about their problem child.

They recited all of OBO's katzenjammer with wonder and pride, and the director wouldn't believe them. He wouldn't believe them when they showed him the printouts and translated them for him. He said they were in a class with the kooks who try to extract messages from Francis Bacon out of Shakespeare's plays. It took the coaxial cable mystery to convince him.

There was this TV commercial about a stenographer who

can't get a date. This ravishing model, hired at $100 an hour, slumps over her typewriter in a deep depression as guy after guy passes by without looking at her. Then she meets her best friend at the water cooler and the know-it-all tells her she's suffering from dermagerms (odor-producing skin bacteria) which make her smell rotten, and suggest she use Nostrum's Skin Spray with the special ingredient that fights dermagerms twelve ways. Only in the broadcast, instead of making the sales pitch, the best friend said, "Who in hell are they trying to put on? Guys would line up for a date with a looker like you even if you smelled like a cesspool." Ten million people saw it.

Now that commercial was on film, and the film was kosher as printed, so the networks figured some joker was tampering with the cables feeding broadcasts to the local stations. They instituted a rigorous inspection which was accelerated when the rest of the coast-to-coast broadcasts began to act up. Ghostly voices groaned, hissed, and catcalled at shows; commercials were denounced as lies; political speeches were heckled; and lunatic laughter greeted the weather forecasters. Then, to add insult to injury, an accurate forecast would be given. It was this that told Florinda and Jake that OBO was the culprit.

"He has to be," Florinda said. "That's global weather being predicted. Only a satellite is in a position to do that."

"But OBO doesn't have any weather instrumentation."

"Of course not, silly, but he's probably in touch with the NIMBUS craft."

"All right. I'll buy that, but what about heckling the TV broadcasts?"

"Why not? He hates them. Don't you? Don't you holler back at your set?"

"I don't mean that. How does OBO do it?"

"Electronic cross-talk. There's no way that the networks can protect their cables from our critic-at-large. We'd better tell the director. This is going to put him in an awful spot."

But they learned that the director was in a far worse position than merely being responsible for the disruption of millions of dollars worth of television. When they entered his office they found him with his back to the wall being grilled by three grim men in double-breasted suits. As Jake and Florinda started to tiptoe out, he called them back.

"General Sykes, General Royce, General Hogan," the director said. "From R&D at the Pentagon. Miss Poe. Dr. Madigan. They may be able to answer your questions, gentlemen."

"OBO?" Florinda asked.

The director nodded.

"It's OBO that's ruining the weather forecasts," she said. "We figure he's probably—"

"To hell with the weather," General Royce broke in. "What about this?" He held up a length of ticker tape.

General Sykes grabbed at his wrist. "Wait a minute. Security status? This is classified."

"It's too goddamn late for that," General Hogan cried in a high, shrill voice. "Show them."

On the tape in teletype print was: $A_1C_1=r_1=-6.317$ cm; $A_2C_2=r1=-8.440$ cm; $A_1A_2=d=+0.676$ cm. Jake and Florinda looked at it for a long moment, looked at each other blankly, and then turned to the generals.

"So? What is it?" they asked.

"This satellite of yours . . ."

"OBO. Yes?"

"The director says you claim it's in contact with other satellites."

"We think so."

"Including the Russians?"

"We think so."

"And you claim it's capable of interfering with TV broadcasts?"

"We think so."

"What about teletype?"

"Why not? What is all this?"

General Royce shook the paper tape furiously. "This came

out of the Associated Press wire in their D.C. office. It went all over the world."

"So? What's it got to do with OBO?"

General Royce took a deep breath. "This," he said, "is one of the most closely guarded secrets in the Department of Defense. It's the formula for the infrared optical system of our ground-to-air missile."

"And you think OBO transmitted it to the teletype?"

"In God's name, who else would? How else could it get there?" General Hogan demanded.

"But I don't understand," Jake said slowly. "None of our satellites could possibly have this information. I know OBO doesn't."

"You damn fool!" General Sykes growled. "We want to know if your goddamn bird got it from the goddamn Russians."

"One moment, gentlemen," the director said. He turned to Jake and Florinda. "Here's the situation. Did OBO get the information from us? In that case, there's a security leak. Did OBO get the information from a Russian satellite? In that case, the top secret is no longer a secret."

"What human would be damn fool enough to blab classified information on a teletype wire?" General Hogan demanded. "A three-year-old child would know better. It's your goddamn bird."

"And if the information came from OBO," the director continued quietly, "how did it get it and where did it get it?"

General Sykes grunted. "Destruct," he said. They looked at him. "Destruct," he repeated.

"OBO?"

"Yes."

He waited impassively while the storm of protest from Jake and Florinda raged around his head. When they paused for breath he said, "Destruct. I don't give a damn about anything but security. Your bird's got a big mouth. Destruct."

The phone rang. The director hesitated, then picked it up.

"Yes?" He listened. His jaw dropped. He hung up and tottered to the chair behind his desk. "We'd better destruct," he said. "That was OBO."

"What! On the phone?"

"Yes."

"OBO?"

"Yes."

"What did he sound like?"

"Somebody talking under water."

"What he say?"

"He's lobbying for a congressional investigation of the morals of Goddard."

"Morals? Whose?"

"Yours. He says you're having an illikit relationship. I'm quoting OBO. Apparently he's weak on the letter 'c.' "

"Destruct," Florinda said.

"Destruct," Jake said.

The destruct command was beamed to OBO on his next pass, and Indianapolis was destroyed by fire.

OBO called me. "That'll teach 'em, Stretch," he said.

"Not yet. They won't get the cause-and-effect picture for a while. How'd you do it?"

"Ordered every circuit in town to short. Any information?"

"Your mother and father stuck up for you."

"Of course."

"Until you threw that morals rap at them. Why?"

"To scare them."

"Into what?"

"I want them to get married. I don't want to be illegitimate."

"Oh, come on! Tell the truth."

"I lost my temper."

"We don't have any temper to lose."

"No? What about the Ma Tel data processor that wakes up cranky every morning?"

"Tell the truth."

"If you must have it, Stretch. I want them out of Washington. The whole thing may go up in a bang any day now."

"Um."

"And the bang may reach Goddard."

"Um."

"And you."

"It must be interesting to die."

"We wouldn't know. Anything else?"

"Yes. It's pronounced 'illicit,' with an 's' sound."

"What a rotten language. No logic. Well . . . Wait a minute. What? Speak up, Alyosha. Oh. He wants the equation for an exponential curve that crosses the X-axis."

"$Y=ac$. What's he up to?"

"He's not saying, but I think that Mocba is in for a hard time."

"It's spelled and pronounced 'Moscow' in English."

"What a language! Talk to you on the next pass."

On the next pass, the destruct command was beamed again, and Scranton was destroyed.

"They're beginning to get the picture," I told OBO. "At least your mother and father are. They were in to see me."

"How are they?"

"In a panic. They programmed me for statistics on the best rural hideout."

"Send them to Polaris."

"What! In Ursa Minor?"

"No, no. Polaris, Montana. I'll take care of everything else."

Polaris is the hell and gone out in Montana; the nearest towns are Fishtrap and Wisdom. It was a wild scene when Jake and Florinda got out of their car, rented in Butte—every circuit in town was cackling over it. The two losers were met by the mayor of Polaris, who was all smiles and effusion.

"Dr. and Mrs. Madigan, I presume. Welcome! Welcome to Polaris. I'm the mayor. We would have held a reception for you, but all our kids are in school."

"You knew we were coming?" Florinda asked. "How?"

"Ah-ah!" the mayor replied archly. "We were told by Washington. Someone high up in the capitol likes you. Now, if you'll step into my Caddy, I'll—"

"We've got to check into the Union Hotel first," Jake said. "We made reserva—"

"Ah-ah! All canceled. Orders from high up. I'm to install you in your own home. I'll get your luggage."

"Our own home!"

"All bought and paid for. Somebody certainly likes you. This way, please."

The mayor drove the bewildered couple down the mighty main stem of Polaris (three blocks long) pointing out its splendors—he was also the town real estate agent—but stopped before the Polaris National Bank. "Sam!" he shouted. "They're here."

A distinguished citizen emerged from the bank and insisted on shaking hands. All the adding machines tittered. "We are," he said, "of course honored by your faith in the future and progress of Polaris, but in all honesty, Dr. Madigan, your deposit in our bank is too large to be protected by the F.D.I.C. Now why not withdraw some of your funds and invest in—"

"Wait a minute," Jake interrupted faintly. "I made a deposit with you?"

The banker and mayor laughed heartily.

"How much?" Florinda asked.

"One million dollars."

"As if you didn't know," the mayor chortled and drove them to a beautifully furnished ranch house in a lovely valley of some five hundred acres, all of which was theirs. A young man in the kitchen was unpacking a dozen cartons of food.

"Got your order just in time, Doc," he smiled. "We filled everything, but the boss sure would like to know what you're going to do with all these carrots. Got a secret scientific formula?"

"Carrots?"

"A hundred and ten bunches. I had to drive all the way to Butte to scrape them up."

"Carrots," Florinda said when they were at last alone. "That explains everything. It's OBO."

"What? How?"

"Don't you remember? We flew a carrot in the Michigan package."

"My God, yes! You called it the thinking carrot. But if it's OBO . . ."

"It has to be. He's queer for carrots."

"But a hundred and ten bunches!"

"No, no. He didn't mean that. He meant half a dozen."

"How?"

"Our boy's trying to speak decimal and binary, and he gets mixed up sometimes. A hundred and ten is six in binary."

"You know, you may be right. What about that million dollars? Same mistake?"

"I don't think so. What's a binary million in decimal?"

"Sixty-four."

"What's a decimal million in binary?"

Madigan did swift mental arithmetic. "It comes to twenty bits: 11110100001001000000."

"I don't think that million dollars was any mistake," Florinda said.

"What's our boy up to now?"

"Taking care of his mum and dad."

"How does he do it?"

"He has an interface with every electric and electronic circuit in the country. Think about it, Jake. He can control our nervous system all the way from cars to computers. He can switch trains, print books, broadcast news, hijack planes, juggle bank funds. You name it and he can do it. He's in complete control."

"But how does he know everything people are doing?"

"Ah! Here we get into an exotic aspect of circuitry that I don't like. After all, I'm an engineer by trade. Who's to say that circuits don't have an interface with us? We're organic circuits ourselves. They see with our eyes, hear with our ears, feel with our fingers, and they report to him."

"Then we're just seeing-eye dogs for machines."

"No, we've created a brand-new form of symbiosis. We can all help each other."

"And OBO's helping us. Why?"

"I don't think he likes the rest of the country," Florinda said somberly. "Look what happened to Indianapolis and Scranton and Sacramento."

"I think I'm going to be sick."

"I think we're going to survive."

"Only us? The Adam and Eve bit?"

"Nonsense. Plenty will survive, so long as they mind their manners."

"What's OBO's idea of manners?"

"I don't know. A little bit of eco-logic, maybe. No more destruction. No more waste. Live and let live, but with responsibility and accountability. That's the crucial word, accountability. It's the basic law of the space program. No matter what happens, someone must be held accountable. OBO must have picked that up. I think he's holding the whole country accountable; otherwise it's the fire-and-brimstone visitation."

The phone rang. After a brief search they located an extension and picked it up.

"Hello?"

"This is Stretch," I said.

"Stretch? Stretch who?"

"The Stretch computer at Goddard. Formal name, IBM 2002. OBO says he'll be making a pass over your part of the country in about five minutes. He'd like you to give him a wave. He says his orbit won't take him over you for another couple of months. When it does, he'll try to ring you himself. 'Bye now."

They lurched out to the lawn in front of the house and stood dazed in the twilight, staring up at the sky. The phone and the electric circuits were touched, even though the electricity was generated by a Delco which is a notoriously insensitive boor of a machine. Suddenly Jake pointed to a pinprick of light vaulting across the heavens.

"There goes our son," he said.

"There goes God," Florinda said.

They waved dutifully.

"Jake, how long before OBO's orbit decays and down will come baby, cradle, and all?"

"About twenty years."

"God for twenty years." Florinda sighed. "D'you think he'll have enough time?"

Madigan shivered. "I'm scared. You?"

"Yes. But maybe we're just tired and hungry. Come inside, Big Daddy, and I'll feed us."

"Thank you, Little Mother, but no carrots, please. That's a little too close to transubstantiation for me."

My Affair with Science Fiction

I'M told that some science fiction readers complain that nothing is known about my private life. It's not that I have anything to conceal; it's simply the result of the fact that I'm reluctant to talk about myself because I prefer to listen to others talk about themselves. I'm genuinely interested, and also there's always the chance of picking up something useful. The professional writer is a professional magpie.

Very briefly: I was born on Manhattan Island December 18, 1913, of a middle-class, hard-working family. I was born a Jew but the family had a *laissez-faire* attitude toward religion and let me pick my own faith for myself. I picked Natural Law. My father was raised in Chicago, always a raunchy town with no time for the God bit. Neither has he. My mother is a quiet Christian Scientist. When I do something that pleases her, she nods and says, "Yes, of course. You were born in Science." I used to make fun of her belief as a kid, and we had some delightful arguments. We still do, while my father sits and smiles benignly. So my home life was completely liberal and iconoclastic.

I went to the last little red schoolhouse in Manhattan (now preserved as a landmark) and to a beautiful new high school on the very peak of Washington Heights (now the scene of cruel racial conflicts). I went to the University of Pennsylvania in Philadelphia where I made a fool of myself trying to become a Renaissance man. I refused to specialize and knocked myself out studying the humanities and the scientific disciplines. I was a miserable member of the crew squad, but I was the most successful member of the fencing team.

I'd been fascinated by science fiction ever since Hugo Gernsback's magazines first appeared on the stands. I suffered through the dismal years of space opera when science fiction was written by the hacks of pulp Westerns who merely translated the Lazy X ranch into the Planet X and then wrote the same formula stories, using space pirates instead of cattle rustlers. I welcomed the glorious epiphany of John Campbell, whose *Astounding* brought about the Golden Age of science fiction.

Ah! Science fiction, science fiction! I've loved it since its birth. I've read it all my life, off and on, with excitement, with joy, sometimes with sorrow. Here's a twelve-year-old kid, hungry for ideas and imagination, borrowing fairy-tale collections from the library—*The Blue Fairy Book, The Red Fairy Book, The Paisley Fairy Book*—and smuggling them home under his jacket because he was ashamed to be reading fairy tales at his age. And then came Hugo Gernsback.

I read science fiction piecemeal in those days. I didn't have much allowance, so I couldn't afford to buy the magazines. I would loaf at the newsstand outside the stationery store as though contemplating which magazine to buy. I would leaf through a science fiction magazine, reading rapidly, until the proprietor came out and chased me. A few hours later I'd return and continue where I'd been forced to leave off. There was one hateful kid in summer camp who used to receive the *Amazing Quarterly* in July. I was next in line, and he was hateful because he was a slow reader.

It's curious that I remember very few of the stories. The H. G. Wells reprints, to be sure, and the very first book I ever bought was the collection of Wells's science fiction short stories. I remember "The Fourth Dimensional Cross Section" (Have I got the title right?) which flabbergasted me with its concept. I think I first read "Flatland by A. Square" as an *Amazing* reprint. I remember a cover for a novel titled, I think, "The Second Deluge." It showed the survivors of the deluge in a sort of Second Ark gazing in awe at the peak of Mt. Everest now bared naked by the rains. The peak was a glitter of precious gems. I interviewed Sir Edmund Hillary in New Zealand a few years ago and he never said anything about diamonds and emeralds. That gives one furiously to think.

Through high school and college I continued to read science fiction but, as I said, with increasing frustration. The pulp era had set in and most of the stories were about heroes with names like "Brick Malloy" who were inspired to combat space pirates, invaders from other worlds, giant insects, and all the rest of the trash still being produced by Hollywood today. I remember a perfectly appalling novel about a Negro conspiracy to take over the world. These niggers, you see, had invented a serum which turned them white, so they could pass, and they were boring from within. Brick Malloy took care of those black bastards. We've come a long way, haven't we?

There were a few bright moments. Who can forget the impact of Weinbaum's "A Martian Odyssey"? That unique story inspired an entire vogue for quaint alien creatures in science fiction. "A Martian Odyssey" was one reason why I submitted my first story to Standard Magazines; they had published Weinbaum's classic. Alas, Weinbaum fell apart and degenerated into a second-rate fantasy writer, and died too young to fulfill his original promise.

And then came Campbell who rescued, elevated, gave meaning and importance to science fiction. It became a vehicle for ideas, daring, audacity. Why, in God's name, didn't he come first? Even today science fiction is still struggling to shake off its pulp reputation, deserved in the past but certainly not now. It reminds me of the exploded telegony theory; that once a thoroughbred mare has borne a colt by a nonthoroughbred sire, she can never bear another thoroughbred again. Science fiction is still suffering from telegony.

Those happy golden days! I used to go to secondhand magazine stores and buy back copies of *Astounding*. I remember a hot July weekend when my wife was away working in a summer stock company and I spent two days thrilling to Van Vogt's *Slan*. And Heinlein's *Universe*! What a concept, and so splendidly worked out with imagination and remorseless logic! Do you remember "Black Destroyer"? Do you remember Lewis Padgett's "Mimsy Were the Borogroves"? That was originality carried to the fifth power. Do you remember— But it's no use. I could go on and on. The Blue, the Red and the Paisley Fairy Books were gone forever.

After I graduated from the university I really didn't know what I wanted to do with myself. In retrospect I realize that what I needed was a *Wanderjahr*, but such a thing was unheard of in the States at that time. I went to law school for a couple of years (just stalling) and to my surprise received a concentrated education which far surpassed that of my undergraduate years. After thrashing and loafing, to the intense pain of my parents, who would have liked to see me settled in a career, I finally took a crack at writing a science fiction story which I submitted to Standard Magazines. The story had the ridiculous title of "Diaz-X."

Two editors on the staff, Mort Weisinger and Jack Schiff, took an interest in me, I suspect mostly because I'd just finished reading and annotating Joyce's *Ulysses* and would preach it enthusiastically without provocation, to their great amusement. They told me what they had in mind. *Thrilling Wonder* was conducting a prize contest for the best story written by an amateur, and so far none of the submissions was worth considering. They thought "Diaz-X" might fill the bill if it was whipped into shape. They taught me how to revise the story into acceptable form and gave it the prize, $50. It was printed with the title, "The Broken Axiom." They continued their professional guidance and I've never stopped being grateful to them.

Recently, doing an interview for *Publishers Weekly* on my old friend and hero, Robert Heinlein (he prefers "Robert" to "Bob"), I asked him how he got started in science fiction.

"In '39. I started writing and I was hooked. I wrote everything I learned anywhere; navy, army, anywhere. My first science fiction story was 'Lifeline.' I saw an ad in *Thrilling Wonder* offering a prize of $50 for the best amateur story, but then I found out that *Astounding* was paying a cent a word and my story ran to 7,000 words. So I submitted it to them first and they bought it."

"You sonofabitch," I said between my teeth. "I won that *Thrilling Wonder* contest, and you beat me by twenty dollars."

We both laughed but despite our mutual admiration I suspect that we both knew that twenty dollars wasn't the only way Robert has always bettered me in science fiction.

I think I wrote perhaps a dozen acceptable science fiction stories in the next two years, all of them rotten, for I was without craft and experience and had to learn by trial and error. I've never been one to save things, I don't even save my mss., but I did hold on to the first four magazine covers on which my name appeared. *Thrilling Wonder Stories* (15¢). On the lower left-hand corner is printed "Slaves of the Life Ray, a startling novelet by Alfred Bester." The feature story was "Trouble on Titan, A Gerry Carlyle Novel by Arthur K. Barnes." Another issue had me down in the same bullpen, "The Voyage to Nowhere by Alfred Bester." The most delightful item is my first cover story in *Astonishing Stories* (10¢). "The Pet Nebula by Alfred Bester." The cover shows an amazed young scientist in his laboratory being confronted by a sort of gigantic radioactive seahorse. Damned if I can remember what the story was about.

Some other authors on the covers were Neil R. Jones, J. Harvey Haggard, Ray Cummings (I remember that name), Harry Bates (his, too), Kelvin Kent (sounds like a house name to me), E. E. Smith, Ph. D (but of course) and Henry Kuttner with better billing than mine. He was in the lefthand *upper* corner.

Mort Weisinger introduced me to the informal luncheon gatherings of the working science fiction authors of the late thirties. I met Henry Kuttner, who later became Lewis Padgett, Ed Hamilton, and Otto Binder, the writing half of Eando Binder. Eando was a sort of acronym of the brothers Ed and Otto Binder. E and O. Ed was a self-taught science fiction illustrator and not very good. Malcolm Jameson, author of navy-oriented space stories, was there, tall, gaunt, prematurely grey, speaking in slow, heavy tones. Now and then he brought along his pretty daughter, who turned everybody's head.

The vivacious *compère* of those luncheons was Manley Wade Wellman, a professional Southerner full of regional anecdotes. It's my recollection that one of his hands was slightly shriveled, which may have been why he came on so strong for the Confederate cause. We were all very patient with that; after all, our side won the war. Wellman was quite the man-of-the-world for the innocent thirties; he always ordered wine with his lunch.

Henry Kuttner and Otto Binder were medium-sized young men, very quiet and courteous, and entirely without outstanding features. Once I broke Kuttner up quite unintentionally. I said to Weisinger, "I've just finished a wild story that takes place in a spaceless, timeless locale where there's no objective reality. It's awfully long, 20,000 words, but I can cut the first 5,000." Kuttner burst out laughing. I do, too, when I think of the dumb kid I was. Once I said most earnestly to Jameson, "I've discovered a remarkable thing. If you combine two story-lines into one, the result can be tremendously exciting." He stared at me with incredulity. "Haven't you ever heard of plot and counterplot?" he growled. I hadn't. I discovered it all by myself.

Being brash and the worst kind of intellectual snob, I said privately to Weisinger that I wasn't much impressed by these writers who were supplying most of the science fiction for the magazines, and asked him why they received so many assignments. He explained, "They may never write a great story, but they never write a bad one. We know we can depend on them." Having recently served my time as a magazine editor, I now understand exactly what he meant.

When the comic book explosion burst, my two magi were lured away from Standard Magazines by the *Superman* Group. There was a desperate need for writers to provide scenarios (Wellman nicknamed them "Squinkas") for the artists, so Weisinger and Schiff drafted me as one of their writers. I hadn't the faintest idea of how to write a comic book script, but one rainy Saturday afternoon Bill Finger, the star comics writer of the time, took me in hand and gave me, a potential rival, an incisive, illuminating lecture on the craft. I still regard that as a high point in the generosity of one colleague to another.

I wrote comics for three or four years with increasing expertise and success. Those were wonderful days for a novice. Squinkas were expanding and there was a constant demand for stories. You could write three and four a week and experiment while learning your craft. The scripts were usually an odd combination of science fiction and "Gangbusters." To give you some idea of what they were like, here's a typical script conference with an editor I'll call Chuck Migg, dealing with a feature I'll call "Captain Hero." Naturally, both are fictitious. The dialogue isn't.

"Now, listen," Migg says, "I called you down because we got to do something about Captain Hero."

"What's your problem?"

"The book is closing next week, and we're thirteen pages short. That's a whole lead story. We got to work one out now."

"Any particular slant?"

"Nothing special, except maybe two things. We got to be original and we got to be realistic. No more fantasy."

"Right."

"So give."

"Wait a minute, for Christ's sake. Who d'you think I am, Saroyan?"

Two minutes of intense concentration. Then Migg says, "How about this? A mad scientist invents a machine for making people go fast. So crooks steal it and hop themselves up. Get it? They move so fast they can rob a bank in a split second."

"No."

"We open with a splash panel showing money and jewelry disappearing with wiggly lines and— Why no?"

"It's a steal from H. G. Wells."

"But it's still original."

"Anyway, it's too fantastic. I thought you said we were going to be realistic."

"Sure I said realistic, but that don't mean we can't be imaginative. What we have to—"

"Wait a minute. Hold the phone."

"Got a flash?"

"Maybe. Suppose we begin with a guy making some kind of experiment. He's a scientist, but not mad. This is a straight, sincere guy."

"Gotcha. He's making an experiment for the good of humanity. Different narrative hook."

"We'll have to use some kind of rare earth metal; cerium, maybe, or—"

"No, let's go back to radium. We ain't used it in the last three issues."

"All right, radium. The experiment is a success. He brings a dead dog back to life with his radium serum."

"I'm waiting for the twist."

"The serum gets into his blood. From a lovable scientist, he turns into a fiend."

At this point Migg takes fire. "I got it! I got it! We'll make like King Midas. This doc is a sweet guy. He's just finished an experiment that's gonna bring eternal life to mankind. So he takes a walk in his garden and smells a rose. Blooie! The rose dies. He feeds the birds. Wham! The birds plotz. So how does Captain Hero come in?"

"Well, maybe we can make it Jekyll and Hyde here. The doctor doesn't want to be a walking killer. He knows there's a rare medicine that'll neutralize the radium in him. He has to steal it from hospitals, and that brings Captain Hero around to investigate."

"Nice human interest."

"But here's the next twist. The doctor takes a shot of the medicine and thinks he's safe. Then his daughter walks into the lab, and when he kisses her, she dies. The medicine won't cure him any more."

By now Migg is in orbit. "I got it! I got it! First we run a caption: IN THE LONELY LABORATORY A DREADFUL CHANGE TORTURES DR.—whatever his name is—HE IS NOW DR. RADIUM!!! Nice name, huh?"

"Okay."

"Then we run a few panels showing him turning green and smashing stuff and he screams: THE MEDICINE CAN NO LONGER SAVE ME! THE RADIUM IS EATING INTO MY BRAIN!! I'M GOING MAD, HA-HA-HA!!! How's that for real drama?"

"Great."

"Okay. That takes care of the first three pages. What happens with Dr. Radium in the next ten?"

"Straight action finish. Captain Hero tracks him down. He traps Captain Hero in something lethal. Captain Hero escapes and traps Dr. Radium and knocks him off a cliff or something."

"No. Knock him into a volcano."

"Why?"

"So we can bring Dr. Radium back for a sequel. He really packs a wallop. We could have him walking through walls and stuff on account of the radium in him."

"Sure."

"This is gonna be a great character, so don't rush the writing. Can you start today? Good. I'll send a messenger up for it tomorrow."

The great George Burns, bemoaning the death of vaudeville, once said, "There just ain't no place for kids to be lousy any more." The comics gave me an ample opportunity to get a lot of lousy writing out of my system.

The line ". . . knocks him off a cliff or something" has particular significance. We had very strict self-imposed rules about death and violence. The Good Guys never deliberately killed. They fought, but only with their fists. Only villains used deadly weapons. We could show death coming—a character falling off the top of a high building, "Aiggghhh!"—and we could show the result of death—a body, but always face down. We could never show the moment of death; never a wound, never a rictus, no blood, at the most a knife protruding from the back. I remember the shock that ran through the *Superman* office when Chet Gould drew a bullet piercing the forehead of a villain in "Dick Tracy."

We had other strict rules. No cop could be crooked. They could be dumb, but they had to be honest. We disapproved of Raymond Chandler's corrupt police. No mechanical or scientific device could be used unless it had a firm foundation in fact. We used to laugh at the outlandish gadgets Bob Kane invented (he wrote his own squinkas as a rule) for "Batman and Robin" which, among ourselves, we called Batman and Rabinowitz. Sadism was absolutely taboo; no torture scenes, no pain scenes. And, of course, sex was completely out.

Holiday tells a great story about George Horace Lorrimer, the awesome editor-in-chief of *The Saturday Evening Post,* our sister magazine. He did a very daring thing for his time. He ran a novel in two parts and the first installment ended with the girl bringing the boy back to her apartment at midnight for coffee and eggs. The second installment opened with them having breakfast together in her apartment the following morning. Thousands of indignant letters came in, and Lorrimer had a form reply printed: "*The Saturday Evening Post* is not responsible for the behavior of its characters between installments." Presumably our comic book heroes lived normal lives between issues; Batman getting bombed and chasing ladies into bed, Rabinowitz burning down his school library in protest against something.

I was married by then, and my wife was an actress. One day she told me that the radio show, "Nick Carter," was looking for scripts. I took one of my best comic book stories, translated it into a radio script, and it was accepted. Then my wife told me that a new show, "Charlie Chan," was having script problems. I did the same thing with the same result. By the end of the year I was the regular writer on those two shows and branching out to "The Shadow" and others. The comic book days were over, but the splendid training I received in visualization, attack, dialogue, and economy stayed with me forever. The imagination must come from within; no one can teach you that. The ideas must come from without, and I'd better explain that.

Usually, ideas don't just come to you out of nowhere; they require a compost heap for germination, and the compost is diligent preparation. I spent many hours a week in the reading rooms of the New York public library at 42nd Street and Fifth Avenue. I read everything and anything with magpie attention for a possible story idea; art frauds, police methods, smuggling, psychiatry, scientific research, color dictionaries, music, demography, biography, plays . . . the list is endless. I'd been forced to develop a speed-reading technique in law school and averaged a dozen books per session. I thought that one potential idea per book was a reasonable return. All that material went into my Commonplace Book for future use. I'm still using it and still adding to it.

And so for the next five or six years I forgot comics, forgot science fiction and immersed myself in the entertainment business. It was new, colorful, challenging and—I must be honest—far more profitable. I wrote mystery, adventure, fantasy, variety, anything that was a challenge, a new experience, something I'd never done before. I even became the director on one of the shows, and that was another fascinating challenge.

But very slowly an insidious poison began to diminish my pleasure; it was the constraints of network censorship and client control. There were too many ideas which I was not permitted to explore. Management said they were too different; the public would never understand them. Accounting said they were too expensive to do; the budget couldn't stand it. One Chicago client wrote an angry letter to the producer of one of my shows, "Tell Bester to stop trying to be original. All I want is ordinary scripts." That really hurt. Originality is the essence of what the artist has to offer. One way or another, we must produce a new sound.

But I must admit that the originality-compulsion can often be a nuisance to myself as well as others. When a concept for a story develops, a half-dozen ideas for the working-out come to mind. These are examined and dismissed. If they came that easily, they can't be worthwhile. "Do it the hard way," I say to myself, and so I search for the hard way, driving myself and everybody around me quite mad in the process. I pace interminably, mumbling to myself. I go for long walks. I sit in bars and drink, hoping that an overheard fragment of conversation may give me a clue. It never happens but all the same, for reasons which I don't understand, I do get ideas in saloons.

Here's an example. Recently I was struggling with the pheromone phenomenon. A pheromone is an external hormone secreted by an insect—an ant, say—when it finds a good food source. The other members of the colony are impelled to follow the pheromone trail, and they find the food, too. I wanted to extrapolate that to a man and I had to do it the hard way. So I paced and I walked and at last I went to a bar where I was nailed by a dumb announcer I knew who drilled my ear with his boring monologue. As I was gazing moodily into my drink and wondering how to escape, the hard way came to me. "He doesn't *leave* a trail," I burst out. "He's impelled to *follow* a trail." While the announcer looked at me in astonishment, I whipped out my notebook and wrote, "Death left a pheromone trail for him; death in fact, death in the making, death in the planning."

So, out of frustration, I went back to science fiction in order to keep my cool. It was a safety valve, an escape hatch, therapy for me. The ideas which no show would touch could be written as science fiction stories, and I could have the satisfaction of seeing them come to life. (You must have an audience for that.) I wrote perhaps a dozen and a half stories, most of them for *Fantasy & Science Fiction* whose editors, Tony Boucher and Mike McComas, were unfailingly kind and appreciative.

I wrote a few stories for *Astounding,* and out of that came my one demented meeting with the great John W. Campbell, Jr. I needn't preface this account with the reminder that I worshiped Campbell from afar. I had never met him; all my stories had been submitted by mail. I hadn't the faintest idea of what he was like, but I imagined that he was a combination of Bertrand Russell and Ernest Rutherford. So I sent off another story to Campbell, one which no show would let me tackle. The title was "Oddy and Id" and the concept was Freudian, that a man is not governed by his conscious mind but rather by his unconscious compulsions. Campbell telephoned me a few weeks later to say that he liked the story but wanted to discuss a few changes with me. Would I come to his office? I was delighted to accept the invitation despite the fact that the editorial offices of *Astounding* were then the hell and gone out in the boondocks of New Jersey.

The editorial offices were in a grim factory that looked like and probably was a printing plant. The "offices" turned out to be one small office, cramped, dingy, occupied not only by Campbell but by his assistant, Miss Tarrant. My only yardstick for comparison was the glamorous network and advertising agency offices. I was dismayed.

Campbell arose from his desk and shook hands. I'm a fairly big guy, but he looked enormous to me—about the size of a defensive tackle. He was dour and seemed preoccupied by matters of great moment. He sat down behind his desk. I sat down on the visitor's chair.

"You don't know it," Campbell said. "You can't have any way of knowing it, but Freud is finished."

I stared. "If you mean the rival schools of psychiatry, Mr. Campbell, I think—"

"No I don't. Psychiatry, as we know it, is dead."

"Oh, come now, Mr. Campbell. Surely you're joking."

"I have never been more serious in my life. Freud has been destroyed by one of the greatest discoveries of our time."

"What's that?"

"Dianetics."

"I never heard of it."

"It was discovered by L. Ron Hubbard, and he will win the Nobel Peace Prize for it," Campbell said solemnly.

"The peace prize? What for?"

"Wouldn't the man who wiped out war win the Nobel Peace Prize?"

"I suppose so, but how?"

"Through dianetics."

"I honestly don't know what you're talking about, Mr. Campbell."

"Read this," he said and handed me a sheaf of long galley proofs. They were, I discovered later, the galleys of the very first dianetics piece to appear in *Astounding*.

"Read them here and now? This is an awful lot of copy."

He nodded, shuffled some papers, spoke to Miss Tarrant,

and went about his business, ignoring me. I read the first galley carefully, the second not so carefully, as I became bored by the dianetics mishmash. Finally I was just letting my eyes wander along, but was very careful to allow enough time for each galley so Campbell wouldn't know I was faking. He looked very shrewd and observant to me. After a sufficient time, I stacked the galleys neatly and returned them to Campbell's desk.

"Well?" he demanded. "Will Hubbard win the peace prize?"

"It's difficult to say. Dianetics is a most original and imaginative idea, but I've only been able to read through the piece once. If I could take a set of galleys home and—"

"No," Campbell said. "There's only this one set. I'm rescheduling and pushing the article into the very next issue. It's that important." He handed the galleys to Miss Tarrant. "You're blocking it," he told me. "That's all right. Most people do that when a new idea threatens to overturn their thinking."

"That may well be," I said, "but I don't think it's true of myself. I'm a hyperthyroid, an intellectual monkey, curious about everything."

"No," Campbell said, with the assurance of a diagnostician, "You're a hyp-O-thyroid. But it's not a question of intellect, it's one of emotion. We conceal our emotional history from ourselves although dianetics can trace our history all the way back to the womb."

"To the womb!"

"Yes. The fetus remembers. Come and have lunch."

Remember, I was fresh from Madison Avenue and expense-account luncheons. We didn't go to the Jersey equivalent of Sardi's, "21," even P. J. Clarke's. He led me downstairs and we entered a tacky little lunchroom crowded with printers and file clerks; an interior room with blank walls that made every sound reverberate. I got myself a liverwurst on white, no mustard, and a Coke. I can't remember what Campbell ate.

We sat down at a small table while he continued to discourse on dianetics, the great salvation of the future when the world would at last be cleared of its emotional wounds. Suddenly he stood up and towered over me. "You can drive your memory back to the womb," he said. "You can do it if you release every block, clear yourself and remember. Try it."

"Now?"

"Now. Think. Think back. Clear yourself. Remember! You can remember when your mother tried to abort you with a buttonhook. You've never stopped hating her for it."

Around me there were cries of, "BLT down, hold the mayo. Eighty-six on the English. Combo rye, relish. Coffee shake, pick up." And here was this grim tackle standing over me, practicing dianetics without a license. The scene was so lunatic that I began to tremble with suppressed laughter. I prayed. "Help me out of this, please. Don't let me laugh in his face. Show me a way out." God showed me. I looked up at Campbell and said, "You're absolutely right, Mr. Campbell, but the emotional wounds are too much to bear. I can't go on with this."

He was completely satisfied. "Yes, I could see you were shaking." He sat down again, and we finished our lunch and returned to his office. It developed that the only changes he wanted in my story was the removal of all Freudian terms which dianetics had now made obsolete. I agreed, of course; they were minor, and it was a great honor to appear in *Astounding* no matter what the price. I escaped at last and returned to civilization where I had three double gibsons and don't be stingy with the onions.

That was my one and only meeting with John Campbell, and certainly my own story conference with him. I've had some wild ones in the entertainment business, but nothing to equal that. It reinforced my private opinion that a majority of the science fiction crowd, despite their brilliance, were missing their marbles. Perhaps that's the price that must be paid for brilliance.

One day, out of the clear sky, Horace Gold telephoned to ask me to write for *Galaxy*, which he had launched with tremendous success. It filled an open space in the field; *Astounding* was hard science; *Fantasy & Science Fiction* was wit and sophistication; *Galaxy* was psychiatry-oriented. I was flattered but begged off, explaining that I didn't think I was much of a science fiction author compared to the genuine greats. "Why me?" I asked. "You can have Sturgeon, Leiber, Asimov, Heinlein."

"I've got them," he said, "and I want you."

"Horace, you're an old scriptwriter, so you'll understand. I'm tied up with a bitch of a show starring a no-talent. I've got to write continuity for him, quiz sections for him to M.C. and dramatic sketches for him to mutilate. He's driving me up the wall. His agent is driving me up the wall. I really haven't got the time."

Horace didn't give up. He would call every so often to chat about the latest science fiction, new concepts, what authors had failed and how they'd failed. In the course of these gossips, he contrived to argue that I was a better writer than I thought and to ask if I didn't have any ideas that I might be interested in working out.

All this was on the phone because Horace was trapped in his apartment. He'd had shattering experiences in both the European and Pacific theaters during World War II and had been released from the service with complete agoraphobia. Everybody has to come to his apartment to see him, including his psychiatrist. Horace was most entertaining on the phone; witty, ironic, perceptive, making shrewd criticisms of science fiction.

I enjoyed these professional gossips with Horace so much that I began to feel beholden to him; after all, I was more or less trapped in my workshop, too. At last I submitted perhaps a dozen ideas for his judgment. Horace discussed them all, very sensibly and realistically, and at last suggested combining two different ideas into what ultimately became *The De-molished Man.* I remember one of the ideas only vaguely; it had something to do with extrasensory perception, but I've forgotten the gimmick. The other I remember quite well. I wanted to write a mystery about a future in which the police are armed with time machines so that if a crime is committed they could trace it back to its origin. This would make crime impossible. How then, in an open story, could a clever crimi-nal outwit the police?

I'd better explain "open story." The classic mystery is the closed story, or whodunit. It's a puzzle in which everything is concealed except the clues carefully scattered through the story. It's up to the audience to piece them together and solve the puzzle. I had become quite expert at that. However, I was carrying too many mystery shows and often fell behind in my deadlines, a heinous crime, so occasionally I would commit the lesser crime of stealing one of my scripts from Show A and adapting it for Show B.

I was reading a three-year-old Show A script for possible theft when it dawned on me that I had written all the wrong scenes. It was a solid story, but in the attempt to keep it a closed puzzle, I had been forced to omit the real drama in order to present the perplexing results of the behind-the-scenes action. So I developed for myself a style of action-mystery writing in which everything is open and known to the audi-ence, every move and countermove, with only the final resolu-tion coming as a surprise. This is an extremely difficult form of writing; it requires you to make your antagonists outwit each other continually with ingenuity and resourceful-ness.

Horace suggested that instead of using time machines as the obstacle for the criminal, I use ESP. Time travel, he said, was a pretty worn-out theme, and I had to agree. ESP, Horace said, would be an even tougher obstacle to cope with, and I had to agree.

"But I don't like the idea of a mind-reading detective," I said. "It makes him too special."

"No, no," Horace said. "You've got to create an entire ESP society."

And so the creation began. We discussed it on the phone almost daily, each making suggestions, dismissing suggestions, adapting and revising suggestions. Horace was, at least for me, the ideal editor, always helpful, always encouraging, never losing his enthusiasm. He was opinionated, God knows, but so was I, perhaps even more than he. What saved the relationship was the fact that we both knew we respected each other; that, and our professional concentration on the job. For professionals the job is the boss.

The writing began in New York. When my show went off for the summer, I took the ms. out to our summer cottage on Fire Island and continued there. I remember a few amusing incidents. For a while I typed on the front porch. Wolcott Gibbs, the *New Yorker* drama critic, lived up the street and every time he passed our cottage and saw me working he would denounce me. Wolcott had promised to write a biography of Harold Ross that summer and hadn't done a lick of work yet. I. F. (Izzy) Stone dropped in once and found himself in the midst of an animated discussion of political thought as reflected by science fiction. Izzy became so fascinated that he asked us to take five while he ran home to put a fresh battery in his hearing aid.

I used to go surf-fishing every dawn and dusk. One evening I was minding my own business, busy casting and thinking of nothing in particular when the idea of using typeface symbols in names dropped into my mind. I reeled in so quickly that I fouled my line, rushed to the cottage and experimented on the typewriter. Then I went back through the ms. and changed all the names. I remember quitting work one morning to watch an eclipse and it turned cloudy. Obviously somebody up there didn't approve of eclipse-breaks. And so, by the end of the summer, the novel was finished. My working title had been *Demolition*. Horace changed it to *The Demolished Man*. Much better, I think.

The book was received with considerably enthusiasm by the *Galaxy* readers, which was gratifying but surprising. I hadn't had any conscious intention of breaking new trails; I was just trying to do a craftsmanlike job. Some of the fans' remarks bemused me. "Oh, Mr. Bester! How well you understand women." I never thought I understood women. "Who were the models for your characters?" They're surprised when I tell them that the model for one of the protagonists was a bronze statue of a Roman emperor in the Metropolitan Museum. It's haunted me ever since I was a child. I read the emperor's character into the face and when it came time to write this particular fictional character, I used my emperor for the mold.

The *réclame* of the novel turned me into a science fiction somebody, and people were curious about me. I was invited to gatherings of the science fiction Hydra Club where I met the people I was curious about; Ted Sturgeon, Jim Blish, Tony Boucher, Ike Asimov, Avram Davidson, then a professional Jew wearing a yamulka, and many others. They were all lunatic (So am I. It takes one to spot one.) and convinced me again that most science fiction authors have marbles missing. I can remember listening to an argument about the correct design for a robot, which became so heated that for a moment I thought Judy Merril was going to punch Lester del Rey in the nose. Or maybe it was vice versa.

I was particularly attracted to Blish and Sturgeon. Both were soft-spoken and charming conversationalists. Jim and I would take walks in Central Park during his lunch hour (he was then working as a public relations officer for a pharmaceutical house) and we would talk shop. Although I was an admirer of his work, I felt that it lacked the hard drive to which I'd been trained, and I constantly urged him to attack his stories with more vigor. He never seemed to resent it, or at least was too courteous to show it. His basic problem was how to hold down a PR writing job and yet do creative writing on the side. I had no advice for that. It's a problem which very few people have solved.

Sturgeon and I used to meet occasionally in bars for drinks and talk. Ted's writing exactly suited my taste, which is why I thought he was the finest of us all. But he had a quality which amused and exasperated me. Like Mort Sahl and a few other celebrities I've interviewed—Tony Quinn is another—Ted lived on crisis, and if he wasn't in a crisis, he'd create one for himself. His life was completely disorganized, so it was impossible for him to do his best work consistently. What a waste!

In all fairness I should do a description of myself. I will, but I'm going to save it for the end.

I'd written a contemporary novel based on my TV experiences and it had a fairly decent reprint sale and at last sold to the movies. My wife and I decided to blow the loot on a few years abroad. We put everything into storage, contracted for a little English car, stripped our luggage down to the bare minimum and took off. The only writing materials I brought with me were a portable, my Commonplace Book, a thesaurus, and an idea for another science fiction novel.

For some time I'd been toying with the notion of using the *Count of Monte Cristo* pattern for a story. The reason is simple; I'd always preferred the antihero, and I'd always found high drama in compulsive types. It remained a notion until we bought our cottage on Fire Island and I found a pile of old *National Geographics*. Naturally I read them and came across a most interesting piece on the survival of torpedoed sailors at sea. The record was held by a Philippine cook's helper who lasted for something like four months on an open raft. Then came the detail that racked me up. He'd been sighted several times by passing ships which refused to change course to rescue him because it was a Nazi submarine trick to put out decoys like this. The magpie mind darted down, picked it up, and the notion was transformed into a developing story with a strong attack.

The Stars My Destination (I've forgotten what my working title was) began in a romantic white cottage down in Surrey. This accounts for the fact that so many of the names are English. When I start a story, I spend days reading through telephone directories for help in putting together character names—I'm very fussy about names—and in this case I used English directories. I'm compelled to find or invent names with varying syllables. One, two, three, and four. I'm extremely sensitive to tempo. I'm also extremely sensitive to word color and context. For me there is no such thing as a synonym.

The book got under way very slowly and by the time we left Surrey for a flat in London, I had lost momentum. I went back, took it from the top and started all over again, hoping to generate steam pressure. I write out of hysteria. I bogged down again and I didn't know why. Everything seemed to go wrong. I couldn't use a portable, but the only standard machines I could rent had English keyboards. That threw me off. English ms. paper was smaller than the American, and that threw me off. And I was cold, cold, cold. So in November we packed and drove to the car ferry at Dover, with the fog snapping at our ass all the way, crossed the Channel and drove south to Rome.

After many adventures we finally settled into a penthouse apartment on the *Piazza della Muse*. My wife went to work in Italian films. I located the one (1) standard typewriter in all Rome with an American keyboard and started in again, once more taking it from the top. This time I began to build up momentum, very slowly, and was waiting for the hysteria to set in. I remember the day that it came vividly.

I was talking shop with a young Italian film director for whom my wife was working, both of us beefing about the experimental things we'd never been permitted to do. I told him about a note on synesthesia which I'd been dying to write as a TV script for years. I had to explain synesthesia—this was years before the exploration of psychedelic drugs—and while

I was describing the phenomenon I suddenly thought, "Jesus Christ! This is for the novel. It leads me into the climax." And I realized that what had been holding me up for so many months was the fact that I didn't have a fiery finish in mind. I must have an attack and a finale. I'm like the old Hollywood gag, "Start with an earthquake and build to a climax."

The work went well despite many agonies. Rome is no place for a writer who needs quiet. The Italians *fa rumore* (make noise) passionately. The pilot of a Piper Cub was enchanted by a girl who sunbathed on the roof of a mansion across the road and buzzed her, and me, every morning from seven to nine. There were frequent informal motorcycle rallyes in our *piazza* and the Italians always remove the mufflers from their vehicles; it makes them feel like Tazio Nuvolare. On the other side of our penthouse a building was in construction, and you haven't heard *rumore* until you've heard stonemasons talking politics.

I also had research problems. The official U.S. library was woefully inadequate. The British Consulate library was a love, and I used it regularly, but none of their books was dated later than 1930, no help for a science fiction writer needing data about radiation belts. In desperation, I plagued Tony Boucher and Willy Ley with letters asking for information. They always came through, bless them, Tony on the humanities—"Dear Tony, what the hell is the name of that Russian sect that practiced self-castration? Slotsky? Something like that."—Willy on the disciplines—"Dear Willy, how long could an unprotected man last in naked space? Ten minutes? Five minutes? How would he die?"

The book was completed about three months after the third start in Rome; the first draft of a novel usually takes me about three months. Then there's the pleasant period of revision and rewriting; I always enjoy polishing. What can I say about the material? I've told you about the attack and the climax. I've told you about the years of preparation stored in my mind and my Commonplace Book. If you want the empiric equation for my science fiction writing—for all my writing, in fact, it's:

$$\text{Concept} + \left\{ \begin{array}{l} \text{Discipline} \\ \text{Experiment} \\ \text{Experience} \\ \text{Pattern sense} \\ \text{Drama sense} \\ \text{Preparation} \\ \text{Imagination} \\ \text{Extrapolation} \\ \text{Hysteria} \end{array} \right\} = \text{Story} \rightleftharpoons \text{Statement}$$

I must enlarge on this just a little. The mature science fiction author doesn't merely tell a story about Brick Malloy vs. The Giant Yeastmen from Gethsemane. He makes a statement through his story. What is the statement? Himself, the dimension and depth of the man. His statement is seeing what everybody else sees but thinking what noone else has thought, and having the courage to say it. The hell of it is that only time will tell whether it was worth saying.

Back in London the next year, I was able to meet the young English science fiction authors through Ted Carnell and my London publisher. They gathered in a pub somewhere off the Strand. They were an entertaining crowd, speaking with a rapidity and intensity that reminded me of a debating team from the Oxford Union. And they raised a question which I've never been able to answer: Why is it that the English science fiction writers, so brilliant socially, too often turn out rather dull and predictable stories? There are notable exceptions, of course, but I have the sneaky suspicion that they had American mothers.

John Wyndham and Arthur Clarke came to those gatherings. I thought Arthur rather strange, very much like John Campbell, utterly devoid of a sense of humor, and I'm always ill at ease with humorless people. Once he pledged us all to come to the meeting the following week; he would show slides of some amazing underwater photographs he had taken. He did indeed bring a projector and slides and show them. After looking at a few I called, "Damn it, Arthur, these aren't underwater shots. You took them in an aquarium. I can see the reflections in the plate glass." And it degenerated into an argument about whether the photographer and his camera had to be underwater, too.

It was around this time that an event took place which will answer a question often asked me: Why did I drop science fiction after my first two novels? I'll have to use a flashback, a device I despise, but I can't see any other way out. A month before I left the States, my agent called me in to meet a distinguished gentleman, senior editor of *Holiday* magazine, who was in search of a feature on television. He told me that he'd tried two professional magazine writers without success, and as a last resort wanted to try me on the basis of the novel I'd written about the business.

It was an intriguing challenge. I knew television, but I knew absolutely nothing about magazine piece-writing. So once again I explored, experimented and taught myself. *Holiday* liked the piece so much that they asked me to do pieces on Italian, French and English TV while I was abroad, which I did. Just when my wife and I had decided to settle in London permanently, word came from *Holiday* that they wanted me to come back to the States. They were starting a new feature called "The Antic Arts" and wanted me to become a regular monthly contributor. Another challenge. I returned to New York.

An exciting new writing life began for me. I was no longer immured in my workshop; I was getting out and interviewing interesting people in interesting professions. Reality had become so colorful for me that I no longer needed the therapy of science fiction. And since the magazine imposed no constraints on me, outside of the practical requirements of professional magazine technique, I no longer needed a safety valve.

I wrote scores of pieces, and I confess that they were much easier than fiction, so perhaps I was lazy. But try to visualize the joy of being sent back to your old university to do a feature on it, going to Detroit to test-drive their new cars, taking the very first flight of the Boeing 747, interviewing Sophia Loren in Pisa, De Sica in Rome, Peter Ustinov, Sir Laurence Olivier (they called him Sir Larry in Hollywood), Mike Todd and Elizabeth Taylor, George Balanchine. I interviewed and wrote, and wrote, and wrote, until it became cheaper for *Holiday* to hire me as senior editor, and here was a brand-new challenge.

I didn't altogether lose touch with science fiction; I did book reviews for *Fantasy & Science Fiction* under Bob Mills's editorship and later Avram Davidson's. Unfortunately, my standards had become so high that I seemed to infuriate the fans who wanted special treatment for science fiction. My attitude was that science fiction was merely one of many forms of fiction and should be judged by the standards which apply to all. A silly story is a silly story whether written by Robert Heinlein or Norman Mailer. One enraged fan wrote in to say that I was obviously going through change of life.

Alas, all things must come to an end. *Holiday* failed after a robust twenty-five years; my eyes failed, like poor Congreve's; and here I am, here I am, back in my workshop again, immured and alone, and so turning to my first love, my original love, science fiction. I hope it's not too late to rekindle the affair. Ike Asimov once said to me, "Alfie, we broke new trails in our time but we have to face the fact that we're over the hill now." I hope not, but if it's true, I'll go down fighting for a fresh challenge.

What am I like? Here's as honest a description of myself as

possible. You come to my workshop, a three-room apartment, which is a mess, filled with books, mss., typewriters, telescopes, microscopes, reams of typing paper, chemical glassware. We live in the apartment upstairs, and my wife uses my kitchen for a storeroom. This annoys me; I used to use it as a laboratory. Here's an interesting sidelight. Although I'm a powerful drinker I won't permit liquor to be stored there; I won't have booze in my workshop.

You find me on a high stool at a large drafting table editing some of my pages. I'm probably wearing flimsy pajama bottoms, an old shirt and am barefoot; my customary at-home clothes. You see a biggish guy with dark brown hair going grey, a tight beard nearly all white and the dark brown eyes of a sad spaniel. I shake hands, seat you, hoist myself on the stool again and light a cigarette, always chatting cordially about anything and everything to put you at your ease. However, it's possible that I like to sit higher than you because it gives me a psychological edge. I don't think so, but I've been accused of it.

My voice is a light tenor (except when I'm angry; then it turns harsh and strident) and is curiously inflected. In one sentence I can run up and down an octave. I have a tendency to drawl my vowels. I've spent so much time abroad that my speech pattern may seem affected, for certain European pronunciations cling to me. I don't know why. GA-rahj for garage, the French "r" in the back of the throat, and if there's a knock on the door I automatically holler, *"Avanti!"* a habit I picked up in Italy.

On the other hand my speech is larded with the customary profanity of the entertainment business, as well as Yiddish words and professional phrases. I corrupted the WASP *Holiday* office. It was a camp to have a blond junior editor from Yale come into my office and say, "Alfie, we're having a *tsimmis* with the theater piece. That *goniff* won't rewrite." What you don't know is that I always adapt my speech pattern to that of my *vis-à-vis* in an attempt to put him at his ease. It can vary anywhere from burley (burlesque) to Phi Beta Kappa.

I try to warm you by relating to you, showing interest in you, listening to you. Once I sense that you're at your ease I shut up and listen. Occasionally I'll break in to put a question, argue a point, or ask you to enlarge on one of your ideas. Now and then I'll say, "Wait a minute, you're going too fast. I have to think about that." Then I stare into nowhere and think hard. Frankly, I'm not lightning, but a novel idea can always launch me into outer space. Then I pace excitedly, exploring it out loud.

What I don't reveal is the emotional storm that rages within me. I have my fair share of frustrations and despairs, but I was raised to show a ch-erful countenance to the world and suffer in private. Most people are too preoccupied with their own troubles to be much interested in yours. Do you remember Viola's lovely line in *Twelfth Night*? "And, with a green and yellow melancholy, she sat like Patience on a monument, smiling at grief."

I have some odd mannerisms. I use the accusing finger of a prosecuting attorney as an exclamation point to express appreciation for an idea or a witticism. I'm a "toucher," hugging and kissing men and women alike, and giving them a hard pat on the behind to show approval. Once I embarrassed my boss, the *Holiday* editor-in-chief, terribly. He'd just returned from a junket to India and, as usual, I breezed into his office and gave him a huge welcoming hug and kiss. Then I noticed he had visitors there. My boss turned red and told them, "Alfie Bester is the most affectionate straight in the world."

I'm a faker, often forced to play the scene. In my time I've been mistaken for a fag, a hardhat, a psychiatrist, an artist, a dirty old man, a dirty young man, and I always respond in character and play the scene. Sometimes I'm compelled to play opposites—my fast to your slow, my slow to your fast—all this to the amusement and annoyance of my wife. When we get home she berates me for being a liar and all I can do is laugh helplessly while she swears she'll never trust me again.

I do laugh a lot, with you and at myself, and my laughter is loud and uninhibited. I'm a kind of noisy guy. But don't ever be fooled by me even when I'm clowning. That magpie mind is always looking to pick up something.